Ordinary
Strangers

Ordinary Strangers

A Novel

Bill Stenson

Mother Tongue Publishing Limited
Salt Spring Island, BC
Canada

MOTHER TONGUE PUBLISHING LIMITED
290 Fulford-Ganges Road, Salt Spring Island, B.C. V8K 2K6 Canada
www.mothertonguepublishing.com
Represented in North America by Heritage Group Distribution.

Ordinary Strangers is a work of fiction.
Names, characters, places, and incidents are the products of the author's imagination or are used fictitiously. Any resemblance to actual events, locales, or persons, living or dead, is entirely coincidental.

Book design by Mark Hand
Typefaces used are New Baskerville and Helvetica.
Cover Photo: Thank-you to the Columbia Basin Institute of Regional History & partnering museum/society for use of the photo #0039.0337: Victoria Ave, Fernie BC 1961.
Inside photo: Shutterstock
Printed on Antique Natural, 100% recycled
Printed and bound in Canada.

Mother Tongue Publishing gratefully acknowledges the assistance of the Province of British Columbia through the B.C. Arts Council and we acknowledge the support of the Canada Council for the Arts, which last year invested $157 million in writing and publishing throughout Canada.
Nous remercions de son soutien le Conseil des Arts du Canada, qui a investi 157$ millions de dollars l'an dernier dans les lettres et l'édition à travers le Canada.

LIBRARY AND ARCHIVES CANADA CATALOGUING IN PUBLICATION

Stenson, Bill, 1949-, author
    Ordinary strangers / Bill Stenson.

ISBN 978-1-896949-70-3 (softcover)

    I. Title.

PS8637.T47O73 2018   C813'.6   C2018-903680-X

For Susan

It doesn't matter what story we're telling,
we're telling the story of family.

–ERICA LORRAINE SCHEIDT

There is no such thing as a 'broken family.' Family is family, and is
not determined by marriage certificates, divorce papers and adoption
documents. Families are made in the heart. The only time family
becomes null is when those ties in the heart are cut. If you cut those
ties, those people are not your family. If you make those ties, those
people are your family. And if you hate those ties, those people will still
be your family because whatever you hate will always be with you.

–C. JOYBELL C.

1

THE FAIR WAS IN TOWN. Hope, B.C. In August-hot weather, leaves on deciduous trees hung as limp and still as the trunks that held them in the air. Families shuffled through the dust, eating cotton candy, waiting for the sun to hide behind the mountains. The unusual absence of wind had cast a lethargic spell upon them. Fewer than a hundred people remained on the grounds, and the sense of exhilaration on faces earlier in the day had been replaced, for now, with fatigue and complacency. The lines for the few available rides had subsided, and the ticket taker at the Ferris wheel put his feet up and rolled a cigarette, long overdue. Soon the sun would set, and a much younger crowd would return the fair to swirls of dust and laughter.

A man and a woman, possibly in their forties, stood out from the lethargy at the close of the day because they were looking for their missing dog, Barker, and this made their vector path helter-skelter and urgent. Sage and Della Howard had inherited Barker as a pup to guard the house. Barker whined when desperate but never barked, and Sage thought his blond retriever was mentally challenged. Despite his misgivings, the dog was worth a search because he belonged to them, which may have been the only reason but reason enough.

Barker, Sage called infrequently and with little conviction, as if he believed a dog that doesn't bark can't hear either. Della went one way, Sage another. The mountains eventually blocked the late-day sun until only the tops of the trees were bathed in lime-green light they could almost taste. Della asked strangers if they'd seen the missing dog and offered a description, but no one could help.

The couple came together again in a copse of fir trees hundreds of years old. They stood still for the first time in a long time, words not needed to express the hopelessness they felt. Suddenly they turned their heads to the sound of a whimpering cry and hurried through the trees to find a toddler, dressed in shorts and tattered top, sweating, dirty and red-faced, turning in circles. When Della picked the girl up, Sage immediately took her away from Della just to feel the weight of her, then he handed over his handkerchief so she could dab the tears and snot from the girl's face. The girl relaxed as Sage held her in his arms, and they walked to a purple car at the edge of the fairgrounds where he strapped her into the back seat. Sage started the car, and the three of them headed into the town of Hope.

They drove several blocks before Sage finally said, The dog may have wandered into town if he smelled food. Can't you get her to shut up for a minute? I'm trying to think.

Della turned to the girl in the backseat. Shush, she said. Sage rolled the window down and drove around, checking the side roads for the dog. Into the town of Hope, then out of the town.

We'll have to inform the authorities, Sage said.

Drive a little, Della said. A moving car can settle a child. I've heard that.

The flow of hot air whistled equally through the windows up front, opened for relief. They both knew what was transpiring, and their cunning wrapped around them with every passing tree and boulder. Sage drove slower than usual. Della noticed and glanced at the speedometer as cars passed them on the highway.

The little girl fell asleep as Della had predicted, but two hours later, she woke when they pulled into Princeton. Sage parked the car in a small community park and walked to the store for something to eat. The girl wasn't interested in eating and wandered fearlessly away from the picnic table and into a field of cavorting dogs. Della scooped her up and took her to the washroom. The girl didn't want to pee or wouldn't pee, Della was not sure which, but she told her everything would be just fine.

As soon as we see a cop shop, we're going to pull in and tell them what's happened, Sage said.

Della said, If we see one. If not, we might as well wait until we get there.

They pulled up to a motel in Osoyoos in the sweltering dark. They stopped at three motels before Della found both a bathtub and air conditioning. Sage had orders to purchase some baby food, something mushy in jars, in hopes that the girl would eat. Della turned on the TV, but the girl had no interest in television, so she drew a bath and placed the squirming child into lukewarm water. The water startled her enough that the crying stopped. Della sang "Hush Little Baby Don't You Cry" even after the child stopped crying. Sage came back with pizza and three jars of baby food and a new outfit, including black patent leather shoes several sizes too big. Della laughed about how everything was the wrong size.

Sage didn't find it funny. I don't know the first thing about buying a kid clothes, he said, so Della said at least they were clothes she'd grow into, then she washed the girl's dirty clothes in the tub and put them on the air conditioner that pumped warm air into the room. The girl, content for the moment, ran around naked.

Do you want a beer with your pizza? Sage asked. I bought

a six-pack. The only time I like beer anymore is when it's hot as hell out.

No thanks. I'm just going to watch the little girl run around.

Late afternoon they arrived in Fernie, new to both of them, a town filled with strangers, and Della and Sage had to wait for the rental house to be emptied. Della said the last people took everything but their dirt, but Sage tried not to concern himself with dirt because in a few days he would start his new life as a coal miner and the thought of it made him sick to his stomach. They stayed in a motel just outside of town because they didn't have any furniture for the house yet. Sage borrowed someone's truck and found enough furniture the second day for them to move in.

For the first three days, the little girl stopped crying only when she was sleeping or being carried somewhere. When they moved her, it was as if she expected to be carried back to the arms of someone she knew. If people heard the child crying, they said to themselves: she's unhappy about something, or hurt or hungry, but no one thought her crying would fill three days of sunny weather or imagined that her favourite place to take refuge was in the dark cavern under her bed. Sage couldn't stand the crying and sat out on the front porch in the evening until the girl finally fell asleep. The two of them no longer questioned the reality of what they had in their possession, but Sage thought they should have stopped in Hope to let someone know. Looking after a dog was one thing, but this was more complicated, with a kid that did nothing but cry, and at first it wasn't clear to him what they'd gotten themselves into. Something had coated the two of them, something transparent and protective at the same time, a film that held their position in place but one they could both see through. After day four, the girl settled, and Sage stopped sitting out on the porch after supper, watching the swoop of swallows.

We've got to do something with her, Sage said.

She's happy now, Della said. She only cried once all day, and she didn't cry long.

Sage understood that for years Della had wanted to have a baby and couldn't, and that now, unless they could find out where the little girl belonged, Della wanted her chance. She wasn't thinking about anything else, he could see that, but he knew she didn't understand the edge of the world the way he did. Even if they contacted the authorities, after so much time, they would be charged with abduction or kidnapping or some other crime. He watched his wife folding the few things the girl owned, and on cue the girl offered up a cooing sound from the bedroom. The doctor had said Sage was shooting blanks, that was the reason they couldn't have children. He didn't like the doctor and wasn't sure he trusted him, but Della believed him and that was all that mattered. His wife never held their circumstance over his head, or at least she never came out and said that she had counted on something else, but Sage understood the space that had been created. None of this would have happened had his dog not wandered off. Bloody useless dog. Always had been.

When the girl was upset, Della thought she needed a bath, so she bathed her four or five times a day. She went shopping before Sage started work and brought back dresses and shorts and pink underwear. Against his better judgement, Sage bought the kid something as well. He didn't bring it in the first day—he left it in the trunk so he could think about what he'd done. The next day he gave it to her, a secondhand Chatty Cathy doll that talked when you pulled the string. It looked grotesque to Sage, and the little girl thought so too. Della pulled the string on the red-headed monster over and over while the girl hid under the bed. *Come play with me. I feel tired. Will someone carry me? I feel hurt.*

Della, eager and persistent about playing mom, refused to give up. They fed her peanut butter on a cracker, which she ate, and Della decided that was her go-to treat, which meant she ate peanut butter three or four times a day for the first week. By day seven, Sage had reported for work, and before he left in the morning, he told Della she had better phone the authorities. Della said she'd think about it, but she didn't think about it for long, and when he got home, she said there had been a breakthrough. With Sage out of the house, her natural instincts had kicked in. She stopped calling herself Della, and because she had been with the girl day and night for such a long time, she thought of herself as Mommy.

Sage watched her with the girl. You didn't phone anyone, did you?

No, I didn't. She's so happy now, if something happens she'll just be upset all over again. I made spaghetti and meatballs, just the way you like them.

Damn it, Della. I told you to phone. You realize what this means?

Yes, Della said. I do.

The transition from Della to Mommy came easy, and she gave several days of earnest thought to what would be a good name for the little girl. She didn't rush because she wanted to get it right. Once you give a kid a name, they wear it until they die. The girl had pale skin, mildly freckled, and bright green eyes that stared out at the world, uneven and suspicious. I think her name should be Stacey Emerald Howard, she said. Though only a suggestion, Della made it sound as if it already had a sense of history.

Emerald's okay, Sage said. Why not call her that?

Emerald for a first name would make her stand out, Della said. That's the last thing we want.

Della believed if they used the name enough it would catch on, but when they threw the name Stacey into the air, the little girl looked toward the door as if she expected someone else to enter.

For the first few weeks, they made rare sojourns into the community. Sage took the car to work, and Della and Stacey stayed confined to the house because Della could never tell when the crying would start again. They had a TV set, but Della was afraid to watch TV. They had a radio, but she didn't turn the radio on, and she wasn't interested in reading the newspaper. Once they had a fixed address, Della joined the local library and soon had books on the floor of every room. Stacey ripped the pages of one book, and Della taped it up immediately. She read to her, but Stacey was in no mood to sit and listen, so Della followed her around the house reading *Curious George* between drags on her cigarette. When Stacey fell asleep, however briefly, Della read *The Complete Book of Children's Needs*. Breakable things once sitting low she now placed up and out of reach. Della said they were learning. Sage didn't say anything.

A breach in her armor occurred, Della was sure of it, several weeks after the girl's arrival. Three things happened in the same week, and Della, who kept a journal of every event that occurred, no matter how insignificant, had three specific events underlined in her writing. First, Stacey ate a whole peach without throwing any of it at anyone. The second thing she did was laugh. Sage came home from work and accidently stepped on a rubber duck, and the duck said something that sounded more like a fart than a quack, and she laughed. Every day after that, when Sage came home from work and before he had a shower, he stepped on the duck, and the little girl got a kick out of it. The third thing she did was speak. During weeks of crying and screaming fits, Stacey refused to say anything and pretended she didn't hear anyone, as if she was a little kid on strike. She pointed a lot and cried and curled up in the fetal position when things didn't go her way, but now she willingly spoke. Not only did she speak, she said the word "mom." Della felt no shame at how important this was to her. She had been yearning for it, and she knew how it had come to pass. *Here, Mommy will help you. Mommy's going to give you a bath now. Mommy loves you. Pass that to Mommy. Good girl.*

The first time Stacey said the word "mom," Della picked her up out of a chair and hugged her, and Stacey began to cry. Della didn't clue in that these early pronouncements were not aimed at her at all. Or maybe they were. Maybe at that age the brain has only a tentative hold on what is real. The next day Della took Stacey downtown and bought her a winter coat, and in some magical way, the coat defined a point of no return. Once the Howards invested in a winter coat, they no longer mentioned finding the authorities and returning the little girl to wherever she had come from—*wherever* the word they both used consistently instead of *whoever*. But perhaps the winter coat wasn't the turning point at all. It could have been a few months earlier. The exact moment may have been when they strapped her into the back seat of their purple car and acted as if she had belonged to them all along.

2

DELLA WAS ONLY NINETEEN when she married Willy Hoffner and Sage stood as the best man at her wedding. Willy had arranged a honeymoon at Lake Louise but hadn't told anyone where they were going, so it was three days after the wedding before Della found out about the tragedy. Her parents, who were divorced but had agreed to travel to the wedding together, had been killed in a collision with a transport truck a few hours after the reception.

The honeymoon had some highlights Della would never forget, but Willy stayed drunk most of the time and acted antsy when sober, so it was her memory of the wedding ceremony that kept her company when they drove back to Vancouver to find out about the disaster that had struck her family. The funeral was a formality. No one knew where Della's sister was, and no one in Vancouver knew her parents. The deaths wiped away any sense of happiness Della had planned to harness in marriage; in a strange way, it was as if the marriage hadn't taken place. Two days after the funeral, Willy's friend Sage got himself a job on a cargo ship, and despite Della's pleas that if ever she needed her husband at her side it was right then, Willy joined him.

Two months after his departure, Della received a phone call.

The reception was poor. Della, it's me. Willy. We made a mistake. You and I both did. We should have never got married. I should have said something, but I knew you really wanted to. So I didn't. Say anything. I'm sorry.

Willy, you must be drunk. Or on drugs or something. Get yourself back here so we can do what we said we'd do. Have kids. Raise a family. Willy? Are you listening to me? There was a silent pause before the line went dead. Della intended to ask him if he'd met someone, but she knew he hadn't. Willy wasn't ready to commit to Della. He wasn't ready to commit to anything.

A week later she received a short letter stuffed with some American money, and that was the last time she heard anything from her husband. Della couldn't remember how long she'd held out hope that Willy would return and they could get back to normal. It may have been months or years. She was completely on her own, not a relative in sight, and depression settled like smog, making time difficult to account for.

Della moved around every few years and had a few acquaintances but no close friends. She was married only in a technical sense but didn't walk around feeling single either. She existed in a confusing purgatorial state that resulted in a shallow social life, and she rarely attended parties of any kind, but it was at one such party, more than nine years after her marriage, where she met up again with Sage Howard. He had grown a mustache but otherwise looked the same, and she told him so. Sage offered no such sentiments when he saw Della after the superseding years, and for good reason. Della had never considered herself beautiful, but for a time a certain grace of form lived within the shadow she cast upon the Earth. Since then she had gained about thirty pounds, and while it wasn't difficult to coax a smile from her, she no longer exuded optimism. She felt like a forty-watt bulb coated with dust. She had worked at a fish processing plant for a while and once overheard some co-workers describe her as dour. Dour

Della, they called her. Della thought she knew what the adjective meant but looked it up when she got to her apartment to make sure. Grim and surly. That's how people saw her. Della worked hard at smiling after that and imagined herself as upbeat and sanguine. She asked herself why she'd let herself go but found no answers, except possibly the notion of hopelessness. Still, wherever Sage had been and whatever doorways had opened and closed over the intervening years, when they finally met again, Sage looked at Della like she was as good as he would ever get.

I just want to get one thing out in the open, Sage said. I know nothing about what's happened to Willy, and at this point I don't care. I don't know where he is. The last time I saw the bastard was in Panama eight years ago. He owes me money. He owes me plenty.

There were only a few suitors pestering Della before Willy came along and not many that weren't drunk after he left, and the emergence of Sage after so many years felt like a blessing or possibly a trick of fate. The two of them never mentioned Willy Hoffner again, and while the party progressed inside, they found seclusion in two hammocks in the backyard. The night was clear, and a sliver of a moon, that looked like a hammock in the sky, shone down on the two of them lounged between the willow trees.

Do you do weed? Sage asked.

Sometimes I do.

Could this be one of those times?

I think it could, Della said.

The two hammocks were about four feet apart so Sage suggested Della settle into his hammock, as it was the larger of the two. Do you think it will hold us both? she asked.

If it doesn't, Sage said, we'll crash to Earth together.

It was a relief that Sage didn't want to discuss the past, only the future. The way he described his vision of the time ahead of him, his confident tone of voice, gave Della the sense that she might be included if it suited her. The weed Sage smoked was the most powerful she'd ever experienced, and she saw more stars out that night than she knew existed. She and Sage giggled like two kids late into a sleepover, and Sage excused himself and went back to the party for something good to eat. That's when Della noticed the smell of him, when he up and left, and while she didn't want to say so out loud, Sage smelled like sage, and she was sifting through whether he had always smelled like sage and that was how he'd got his name, when a sniggering Sage returned with four apple fritters wrapped in a paper towel, and they settled into the hammock again.

Is Sage your real name?

Yeah, why?

Just wondered. I like the name Sage.

Della didn't know the couple that owned the party house, but Sage did. The man let his dog out for a pee, and he bounded out to the hammocks and licked the remnants of apple fitter off their hands. Soon the owner, Bobby, came to the backyard with two beers.

Thought you two would like something to drink, he said.

Thanks, Sage said. What's your dog's name again?

Barker, Bobby said. He's just a pup, can you believe it? He's still growing.

The man didn't have anything more he wanted to say and took his dog inside, and Sage and Della lay there drinking their beer. Too sweet or something, it didn't taste like beer to Della, and halfway through drinking hers, she said, I've got to pee, but I don't want to go in there.

Sage didn't want to go back inside either. He only had one joint left, and he wanted to keep it for the both of them. Pee over there, Sage said. Behind the tree.

It's easy for you being a man. You just pull out your extension cord whenever you need it and you stand on your feet.

You don't stand on your feet when you pee in the house, do you?

No.

Well, then. What's the difference? Just pull off your panties and squat like usual. Come on. We'll pee together.

The two of them peed in earnest and then giggled again. They lay in the large hammock and smoked Sage's last joint. A late summer breeze pushed its way between the houses and trees and gave them reason to snuggle closer together. I like that dog, Sage said.

This has been a good night, Della said. The best I've had in a long time. Their voices grew soft and mellow like they were engineering something that was no one else's business.

Doesn't it feel like a long night, though? Sage said.

It does. I feel like I've been lying in this hammock for the last ten years.

I'd like to go on a road trip, Sage said. Do you want to come on a road trip with me?

Where are you going? I've got to work on Monday.

Las Vegas.

Las Vegas? What will you do in Las Vegas?

I'm getting married.

Married? What do you mean you're getting married?

I'm getting married, that's all. I want to marry you. Della started laughing out of control. She could hardly breathe. You think I'm kidding, don't you? If you don't say yes, I'm going back into that party and I'll find someone else.

But I can't get married. I'm already married. Technically anyway.

Hell, that won't matter. This is Vegas we're talking about. If you've got the money, they've got the show. Maybe I'll marry the damn dog. I'm leaving early. Eight in the morning. You coming or not?

Most of what happened for the rest of the night Della could not fathom. She woke with sore hips in a double bed in a room she didn't recognize, the smell of coffee in the air. A note on the bed read, Shower if you want to. Gone to get supplies for the road. The car is packed.

She got up and looked out the window. A light rain had been falling for some time by the look of it. They would be driving away from the rain. Away from the rain and into something else.

3

HART FERGUSON AND HIS WIFE, Molly, had lived in Fernie for almost twenty years, Molly for forty years because she was born there. Her sister had escaped to Calgary when she graduated from high school, and she lived in the big city now, happily married, or so she said, with two kids and a well-paying job. Molly always thought she too would live in Calgary; in fact, there were days when she still thought she'd like to. She met Hart in Calgary, and when they married, she assumed Calgary would be their home, but when Hart came to meet her family in Fernie, he fell in love with the place: the proximity of the Rocky Mountains, the Elk River, the nearby lakes. Calgary hadn't yet bulldozed its way into the 20th century, but Hart saw it coming. In Fernie a man could wake up in the morning, stare up at the Three Sisters and fill his lungs with freedom.

Molly had a reputation as a know-it-all, and she'd lived in Fernie so long she figured she deserved the title. People moved in and brought with them expectations of where they'd come from, and over time their outlook changed. When they ran into Molly, the change hastened considerably. Molly had married a dreamer, and for the first ten years living in Fernie, Hart would stand outside in all four seasons, his mouth gaping in awe, living the dream. The Fergusons had a boy, and for awhile it cemented them to the community. They lost him soon after he turned eight, and because they had no one in particular to blame for his drowning, Hart and Molly took turns blaming each other or feeling guilty, sometimes both at the same time. They didn't discuss having a second child. Raising a child wasn't like owning a dog. You didn't grab another child and hope it would make things better. A second child would only be a reminder of the one that had got away.

I see the new neighbour moved in today, Hart said.

I noticed. I guess I'd better make a pie and take it over.

I guess you'd better, Hart said.

Hart did his share of talking when selling life insurance. In the past he had talked a lot to his wife, but over the years, he was less inclined to. Most of the words uttered around the house came from Molly, and because he had been out most of the day, he received a play-by-play description of the move next door.

They have a TV, she said. It's a small one though.

I've been telling you for years we ought to get one, Hart said. Even the secretary in our office has a TV. If something happens in the world, you hear about it within the hour instead of the next day. They show movies too. Same ones we see in the theatre downtown. Just later is all.

Molly knew this was the real reason her husband wanted a TV. Four or five times a year, a Western played at the local cinema, and Hart always went. Sometimes twice. Molly figured they'd get a TV of their own eventually, but she was in no rush.

I see they have a little girl with them. The move has been hard on the little girl.

And how do you know that? he asked.

She cries like a fire hydrant. If you stick a sucker in a mouth like that, it generally does the trick. I guess they don't know that.

The next evening Molly took a pie next door. The husband

and the wife and the little girl were inside unpacking, and she heard laughter when she stood at the front door, knocking. It was good to hear laughter in the neighbourhood. She introduced herself and pointed to her husband, Hart, who waved from where he was fixing the lock on their front door. Sage and Della were their names. Different names for sure, especially Sage. Molly wondered, if with a name like Sage, he was all caught up in the Western thing. That was all she needed: a neighbour coming over and encouraging her husband who already thought he was John Wayne. She didn't catch the child's name because soon after she arrived at the door the girl cried. Some kids didn't take well to being moved around like that, Molly thought.

Hart lay on the couch reading a Western novel when Molly got back. He didn't ask for a full report, but he got one. The husband was to start work at the mine, and the wife would mind the child. Molly suggested Hart should drop in some night after supper and ask if they had insurance or not. Hart said, No, he wasn't about to do that. Someday they'll find out I sell insurance, and if they're interested in buying some, they will, he said.

That was the type of man Hart was. Half the town probably didn't have insurance of any kind, and he knew that, but for some reason it didn't bother him. His wife liked to have something to worry about, and she was always going to be better at that than he was. She read the newspaper daily, and once she'd read the catastrophic headlines common to the front page, she consumed the rest of the news with a modest smile on her face.

She's a stocky woman, Molly said. Her name's Della. She wouldn't have trouble staying on course in a north wind. The husband's built like Ichabod Crane. Funny what brings two people together, isn't it?

Hart mumbled something from behind his book. It sounded like agreement and was enough to satisfy Molly. She found she liked going to bed earlier and earlier the older she got, and she was ready for bed now. She liked to be up before anyone else, as if that gave her some kind of privilege on a new day.

Many things that happen to you when you're little will warp you one way or another, but you don't necessarily find out what they were. If raised by mean parents who locked you in your bedroom for months on end until you were ten years old and finally escaped, you could find someone to help and explain what had happened, but parents can get away with almost anything for the first three or four years, and as long as they smarten up after that, no one knows the difference. This applied to the raising of Stacey Emerald Howard since neither Della nor Sage had experience with child-rearing and no parents or relatives lived nearby to offer suggestions. That left the door open for Molly to fill the breach in the advice department.

The next-door neighbour, who Sage early on dubbed Molly the Nose, didn't like the way Stacey's skin broke out in hives every week or ten days. Sage said the rash was just a phase that would pass in time, and Della hoped that was the case, but it wasn't.

Tell Molly the Nose to go piss up a rope, Sage said.

Don't talk that way around the house. Stacey doesn't need to hear that kind of talk.

Then ask me to step outside the next time you want me to talk about Molly the Nose.

Molly the Nose understood persistence, and so it came time to take Stacey to a doctor. Della chose ancient Dr. McMillan, thinking he wouldn't ask questions about someone he would probably never see again. Thick glasses rode part way down his nose, and he couldn't seem to make his mind up, despite years of practice, whether to look through them or over them. He wrote a prescription for a salve of some kind, and despite the letters being large and rudimentary, Della had no idea what he'd written. He said the hives were likely a reaction to something Stacey had been eating. Had anything new been added to her diet, he wanted to know. They had no sound answer to that one nor to the question of whether her shots were up to date. The appointment came at the end of the working day, and Sage had made sure to accompany Della because he didn't trust her to not say something stupid. Let me do the talking, he had said before they went in, then explained to the doctor that Stacey was born during a short stint of living in Ecuador and that while he thought she'd had some shots over the years, they'd lost the records because of a house fire. Then he asked if the shots were free. The whole time he spoke, Della stared earnestly at the black and white tiles between her feet until the doctor looked there too, as if he thought something must have dropped on the floor. While the doctor listened, he may have considered Sage's story a tall tale, but he seemed willing to absorb it regardless of the consequences. He opened a file on Stacey's behalf and made a series of appointments at the local clinic. Stacey never did come down with smallpox or TB, and such diseases didn't stand a chance because she'd been pricked in the arm many times over. Della felt proud that if they handed her a sucker as a diversion, Molly's suggestion, she never cried once getting her shots.

The whole hives-prevention scenario set off other alarm bells for Della and Sage. They had no legal proof that the little girl *was* Stacey Emerald Howard, which meant they couldn't travel out of the country with her in tow, and school was on the horizon. Della got in a flap and refused to leave the house for a few days just thinking of the consequences, but Sage stepped in and began a letter-writing campaign with Vital Statistics in Vancouver. He said he knew how to handle dumb-ass bureaucrats, and eventually a birth certificate materialized, one that laid claim to Stacey Emerald Howard, a document that looked mutilated from the start and after a time went missing.

The hives disappeared once they stopped feeding her peanut butter three or four times a day, and Molly the Nose, satisfied with the result of her intervention, kept herself on alert because she sensed she now lived next door to a family looking for answers.

The Howards owned one car, and Sage needed it every second day to get to work, since he'd found Emery to carpool with, so Della had use of the car often enough to take Stacey places if she wanted to, primarily to the grocery store because she needed cigarettes. Della refused to buy a whole carton at a time in case she decided to quit. She knew how to drive in the snow but didn't like to, so if more than three or four inches fell on the road, they got to town with Della on foot and Stacey in a sled during the winter months, and often the only reason they ventured out was a fading supply of Players Mild. In town, Della kept close watch on mothers tending to their kids in case she discovered what she ought to be doing that she wasn't. On the days when they had a lot of snow but it wasn't that cold, Della dressed Stacey in a jumbo snowsuit and left her out in the yard, where she entertained herself for a couple of hours. A two- or three-year-old could do a lot in a snowbank by herself. Della checked on her from the window once in a while and waved her way, and while Stacey didn't seem thrilled by that part of her day, she did learn to be the kind of person who could spend time alone. Molly the Nose approved of the fresh air but said she needed to be around young kids or delayed language development would result. When Della explained the theory to Sage, he said maybe that was why Barker never learned to bark because they'd lived out in the country that first year, miles from other barking dogs.

Della decided Stacey should watch *Sesame Street* every morning, and Della and Molly the Nose watched it with her. Stacey got up and danced when lower case *n* sat lonely on a mountain top with no wind, or a crew who lived inside capital *I* came out for daily cleaning, and she always stared transfixed when Grover had a hissy fit, while outside the snowflakes continued to fall on top of one another so Della couldn't drive anywhere.

Sage always, and Della sometimes, smoked dope at night. The summer before they found Stacey, Sage wanted to drive all the way to Woodstock, but Della said it was too far to travel. Sage insisted this was a chance of a lifetime and threatened to go by himself, but still Della refused. He told her she was stubborn as a mule, and Della asked when was the last time he'd ridden a mule? When he didn't respond, she told him it was better to be stubborn as a mule than dumb as an ass. Sage never forgave Della, and to make up for not going, he smoked dope nightly and listened to The Who, Creedence Clearwater, Jefferson Airplane and Jimi Hendrix. It wasn't the same, though. People who made it to Woodstock were permanently branded in a way Sage could only dream about.

Della always had cookies around the house, chocolate chip cookies, some made with peanut butter, and lately, some without. The music never bothered Stacey. When she was tired, she went to bed and fell asleep without a care. Marijuana smoke lay thick in the air of the house, but no one factored this into Stacey's compliant behaviour. Sage never had a problem finding enough dope to smoke, and others in Fernie liked to hang around the Howard house on weekends because they knew Sage was always well-supplied. Sage didn't sidle up to people easily but was never happier than on party nights, when all the blemishes of humanity had soft edges and grew tolerable. Most of these people were younger than Sage and Della and didn't have kids of their own, so everyone took turns giving Stacey her a nightly bath, and they brought so many toys and stuffed animals, as compensation for the dope, that soon Chatty Cathy had plenty of friends to talk to in her crowded room. Stacey had memorized everything the doll had to say, and Chatty Cathy had family around her now, willing to listen, but they had to listen carefully because Sgt. *Pepper's Lonely Hearts Club Band* played louder than usual in the room next door.

4

SOME OF THE MEN Sage worked with in the mine liked being there, but he thought that was only because they'd gotten used to it. Some of the jobs appealed to him, too, but the men who owned them had worked twenty years or more for the privilege. Della was against his taking a job there in the first place. She imagined Sage on his hands and knees with a pick and shovel, exposed to noxious gases and coal dust that would graduate to black lung. Only parts of her idea of coal mining were true. Gases floated around, and despite the efforts of safety precautions, coal dust was unavoidable, but with continuous mining, the days of massive crews with picks and shovels had ended. Sage wasn't employed in the act of mining anyway. To begin with, he worked as a labourer on construction and maintenance, keeping the mine safe for those running the machines that did most of the work. He came home dirty and tired every night, but he carpooled with Emery, who had been certified in first aid and spent most of his day at the mine in a clean and climate-friendly office. Emery kept a blanket on the passenger seat of his car for when he drove Sage home. It didn't take much convincing for Sage to consider taking courses on Saturdays so that one day he too could walk out of the mine looking clean.

Had they not found Stacey, it might have only taken a few weeks for Sage to quit the mine and look for something else. He'd done just about every kind of job a man could do over the last fifteen years, and restlessness always sent him looking for another occupation with better pay or better working conditions or something else. But now things had changed. His marriage had flattened out, and he knew it. Now that Stacey lived in the house, Della had come back to life, back to a different version of the woman she had been when Sage had married her. Stacey wasn't his biological daughter, but the roles he and Della worked at were the ones his wife had planned all along, so Sage considered the family matter closed.

Emery played pool better than Sage, but even so, it became a ritual after their Friday shifts to stop at the pub and play a few games and drink a few beers.

Will that be all for you fellas? Selma said, bending over and moving two glasses of beer from her tray to the small table where Sage and Emery sat, pool cues in hand. Emery always sat before the beer arrived. Selma had what Emery described as outstanding knockers, and the tops of them, threatening to rise like the morning sun out and onto the table, came into full view when she bent over. Emery always ordered small glasses of beer so Selma's service to humanity would be as frequent as possible.

We'll run a tab, love, Emery said. He slipped a dollar bill into her bosom. That's just so you'll remember to come back again. Selma retrieved the dollar bill and adjusted the balance of her main attractions before heading back to the bar. Sage's game had been improving of late, and Emery had talked him into considering the weekly afternoon beer a wager. Most times this meant Sage paid for every beer they consumed.

What a man wouldn't do to fall asleep with his head buried between those soft pillows, Emery said. I wouldn't care if I ever woke up again.

Your wife might have something to say about that, Sage said.

I know. I know. I'm just saying. A man should never stop dreaming.

Foremen are assholes, Emery said after Sage told him that no matter what he and the carpenter he worked with did, they could never satisfy Brigsby, the foreman in charge. Being an asshole is the first thing they look for in a foreman. That's why I've got my ticket in first aid. There's no one breathing down my neck, and everything I do comes with some kind of appreciation. A fellow came in a couple of months ago with a finger from his right hand sitting in his left hand. I wrapped it in ice and sent him off the hospital, and they sewed it back on. He came in four or five times after that on his way to work to thank me. I told him it was just part of my job, and he looked at me like I was a god.

I see they hired a woman a few weeks ago, Sage said. First time ever, so I'm told.

She's a looker, Emery said, but you've got to be careful with a woman that wants to work in a place like that. My guess is she's loaded with male hormones and prefers women over men.

But you don't know that.

I'm just saying. They're out to prove something to the world. Mind you, it'll make my day if she's injured down the road. I might not be in such a hurry to send her off for repairs.

Most of the time Sage and Emery talked, the results felt less than satisfactory. Everything Emery said seemed skewed, and Sage couldn't quite own his part of the conversation. When Emery got his mind all wrapped around a topic, his pool playing suffered; Sage was down to one ball but missed, and he stood by and watched Emery put an end to the game. I should get going, Sage said. He felt he had a right to say that because he was driving that day, and Emery never put up an argument so long as he had two beers paid for. Sage handed his friend the money because Emery liked to be the one to pay Selma. Sage stood for a moment at the door and imagined Stacey growing up to be a woman needing work. He wouldn't want her to end up working in the mine. He wouldn't be too fond of her being a barmaid with her tits hanging out, begging for tips, either.

Della had been employed in the past. The longest she had stayed in one job was at a fish-packing plant in Prince Rupert, but that was a long time ago. She wanted the best for Stacey so she didn't argue with Sage's mounting campaign that she find a job. Most of the couples they knew had two jobs, sometimes three. Still, she struggled to contemplate any other life than that of a stay-at-home mom.

Della could only relate to numbers that represented amounts of money she could spend. She had heard about the new math they were teaching in schools but doubted she would like it any better than the old math that paralyzed her growing up. She liked the phrase "new math" because it suggested that the old math, which she had no use for, had been a mistake all along. Following her husband's counsel, she reluctantly applied for and got a job posted at their local Bank of Commerce.

The job would be part-time, which suited Della just fine, but it required a full week of teller training. Molly the Nose offered to look after Stacey while this happened, but it didn't happen for long.

Della lasted halfway into her second day before the manager decided banking and Della weren't compatible. She came home when Molly the Nose and Stacey were halfway through *Sesame Street* and said she hated banking and had quit. Molly the Nose frowned because she had already imagined the new curling iron she planned to buy with her babysitting money. Sage had the family bank account at the Bank of Commerce, but Della insisted he switch to a different bank. She wouldn't walk back in there every month to take money out.

Losing the job opportunity at the bank felt to Della like coming down with a serious virus. She hung around the house for the next week, claiming faintness and no energy. She also found the behaviour of her neighbours disturbing. Hart from next door had been lobbying for weeks to get a TV so he could watch his Westerns, but Molly the Nose had resisted because she thought they were cliché and she didn't want to encourage Hart's fetish. But with Della laid up for a week of employment-failure-recovery, Molly the Nose had to miss her daily fix of *Sesame Street*, and that was the catalyst that caused the Fergusons to finally get a TV bigger than the one the Howards owned. That hastened Della's recovery. A week later she tried another job on for size at a bakery downtown.

Della loved to bake and loved being around the smell of baking, so it was a perfect fit, especially the part where she had to go in early and help stock the glass cases with breads and delectable treats. As a bonus, she brought home bread and Eccles cakes and whatever else hadn't sold during the day.

So long as customers came to the store in an orderly manner and she could deal with them one at a time, everything worked out fine, but once the store filled with three or four people, pointing, asking questions, their kids smearing their hands on the glass cases (which she was somehow supposed to prevent), the job became too stressful, and by the end of her fourth day, before her kind and mostly patient boss could intervene, Della told him she wouldn't be back the next day. Molly the Nose was doubly disappointed because once again her source of babysitting money had disappeared along with the supply of free doughnuts she had come to rely on.

Another week in bed resulted, and twice Sage had to cook dinner. He complained about it and headed to the pub to fill the evening in protest, and Della felt like a complete failure. If Sage hated anything more than a bad thing happening, it was when two or three came one after another, creating an overriding sense that others were waiting in queue. They needed an influx of something that didn't smell of defeat, and he came home late from work with a dog in tow. Sage claimed he brought the dog home to lift Della's spirits, to get her out of bed at least so she could be functional again, but he also missed Barker. The new dog, already four years old, had a name, but Sage decided they should call him Hart. This didn't go over well with Molly the Nose, who felt slighted because whenever they called Hart in from digging in the yard, everyone thought they were calling their next-door neighbour. But Hart the neighbour didn't mind. He liked the name Hart, and sharing it with a dog didn't seem unreasonable.

Hart the dog looked as if he had every breed of dog mixed in him somewhere, and Sage had got him for nothing because one of his co-workers had to give him up when he and his wife had a child. Hart was the colour of Neapolitan ice cream, and if Stacey stood close to him in the summer, his happy tail cooled her off. Hart slept on the linoleum in Stacey's bedroom every night despite Sage laying a dog blanket next to his bed. Della complained about Hart daily in her journal because the dog shed hair everywhere and left slimy dog toys underfoot for her to trip over. Sage just laughed when she said anything. It was like having another kid in the house, he said. They say a dog is man's best friend for a reason, he claimed, and Della said because a man is never around to clean up after them.

Sage stopped pestering Della about getting a job of any kind once he got Hart, almost as if the dog made up for their relative poverty, but a few months later, the dog came down with distemper and wandered off to a nearby pond to die on his own. His disappearance left a discernible emptiness around the house. Della felt it as much as anyone, and while she adored her mothering role, she decided that rather than take a job with a thankless boss serving people who treated her as a slave, she would stay at home and babysit at the same time. Sage thought this was a great idea and said if the money she brought in paid for her cigarettes and his dope and kept the purple car on the road, then they might have a chance to build a future after all. He wanted to celebrate, but they didn't know anyone who might pop in for a few hours to babysit except Molly next door and Sage refused to ask her, so he set off for the pub on foot to celebrate by himself.

And so began a series of surrogate brothers and sisters living at the Howards during the daytime and sometimes overnight during a weekend. Della documented every one of them and devoted two or three pages in her family album to people like Edwin the red-headed baby or Laura the little French girl who wanted to grow up to be an Irish dancer. Pictures of the kids' parents shared space in the album along with pictures of the kids with Stacey at various stages of development. Stacey asked why the pictures in the album didn't go back to when she was little, and Della said because the book that had all of her baby pictures went missing on one of their moves and that was a sad loss, not having a record of all those years, a most sorrowful loss she was still coming to grips with.

Some kids she babysat for a month or two and some over a period of several years. The end of their street became a haven for young kids because Molly the Nose still wanted that curling iron and she started taking in kids in as well. Sage built two swings under a tree in the backyard, and Hart next door put in a teeter-totter and built a playhouse, which looked like a fort from the days of the Wild West. Molly the Nose was okay with the fort but was against war and violence, so all the toy guns had to stay on Howard property, a long way from the fort, which didn't make sense to most of the kids.

Della called these kids her clients. She saw her job as important, as if she were an informal social worker toiling to improve society. She kept notes on anything she considered significant during the day. *11:45. Meghan complained of being hot and feverish. Temperature taken. 100.1. Napped on the outside cot for half an hour (cool cloth on forehead) and seemed fine after.*

Her clients came in two categories. Those who could walk and talk and play, and helpless babies that got served first and took up most of Della's time. Stacey preferred walking, talking clients as she got older, preferably girls her own age, though boys were fine too because they played mostly with the boy toys Della had around the house and were less prone to hogging her favourite dolls and stuffed animals. Tommy was one such boy, and the two of them drank Kool-Aid daily, laced with Fizzies tablets, and went out to the woodshed and had burping contests.

Most burps wins, Tommy said. You go first. Stacey didn't like the taste of the Fizzies tablets because they added a root beer flavour to perfectly good Kool-Aid. She waited until her stomach settled a little so she wouldn't barf all over the woodshed. She managed seven burps, enough that Tommy didn't laugh in her face like he usually did. Tommy popped his Fizzie tablets and downed the Kool-Aid and started his burping saga immediately. Stacey always expected him to get sick, but he never did. Tommy tied his previous record of sixteen burps and looked disappointed when he finished. This common ritual amused them for most of one summer, but then Della couldn't buy Fizzies anymore because it turned out they were bad for you, according to someone.

Stacey knew there had to be something she could do better than Tommy, and one day when they were helping Della make lunch, she discovered her talent. Just a whiff of onion, and tears streamed down her face, and so began another daily challenge where the two of them went to the woodshed and cut an onion in half to see who could cry the most. Tommy didn't take to Stacey's idea easily, and when he couldn't match her river-on-demand tear production, he decided they should see who could hold an onion under their nose and cry the least. I don't see why we have to change the rules, Stacey said, but went along with it anyway. Still, she could only compete if she followed Molly the Nose's recommendation and surreptitiously started off with lemon juice dabbed around her mouth and nose and a piece of bread hidden under her tongue.

Birthdays were a big deal for anyone in Della's flock. She baked a cake, even if the kid was too young to eat any of it. She went all out: presents, goody bags, balloons. She tried to impress the parents more than anything, but she disguised it well. Stacey's birthday, deliberated upon soon after they got her, was September 7th. They'd missed her first two birthdays, they guessed. Stacey's birthday presents every year came from a specific category. Sage always bought something she could play with, and Della gave her store-bought clothes to wear. Sage bought her a series of tricycles sized to fit her growth spurts but scabby in places, though one year he went all out and Stacey woke to a new tricycle and, sitting on the seat, a blue-eyed Stacey Doll with long red hair dressed in a provocative blue and pink party dress that looked more like a negligee. Stacey held the doll in her hands but didn't know what to make of it and neither did Della. Sage explained that the doll had a bendable waist, legs and arms and came with real eyelashes. She's the real deal, he said.

As time passed, they marked Stacey's growth on the door frame leading into the kitchen, and with every passing year, Della's journals reflected hope and contentment and a sense that life was as it should be. Life as a surrogate mom in various extensions matched Della's employment needs perfectly, so that she felt content and satisfied, but as the precious years melted into the past, Sage could not say the same.

5

ONE THING GUARANTEED to send Sage into a rage was seeing
a bunch of men in suits and ties standing around the jobsite
discussing esoteric bullshit like market value, safety, govern-
ment regulations or whatever else they thought was so damn
important. Most of these men, he knew, had never worked a
blue-collar job in their life and never would. Last week he'd
watched three of them get a tour of the mine, an escorting of
Japanese businessmen similarly attired: blue suits, yellow ties
and the mandatory white hard hat in case, God forbid, something landed on their head to disturb the intellect deemed
so vital to the operation. This week management toured two
men and a woman, and added together, the three didn't look
as old as Sage. He understood the company had important
decisions to make in the name of profit, but once the coal was
located, the means to extract it determined, the method of
transporting it to the hungry freighters waiting at the coal port
in Delta decided and the price set, then what else was there?
What important job did they fulfill on a daily basis while those
who toiled at the mine showed up like sheep day after day?
He wondered how they filled their time and imagined most of
them had a flask of something in their desk drawers, something

that would keep their system moving when things went quiet. Some of the suits that floated around the mine held degrees, he understood that, but many did not. Some had worked their way into their positions of privilege by one means or another, and when Sage asked himself if he would relish the opportunity to do the same, he had to say yes.

The jobs Sage dreamt of having he didn't completely understand, and he wasn't convinced they suited him or, deep down, if he even wanted them for what they were; he thought he might only want what he didn't have. The road to personal disenchantment he'd been down many times in the past: a road well-worn and in need of repaving.

It was a Friday, and Emery's turn to drive, but for some concocted reason, Emery didn't want to stop for a beer and play pool and stare at Selma's tits, so Emery dropped him off and entered the pub alone. Last week he'd beaten Emery two out of three, and this week there'd be no pool playing. Emery was wily that way, but Sage didn't feel like playing pool anyway; he was content to sit and brood on uncertainty. If management got together at the end of the week for a drink, he had no idea where they went, but he never saw them at the pub. They must be huddled together someplace in town with better things to talk about than mining.

Sage sat alone finishing his second beer. A man he'd never seen before sat a few feet away, also alone. Selma came to the man's table and asked if he wanted a refill, but the man said no and threw a ten dollar bill on the table. Selma dug into her pouch for change, and the man said to forget it, then as she thanked him and turned toward the bar, the man grabbed her and pulled her onto his lap. A large tip must be worth something, he said, and Selma tried to get up, but the man held his hands, as if in prayer, around her hips.

Sage finished the last of his beer and stood up. The man was in no hurry to let her go. Sage walked over to his table. Hands off her, he said. Selma squirmed for her release, and her elbow caught the man on his jaw.

You stupid bitch, the man yelled.

It's time for you to go home, Sage said. The man set the waitress free and looked at Sage, trying to calculate his odds, then he got up, waving his arms over his head like the world had gone crazy, and walked outside.

Thanks, Selma said.

Sage went to the washroom before leaving, but when he got outside, the man was waiting at the corner of the building and jumped him from behind. Sage hit the pavement hard, and a sharp pain bolted down the back of his neck. The man kicked him once in the ribs and then ran off down the street.

No one else was in the parking lot. Sage didn't get up because he'd never experienced such sharp pain before. He rolled onto his back and lay there until a car pulled into the parking lot and almost ran him over. Two young men got out and walked over to where he lay prone on the pavement. Hey, bud. You okay down there?

Yeah, Sage said. I'm perfectly fine.

The two men helped him up, and Sage thanked them. He hobbled out to the road that would take him home.

Della had dinner ready when Sage walked in the door. I guess that was good timing, she said. Franky's parents picked him up late, and I just finished cooking.

After years of practice, she had become fluent in deciphering her husband's moods. Despite her best attempt at a cordial welcome, she sensed something out of balance.

Fuck, Sage said. He grabbed a beer from the fridge.

What's *your* problem? Della said. Sage said fuck one more time and went into the living room. Hey, mister. You might have had a rough day, but that doesn't mean you can wear your boots all over the house.

Sage stood in front of the TV. Stacey sat watching a nature show about how beavers build their dams. He changed the channel until he found the news. What's the matter with you? Della said. She was watching a show and minding her own business.

I want to watch the news, Sage said.

You want to watch the news, so you just come in here and change the channel. God wouldn't change the channel without asking. Put her program back on.

Stacey grabbed the blanket layered on the back of the couch and wrapped herself into a tight ball, watching. Sage didn't move. Nobody moved. The pain in Sage's neck had softened on his way home, but now it was building again. He lunged at the TV with the heel of his boot, sending it skittering sideways. The channel tuner spun around on top of the TV, twirling there like some kind of magic trick, then the TV emitted a smoky vapour out the back. Stacey cried.

What the hell's gotten into you? Della went to Sage, who seemed frozen to the linoleum. Did you hear me? How could you do something so stupid? That's the family TV you just ruined. Della pushed Sage on the shoulder to get him to turn around. To say something. The pain shot up his neck, and his head throbbed again. He turned around and grabbed Della by the hair and threw her across the room, where she lost her balance and landed on the couch on top of Stacey.

Sage didn't turn to see if he'd hurt anyone. He returned to the kitchen and grabbed his coat from the back pantry. This time of year, it got cold soon after the sun went down, and he had no idea how long he would be away.

6

MOLLY THE NOSE DECIDED ON A WHIM to visit her sister living in Calgary, and she suggested Della and Stacey go with her to visit for three days. You can't keep a kid in a small town forever, she warned. If you do, they'll grow up thinking that's all there is. Most of the young people in this town move away as soon as they can. It's their only hope.

Della could see her point. She told all her babysitting parents ahead of time she would not be available on Friday, and that would give her a three-day weekend of escape. She felt guilty explaining things because she'd never taken a day off, except for weekends, in three years of babysitting. But Stacey was starting kindergarten in the fall, and she'd heard about Calgary. Someone told her the city was almost as big as New York, and she hoped they could go to the zoo.

Molly the Nose didn't drive at all, so that meant Della needed the car. Sage suggested they take the bus, but Molly the Nose said the bus took forever and would cut into their trip. Why isn't Daddy coming? Stacey asked, and Della told her this was a girls' weekend away and men weren't invited. It's good for men to be alone occasionally, she said. They take things for granted otherwise.

Della needed a break from everything around the house,

Sage in particular. It took months, but they finally got a new TV, ordered from Sears and delivered as a peace offering meant to sweep away the past transgressions for good. Drive carefully on that highway, Sage said, handing her the keys. Some maniacs out there don't give a damn. And check the oil as soon as you get there. It burns a little oil. He opened the hood and showed her where to find the dipstick. Della watched with mild interest. She would get a gas jockey to check the oil once she got to Calgary.

Della dropped Sage at work and left in the morning light on an adventure that, now she was on it, felt long overdue. She left two frozen dinners in the freezer and reminded him that Saturday was vacuuming day if he didn't have plans.

After a year of studying, Sage had earned the right to be a first aid attendant at the mine, and he had worked shift work and weekends for the last few months, but with Emery on holidays for the next two weeks, Sage had his day shift. When he got home on Friday, he showered and sat in front of the TV to eat supper. The TV was bigger than their last one, but somehow the colour didn't look as good. He had a beer to wash things down and smoked dope and sat by himself to do some thinking. Nothing interesting came to mind, so after nine he walked to the pub, thinking maybe some of his co-workers would still be there. Most of the fellas at work went hunting and fishing. Fishing he might like. It would be better than shooting something, and he didn't fancy being a man who owned a gun. He might run into someone who would show him the ropes, and sure enough he ran into Bart Sanderson, the accountant at the mine, and listened to fishing stories pour out of the man's mouth one after another until none of them seemed plausible. Landing a twenty-inch Cutthroat or a thirty-inch Bull Trout with a dry fly is better than sex any day, he said. Sage heard Bart was married for a few years, but he wasn't anymore. Maybe for him the sentiment had some truth.

Before he knew it, no one else sat at the bar, and the bartender had cashed out and gone home. You're a late-nighter, Selma said. She busied herself scrubbing the bar and loading the huge dishwasher. Here, she said. It's too late to legally sell you any beer, but this one's on the house. She passed him a beer and leaned against the bar, her head in her hands, and stared into his face.

Thank you, Sage said. I won't keep you. You have to make your way home.

You don't have to worry about me. I live close by. She pulled up some chairs and turned them upside down on the tables so Sage got up to help. You're a real gentleman. You know that? Not like most of the people that hang around here.

I don't know much about you, he said. About your past I mean.

You a man who likes to hear good news stories or bad news stories?

Good news, I guess.

Well that settles it then. You don't want to hear anything about Selma Divjak.

Once the chairs were off the floor, Selma emptied her tip jar onto the bar, then added it up and put half into an envelope and slid it under the cash drawer of the till. That's the bartender's half, she said. He trusts me to divide it equally. Most of the time I do.

You live close by?

Sure do. I live upstairs. Come on, I'll show you.

Sage finished his beer, and Selma put his glass in the dishwasher and started the machine. She checked the back door, and at the main door, she turned off the lights except for one that cast a blue tinge over the bar and made it look more welcoming somehow. It smelled like a bar, but it looked like heaven.

They walked around to the back of the building and up a set of stairs. Sage had seen the stairs before but hadn't thought at all about where they led. When they got to the top of the stairs, Selma leaned against the door with her shoulder and he followed her inside.

You don't lock up?

The lock doesn't work. Most people assume the door is locked, so I don't worry about it.

It's cozy the way you've got it. Sage didn't know what else to say about the old couch covered with a grey blanket and cushions all over the floor. He'd never seen so many cushions in one place except maybe at a store that sold cushions. A small white fridge and stove squatted on either side of the sink, and only a ratty poster of JFK hung on the wall. He couldn't see the bedroom from where he stood, but if she owned a TV or radio, that had to be where she kept them. He noticed that all the dishes were washed and sitting in the drainboard, ready to be put away.

This place could use a few windows, he said.

They don't charge much for an apartment with only one window, she said. I never drink on the job, but I treat myself to a nightcap before I go to bed. Care to join me?

Sage said he thought that would be all right. She never asked him what he wanted or gave him a choice of drinks, but she turned away from him and leaned over the sink and pulled two clean glasses from the cupboard, even though similar ones rested on the drainboard ready to go. Sage walked up behind her and put his hands on her shoulders. She turned to face him. I want you to start at the top and work your way down, she said. I want you to take your time.

7

EARLY SUMMER, HOTTER THAN USUAL, and with only one child to babysit, Molly the Nose decided it would be a fine day to walk to the corner store for an ice-cream cone. She invited Della, but she declined. Della had Stacey and Tommy to contend with but also a one-year-old baby who needed a nap in the middle of the afternoon. Stacey and Tommy felt ripped off. Della said she had a headache and lay down beside the day crib in the hottest part of the afternoon.

Stacey and Tommy busied themselves building irrigation ditches in the backyard. Tommy was five, and Stacey wouldn't be four much longer. In parts of the garden where nothing had been planted, they dug a trench and fed the garden hose into the channel. When filled with water, it looked just like an irrigation project they'd seen on TV the week before. They left the hose running because they wanted to see if a natural lake would form.

In no time at all, I think we'll have a big lake out here. What do you think? Stacey didn't offer a response. She stared at the grass.

They had nothing to do until the flow of water proved them right or wrong, so they climbed through the fence to the backyard belonging to Molly the Nose and Hart Ferguson. Tommy figured if they were there when Molly the Nose returned, they might get a lick of ice cream, a bite if they were lucky. Maybe she would even bring two extra ice-cream cones back with her.

You kids looking for someone to play with? Is that it? Hart had come onto the back porch and found them wandering around, looking lost. Molly's not home yet. Come on in, and I'll get you some lemonade made this morning.

I've never been inside their house before, Stacey whispered into Tommy's ear. I don't think we should go.

Don't be stupid, Tommy said. He's got lemonade.

Hart told them to sit themselves down at the table. He poured the lemonade into two glasses and put a plate on the table that held two cookies, making Stacey glad they'd accepted.

Won't be long before you two head off to school, Hart said.

Tommy already goes to kindergarten in the mornings. I'm going next year, and I can read already.

You cannot, Tommy said.

I can read some.

They munched on their cookies and looked around the kitchen. The grey Arborite table matched the grey walls. The floor was black tile, and the ceiling was shiny white. Stacey liked her own kitchen better.

You kids might be interested in some of my collections, Hart said. Stacey and Tommy exchanged glances but remained silent. Hart stood up and walked to the side of the house, and they both followed. Guns are my favourite thing in the world. I don't shoot nothing with them. I just like the idea of them. I don't keep a lot of guns, but the ones I own are important. Here, take a hold of this revolver. Stacey took a step back, and Tommy hesitated. Don't be afraid. There're no bullets for it anyway. That there is a Remington from 1875. If you haven't heard of Jesse James you will someday. Wild outlaws the James gang. Jesse's older brother, Frank James, this is the gun he used. Took only one bullet at time is all. Heavier than you'd think, isn't it?

Tommy aimed the gun against the wall with both hands and pulled the trigger. Stacey took the gun in her hands then passed it back to Hart.

They call this here rifle a Winchester. They call it the gun that won the West. I don't have bullets for it either, but it's capable of shooting off seventeen rounds at a time. Makes sense it won the West, when you think about it. You've heard of the Battle of the Little Bighorn haven't you? Well, maybe not. Anyway, the Indians won that one because the army only had single-shot rifles and the Indians had all sorts of guns, including ones like this that could shoot over and over. Success in war is about technology and always has been. Look over here. This case has genuine Indian arrowheads found out on the Plains. They knew how to put poison on the end so the animals they hit tightened up and couldn't run away.

Stacey and Tommy followed Hart's voice around the room. He showed them what he claimed was a genuine Indian tomahawk, though it looked hardly used, and a single spur once worn by Bill Miner, the gentleman train robber. Tommy found the tour more interesting than Stacey did. She figured even if Molly the Nose brought back extra ice-cream cones, they would have melted by now.

Hart showed them a chair he had made with a saddle in the big bedroom then told them to take a seat on the couch because in fifteen minutes the movie *High Noon* would be on channel 2. He got them each another cookie and more lemonade to pass the time while they waited.

What are you three doing in here? Molly the Nose yelled.

We're about to watch a movie, Hart said.

Don't you know Della has been having a conniption? She walked the baby in the stroller all the way to the store and back looking for these two. Molly the Nose went to the front door. Della, they're in here. They're watching TV with Hart. Without being asked, Stacey and Tommy got up and walked out to the front porch to join Della.

Hart sat on the couch looking confused. Come back once you're both in school, he said. I'll teach you how to make a bow and arrow.

Della didn't say a word until they got back inside their own house. How many times have I told you it's this house or the yard?

We're sorry.

Sorry? I nearly had a fit. Here, play with the baby on the couch. I need a drink of water.

Stacey and Tommy put the baby between them and took turns making cooing noises. The yelling bewildered the baby, her eyes darting back and forth between them. Della returned with a cigarette in hand.

What were you two doing over there?

We just went to play for a minute. And to see if there might be ice cream from the store. We didn't stay long. Hart was nice to us. He gave us cookies and lemonade and let us hold his guns.

His guns? He let you hold his guns?

They're heavier than you'd think, Stacey said, trying to make it sound like an informative trip. Tommy pulled the trigger, but I didn't. I just held it.

Never again. You hear me? Never again. Now go out in the backyard. You've got an hour before Tommy's mother gets here.

With visiting Hart next door, they'd forgotten about the hose and the irrigation. It hadn't formed a lake like they'd thought it might. Instead, every inch of the garden was soaked, and some of the plants were floating in puddles. Stacey ran and shut the water off.

I hope it dries out before they see it. My dad can get mad sometimes.

You worry too much, Tommy said. It sure is a lot of water out there. It's like a real irrigation ditch. As soon as you start school,

I want to go back there because that guy says he'll help us make our own bow and arrow. Stacey stared at a radish floating in the irrigation project and covered in mud. That was the problem with vegetables. They grew in dirt and came out dirty and needed to be thoroughly cleaned. She liked apples and plums better. They showered when it rained and were ready to serve when you picked them. She picked the radish up and pushed it back into the muddy dirt so it almost looked like a normal radish.

With a house full of kids weekdays, Della found it hard to keep her home as she liked. She was in survival mode most of the time. Her last client wasn't picked up until 5:30, and then she had supper to worry about. Most Saturdays started off with what Della called getting the house shipshape. Sage helped if he was around, but most of the time, he had something like an oil change or a tune-up scheduled for Saturdays. That left Stacey at home to help with cleaning the house. She could watch cartoons between nine and ten and then had to help put the house in order.

Stacey didn't mind Saturdays so much. She liked things in order. Sage had built her two long shelves that ran along one wall of her bedroom. One for books and one for stuffed animals. Because Della knew she wouldn't get an argument from her about cleaning her room, she assigned her vacuuming and dusting the living room, and then she got to tend to her own affairs. So that was how Della and Stacey passed a Saturday with light snow falling outside. It was still early winter, and like every year, the snow began like a rumour that might or might not stay, a rumour eventually confirmed. It didn't matter to Stacey. She didn't start school until next year, and if she wanted to play in the snow, she only had to open the door any time she wanted for the next four months.

Sage, why do you keep leaving your coat on the back of a chair when you come home? We have hooks in the porch for coats.

Sage had something on his mind and wasn't in the mood to fight; instead, he accepted Della's comment and returned his coat to the rack that sat beside the back door.

We've owned that car for what? Six or seven years now?

How would I know? Della said. We bought it four years before we had Stacey is all I know.

That makes it eight years then. Arnie down at the garage says it will burn oil worse and worse unless we rebuild the head. I'm wondering if it's worth it. Caught up in that important decision, he forgot to take his boots off until he'd already walked halfway across the kitchen floor. He went back to the porch to take them off but not before Della came into the room.

Look at that, she said. We can't even have a clean house for two days a week. Why can't you be as neat and tidy as your daughter?

Stacey?

Do we have another daughter?

Since when is she Miss neat and tidy?

Well, if you were around more on Saturdays, you'd see what she can do for someone her age. She doesn't complain about it either. She's outright finicky. The other day one of her stuffed animals had fallen on the floor, so I went to put it back again and noticed she has them all in order, shortest to tallest. Her books are the same way too.

Sage got up from his chair in the kitchen and went to her bedroom door. Well I'll be damned, he said. Where is she?

Next door. I made a batch of cookies, and she took some over to Molly and Hart.

Since when are we cooking for those two?

You know, Sage, you should look around and be thankful for the friends and neighbours we have in this town. Molly has always been there for us whenever we need her. She's invited me to go to church with her tomorrow, and I'm going. You can come with us if you want.

No thanks. Hart doesn't go to church, does he?

No. But that doesn't mean you can't. Come here. I want to show you something. Della walked into Stacey's bedroom and took the second-largest stuffed animal and moved it about half-way down the pecking order. You watch, she said. Before bedtime she'll have them all lined up again.

She had a choice, on Sunday, to attend church with her mother and Molly the Nose or go for walk to the river with Sage. Her dad told her once that Jesus Christ didn't have a sense of humour. Sage liked to watch the snowflakes fall into the river. She chose the river.

Not much presented itself in Della's closet as formal, so if she liked going to church, she would have to look around the secondhand stores for something else to wear because if you met the same people in the same place once a week, you couldn't wear the same thing forever. Molly's friend, Rose Schultz, picked them up at 9:30. By then the snowfall had let up.

I feel good about today, Molly said. I've wanted to invite you to give our church a try for the last two years, and I finally got around to it. Knox United doesn't have a huge congregation, but it's peaceful.

I know little about the United Church, Della confessed. I went to a few Catholic services with my mother when I was much younger. Easter and Christmas normally.

Well, Molly said, think of it as somewhat similar to the Catholic Church but with less fanfare. No rosary beads and no fish on Fridays.

No fish on Fridays, Rose said. That's a good one. Della could see why Molly liked Rose because Rose found anything Molly said funny or interesting.

Knox United was huge compared to any church Della had ever set foot in. The windows along the side let in the glare of winter light that reflected off the newly fallen snow. The worn sheen to the pews and the elegance of the pulpit reflected a more prosperous time in the history of the town. And the smell. Every church Della had ever entered had what she assumed was a church smell, and Knox United was no exception. She now thought of it as the smell of sin, the result of decades of church attendance by those who walked in with their sins and left them behind when the service ended.

Molly insisted they get there early and sit close to the front. The church appeared to hold at least a hundred and fifty church-goers, and yet when the minister, who hadn't been identified by Molly or Rose, got up to the front to welcome the congregation, no more than twenty-five parishioners sat before him. And with the church only slightly warmer than the outside world, many kept their coats on. Della wondered if the church was ever full. At Christmas perhaps. Or for a wedding. She didn't ask because she knew the question would sound like a slight to Molly the Nose.

The minister had a resonant voice that made everything he said sound truthful. He talked about God and salvation and how winter was a time for internal contemplation. He led three or four hymns, but with so few trying to keep up with the organ, the result was faltering. Toward the end, all but two of the attendees, Della and a young girl who sat at the end of her pew, rose to accept communion. Entering a church was a big enough step, and Della didn't feel the need to consume a Christian vitamin her first day.

The minister stood on the landing at the front of the church as they departed. It took time to leave because he had a brief conversation with each of his regulars. Molly introduced Della, explaining her newness to the community, and the minister held her hand in his hands and looked into her eyes and welcomed her with such deep earnestness that Della felt compelled to return the following week. Out on the street, where the snow fell more deliberately than before, the people looked vulnerable, like field mice out in the open, while inside there had been a sense of comfort and safety that Della still carried with her.

Rose Shultz only lived a block and half from the church, but because of the soft snow on the ground, they drove to Rose's for tea after church. Our ritual, Molly said. Do you mind? I'd love to sit and have a cup of tea, Della said. I don't get out much.

Once Rose had seated them in the wallpapered dining room, she brought out an ashtray for Della. I don't smoke, she said, but my understanding is you do. So far, Della liked this Sunday ritual. It beat watching snowflakes fall into the river. It beat a lot of other things she could think about too.

8

TOMMY'S PARENTS HAD A MEDICAL EMERGENCY in their family that meant they had to drive to Calgary, and since Della had taken a Friday off earlier in the year, Tommy's parents asked for the sleepover in a way that suggested Della couldn't say no. The house the Howards lived in had only two bedrooms and a smaller spare room with no bed, so Tommy would have to sleep in the same bed as Stacey for the night. Everyone agreed that would be okay. Woohoo, Stacey said in response. Tommy, who she fought with half the time Della babysat him and played with heartily the other half, would be the first friend to sleep overnight at her house.

When Tommy's parents dropped him off early Saturday afternoon, the day was clear and crisp after two days of snow. Della didn't feel right about assigning housekeeping duties with Tommy there, so she told them they could watch an afternoon movie on TV but that they needed fresh outside air for two hours first. The two of them busied themselves building an igloo and forgot about coming in for the movie.

If we build it right, maybe we could stay out here overnight, Tommy said. Eskimos live up north in igloos, and they sleep in them and everything.

It would be cold, don't you think? And it would be so dark out at night, how could you read when you went to bed?

I guess they read in the daytime, Tommy said. Or they must have lanterns that burn blubber.

A crust had formed on the top of the snow, but the snow underneath was wet enough they could roll balls a foot in diameter, shave them off to approximate squares, then lift them into place along the four walls. They only stopped once for hot chocolate, and by dark they had four walls built as tall as Stacey, but they hadn't thought to make a doorway into the house. They turned the porch light on and worked a while longer, but they couldn't lift the heavy snow above their heads.

Why don't we use some of the fresh snow in your front yard? It's like new.

I like to leave the front yard that way. Right now it's even on both sides of the sidewalk. When Dad gets home, we'll get him to help. He's strong enough to help us build it higher. But what can we do about the roof?

I don't know. They must have used boards or something. Do you have any boards lying around?

They looked behind the garage and found some one-inch boards under the eave, out of the snow. Soon they had a small igloo with boards stretching overhead from wall to wall. We'll get your dad to help us finish, Tommy said. By the time we're done, no one will know the difference.

Behind the Howards lived the only neighbours they didn't know well. A broken-down wooden fence separated the two yards, and they often heard yelling and swearing coming from the house. Molly the Nose said the Browns lived there, or some of them. Mr. and Mrs. Brown hadn't decided whether they should live together, she said, and every time Mr. Brown came back, it lasted for a day or two until more yelling and swearing left only Mrs. Brown to look after the two sons, twins, either fourteen or fifteen. Molly said that even though they were twins, they had been born in different years. One before midnight and one after. Della didn't know what to think about that, but she had heard a big blow-up the previous fall and had brought Stacey in from the backyard and told her she could watch whatever was on TV. Molly the Nose didn't know the twins' names, but she thought they both began with D.

In the afternoon, the twins stood at the fence, watching. They asked what Tommy and Stacey were building, and Tommy told them it was an igloo. Then an hour later, the two boys hid behind the part of the fence still standing and threw snowballs at them while they worked.

Stacey told Tommy some D-twins stories she knew and called them disgusting. Tommy said Eskimos had enemies too, and once they got their igloo finished, they wouldn't have to worry about them anymore.

Sage had covered for someone at work and didn't get home until late, but Della had dinner ready when he finally got in. The whole time they ate, Stacey and Tommy pleaded with him to go back out and help finish the igloo, but Sage had numerous excuses, such as it's dark out there now, I'm too full to build an igloo and I'm dead tired from working all day. Stacey knew her dad didn't work on Saturdays but said nothing because she hoped to appeal to his sunny side if she could find it. The debate got them nowhere, and Della suggested Sage could help them in the morning when she went to church. Tommy thought that would be all right, but Stacey wasn't satisfied. This was no way to treat a guest, she said. Della said she would make them another hot chocolate and they could each take a piece of chocolate cake and eat out by the unfinished igloo for half an hour before a bath and bed. Tommy thought this would be a great adventure and took charge of carrying a tray with the cake and hot chocolate, and

Stacey had a flashlight so they could see what they were eating. That should have been a perfect ending to an almost perfect day, except that when they got out to the backyard they found their igloo trampled to the ground. The boards lay akimbo, and none of the remaining walls stood more than a foot high.

Wow, Tommy said, as he'd never experienced such destruction. Stacey cried and Della and Sage came out to the backyard.

It's the D-twins, Stacey said. They were watching us and throwing snowballs at us all day. They're the only ones who knew what we were doing.

Della gave Stacey a hug and patted the toque on Tommy's head. You'll have to go over there, Della said, meaning Sage. If that woman doesn't know how to raise kids, someone's gotta tell her. They worked hard to build this and now look. If you don't go over there, I will.

I'll go, Sage said. I'll see what's up. We didn't see them, that's the problem.

Della took them both inside and let them eat their cake and watch the second half of *Bridget Loves Bernie* while Sage followed signs of foot traffic in the snow between the fence and his backyard. He went through one gap in the sagging fence and up to the back door of the Browns' house, where every light they owned seemed to be on, and even from the back porch, he could smell cooking grease. He knocked on the door and one of the boys answered. Is your mother in? I need to talk to her. The boy looked sideways at Sage, as if the request were unreasonable in some way or had never before been made.

Mom, a man wants to talk to you about something.

Sage heard broken glass and some cussing, and then Mrs. Brown appeared at the back door. She looked dressed up as if she might be going out somewhere. It's you, she said. What do *you* want?

The kids built an igloo in the backyard this afternoon, and

while we were eating supper, someone came over and trashed it. I'm wondering if your two boys know anything about it.

Are you accusing them of something? she said.

No, I'm just wondering if they know anything about it. The kids are heartbroken.

Donny! Dickey! Get your asses out here this minute. Mrs. Brown glared at Sage while they both waited. Sage jammed his hands into his coat pockets. Do you two know anything about smashing an igloo over at this man's house? Both boys said they knew nothing about it, then stood there staring at Sage as if his allegation was preposterous. He wondered how two kids that came from the home they did could learn such confidence.

I thought they might, Sage said. We had fresh snow yesterday, and footprints go between the broken fence and the igloo.

Look Mister, both my kids said they don't know a thing about it. End of story. Sage didn't know what else he could say. Mrs. Brown turned and waved the two boys back into the house, and then she pulled the door behind her and stood out on the back porch facing him. She wrapped her arms around herself to brace against the cold.

Look, Sage said. You can see the snow trampled down the middle of the backyard. Of course I didn't see them smash the igloo, but it seems obvious by the footsteps.

Footsteps? You want to talk about footsteps? I know a few people in this town. I've lived here a long time. Some people I know have been watching your footsteps on Sundays. Up the stairs at the back of the pub. If you're so concerned about where people are walking, Mister, you might consider where your footsteps have been lately. She turned away from Sage and closed the back door between them.

What happened? Della wanted to know. Stacey lay curled up on the couch, a pillow under her head. Sage could hear water running in the bathroom.

She said her boys know nothing about it. I'm sure it was them, but we have no proof. Why isn't Stacey having her bath?

Because Tommy's in there having his bath. When he's done and in his pyjamas, it will be her turn.

I don't see why they couldn't share the same bath.

A year ago, they wouldn't have known the difference, Della said. This is what happens when kids get older.

9

SAGE KNEW HE HAD HOLES in his moral fiber. He always felt dissatisfied and could never stick with one thing. Going somewhere, climbing the proverbial ladder all the way to the top, that was something he could only dream about. He tried to settle, but as soon as he recognized a comfortable balance, he was overcome by a craving as familiar to him as a next-door neighbour. Now, in his mid-forties, it was happening again. He hated his job, and he wanted a change. You had to be a certain person, like Emery, to be a good first aid man. Emery could embrace tragedy and then pretend it hadn't happened. You had to have the ability to be on guard and yet live as though you were a normal person.

He'd had a job with a paving company in Vancouver that he didn't mind for a while. He had started out on the end of a shovel and eventually had run the roller that did the finishing off. His boss liked him a lot, a man who promoted him to running the roller because he didn't turn up hungover most days. But then the owner made a decision. To play with the big boys, he would need to invest in new equipment and risk contracts not showing up to pay it off. So he sold out and went small. Driveways in the metro area, something the owner and his brother could handle by themselves. But he knew people in Fernie, which was why Sage had ended up there.

But it wasn't just the job. Sage was addicted to restlessness, a man who followed a crooked path and didn't know what to do about it. Every time something changed in his life, he felt excited. But the excitement didn't last long. A few days maybe. Then after a time, months sometimes, tension built, and he wanted a bigger world. He felt no different from someone addicted to cigarettes. After a time, you get what you want, or you're filled with anxiety because you don't.

Della was as good a wife as any man could expect. She thought of important things before he did. She beamed in her role as a mother, and Della was the only woman he loved. He wasn't sure he could have made that claim the day he married her, but he loved her now the only way he knew how.

After that first night Sage visited Selma in her small apartment above the pub, nothing happened for a long time. He wasn't the type to hang out at the bar for hours on end. Not a man who closed the bar down. Maybe when he was younger, but he had no desire to drink himself silly in middle age. Then Stacey went to church with Della. They had a small Sunday school class Stacey went to while Della took in the service. Stacey didn't like the class much, but she often went with her mother to the church service itself. She liked the sound of the organ and the tidiness of the church, and she particularly liked it when she and Della had a pew to themselves.

Sage had no interest in attending church. He said he would rather go for a walk along the river, which he did the first Sunday they were both at church. Then the following week, he visited Selma again. She slept in everyday of the week, and he woke her on Sunday just after nine. Her smell drew him in. The taste of her. He didn't know Selma's exact age, but she was much younger than he was, and he wondered if he'd forgotten what younger women smelled and tasted like. He never stayed long Sunday mornings, and she didn't want him to. If he didn't show up, she never mentioned his absence, but every time he arrived, she welcomed him.

Feelings stormed through him as he walked through the town now. He wanted to punch and hurt someone, an enemy of some kind, but Sage didn't have an enemy. He wanted the people around him to stare at him, incredulous that he would loiter downtown without purpose, but nobody noticed him. He wanted to sit by the side of the river and drink a bottle of whiskey until he didn't know where he sat. When he stood in one spot and watched the people filled with expectation coming and going, smiling, chatting, kicking an empty pop can down the snow-scraped street, it made him feel like crying. He knew he needed help, but he didn't know where to turn.

If someone like Mrs. Brown knew who he'd become, she might not be the only one. For most of the morning, he'd rebuilt an igloo, and then Della had come home from church and he couldn't face her. She seemed happier than usual. Maybe the sermon had suited her, or maybe she was glad because he'd helped the kids like he said he would. He tried not to think of Selma, if even for a full minute, but found it hard to do. When he thought of Selma, the image of Mrs. Brown's indignant face and orange lipstick took over unless he looked at something specific and thought about the thing he looked at. That's why he had told Della he needed a walk to clear his head.

He walked past the florist and then stopped and turned around. A large brown dog passed him in a hurry without looking up. The dog didn't look hungry, just intent on where he was heading. Even the dogs in this town know where they're going, he thought. The sun was out, and the flower shop had filled with light and colour, a store long and narrow and smelling like a summer day. The woman behind the counter was older, possibly the owner willing to work on Sunday. Something about the store, the smell of it and the woman behind the counter, made Sage not want to leave and get back on the street.

How much is that bunch over there? he asked.

Those are lovely, aren't they? I'm afraid you've got good taste. That's the last grouping like that in the store. It costs eight dollars.

She asked Sage if he wanted them specially wrapped, and he told her as special as she could make them. You'll want a card, she said. What do you want the card to say?

Sage thought about it. Put down "Just because," he said.

Oh my, the woman said. I don't believe I've ever had anyone say that in all the years I've been selling flowers.

When he got back, he could see from the road that Della was on the couch reading to Stacey and Tommy. He wanted it to be just Della at home when he presented the flowers, but that wasn't going to happen. In the porch enclosure, he hung up his coat, took his boots off and walked into the living room. I bought you something, he said.

Della got up off the couch and made a big fuss over the flowers. I'll get these in water right away, she said. This is amazing, and it's just like the sermon at church. The minister said if we have faith and just sit back without expectation, providence will come among us. She deserved to be happy, Sage thought, happy his wife liked what he had done. He wanted to say something to make it clear the flowers were his idea, not God's.

You know? Della said. I can't remember the last time you bought me flowers. Sage didn't say anything. He thought about it too and realized he never had.

Stacey didn't have brothers or sisters to play with, but she didn't need any. Della had four kids on the go one spring, the youngest only sixteen months, so it was as if Stacey were being raised in a large family. Tommy, the flat-nosed boy, was a year older; Leah, who had to be reminded to speak English not French, was close to Stacey's age; Gobinder, who didn't smell—but only ate a lot of curry—Della explained to Stacey, was a year younger and only wanted to watch TV; and then there was the baby who everyone, including Della, called Baby.

Della had extra toys around the house, bought so all the kids could play together, and most of the time, Stacey didn't mind if others played with her personal toys. But she took her Pippi Longstocking doll, her favourite, to bed with her each night and hid her under her pillow in the morning so no one else would touch it. Everyone, including Della, waited for spring to take hold so playing outdoors was feasible, but for three days in a row, it had rained and everyone, on the tail of winter, felt housebound.

Mid-morning, Tommy and Leah went into Stacey's bedroom, and Tommy decided it would be fun to have a pillow fight, which led Leah to discover Pippi Longstocking. When Stacey noticed, she demanded the doll back, and Leah either didn't understand because of her developing English skills or because everything else in the house was first come, first served. Leah didn't give the doll back, and Stacey punched her in the nose, and soon blood ran all over Leah's frilly white blouse. Leah stepped back, stunned and confused. Tommy screamed at the sight of blood.

What's going on in here? Leah, what happened?

Della had Baby in her arms and put her on Stacey's bed and told her to make sure he didn't roll off. She tilted Leah's head back and told her to pinch her nose and went to the kitchen for a wet cloth.

Stacey punched her, Tommy said. She punched her on the nose.

Della only half listened as she busied herself cleaning the blood off Leah's face. Stacey pinned Baby to her bed with one hand and looked down at the floor, crying. Della said, let's get that blouse off you and put it in cold water. There's blood every-where. She removed the blouse, and when Leah saw the blood stains, she cried too. Della grabbed a red plaid work shirt from Sage's closet so Leah would be warm. It hung past her knees.

Right on the nose, Tommy continued. She hit her right on the nose.

Gobinder heard the kerfuffle but remained in the living room watching *The Jetsons*.

The bleeding stopped, so Della propped up pillows on Stacey's bed and let Leah lie back and look at the ceiling with a fresh wet cloth on her face. She rinsed the blouse, and most of the blood had vanished, but in places you could see where it had been. She added salt to the cold water and left it to soak. Della told Tommy his report had been thorough enough and that he should watch TV while she sorted things out.

I don't want to go to my room, Stacey said. She's in there bleeding and taking up the whole bed. Della dragged her into the room and shut the door. Neither girl wanted to explain what had happened so Della said she would wait until they were ready to talk. She picked up a book from the floor and read it like it was a novel she was halfway through. The robins in the backyard didn't mind the rain. They were busy sorting out who to make babies with.

She stole my Pippi, Stacey said.

She was playing with it, you mean. Is that right, Leah? You were playing with Pippi? Leah nodded.

Playing with a doll is a lot different from stealing a doll. You can't punch someone in the face for something like that. If people acted that way, half the town of Fernie would walk around with bloody noses.

Whether Leah understood the words or not, she giggled, lying there on the bed.

I can understand if you don't want the other kids to play with

Pippi. We'll just have to find a better spot to keep her. I think it's time to say you're sorry, young lady.

There's blood on Pippi's leg. See it?

Della tried again. And again. Stacey wouldn't apologize, so Della picked Leah up and carried her to the living room and told Stacey to stay in her room. I don't care, she said. I don't want to play with those dumb kids anyway.

Della rinsed the blouse out with salty water two more times until the stain became almost invisible. She filled the sink with warm water and bleach and got lunch ready. She asked Stacey again if she wanted to apologize, and when she said no, Della left her egg salad sandwich on a plate just inside her bedroom door.

You sure bleed a lot when you're punched on the nose, Tommy said.

Yes, Tommy. Enough about bloody noses. After lunch I think we could colour some pictures. We got a new set of crayons. Sixty-four of them.

Stacey heard the cheering that resulted. She didn't want to crayon anyway.

The afternoon passed more slowly than normal, and everyone felt the tension in the air. Tommy went to Stacey's bedroom door at one point and told her to hurry up and get out here. Stacey told him to shut his big fat mouth.

Sage, on an upgrading course, had said he would be home for dinner but he might be late if he went out with the others for a beer. Della cooked fish sticks, chips and made coleslaw, something both he and Stacey loved. She waited until six-thirty, and when Sage hadn't returned, she ate hers at the kitchen table and put a small serving on a plate and took it into Stacey's bedroom. Stacey turned away from her on the bed and faced the wall, still refusing to apologize. Della picked up the sandwich, which hadn't been touched. Your dad's not going to like hearing about what went on here today, Della said. Stacey refused to respond.

Sage didn't get home until almost nine. Della could tell he'd had more than one beer. He sat down at the table to eat his portion of fish sticks and chips, and while he ate, Della filled him in on what had happened.

I'll go in and have a talk with her, he said. I might not be as nice about it as you were.

Trust me, I was firm. You'll have to wait until morning now. I haven't heard a peep out of her for more than an hour. I'm sure she's exhausted.

Sage went to the bedroom door, and Della followed. They turned the light on. Stacey had taken off all her clothes but had not bothered with pyjamas. She lay in bed, only partially covered by the sheets. Neither Sage nor Della said anything for a few minutes, trying as they were to take in what they saw. Stacey had found leftover crayons and had drawn all over one wall of her bedroom. A girl with light brown hair and a white blouse stood out in the drawing, as did an excessive amount of blood depicted as splattered all over the room. The likeness to the little girl was uncanny.

The next morning was a Saturday, a day that Sage did something that suited him, and Della and Stacey cleaned up the house and went somewhere. When Sage left, Della still had heard nothing from Stacey's room. She opened the bedroom door and found Stacey lying in bed reading, Pippi Longstocking cradled in one arm. The fish sticks from the previous night had drawn the attention of several flies.

I hope you're pleased with yourself young lady. Your dad was ready to bust in here and tan your hide, but I set him loose. I was planning on the two of us shopping this afternoon, after we got the house tidied. Now you've ruined that too. Do you have anything to say for yourself?

Stacey turned a page over. Della bent down to pick up her

untouched supper, and her knees cracked. When she turned to leave, Stacey turned toward her for the first time. She stuck out her tongue, but her mother never noticed.

Della thought about the house, what had to be done and about getting on with it. Stacey had to be hungry. She hadn't eaten for almost twenty-four hours. Della liked being around pleasant people, and she thought she'd been raising a daughter that would be that way too. What set of circumstances had convened to suggest it was okay to punch another child on the nose over a doll? Maybe going to school, the only thing on the horizon about to change, had her worried. Della thought about Stacey not eating and of the reports of anorexic kids in the news. Was this how it started? Going on a hunger strike to establish power? The last thing she wanted was for Sage to step in and, in his words, set her straight from a man's perspective.

All right, young lady, enough is enough. You can't live here and think you can lounge around in bed all day. You can leave your room a mess if you want to, but the vacuuming and dusting are your responsibility and you can get at it. I've saved you once, but I won't do it again.

Della left the bedroom door open, turned on the radio and washed the kitchen floor. She sang along when she knew the words. Stacey came out of her room and started the vacuum cleaner. She knew she should dust first and vacuum later, but at least she was doing something. She finished and took her book and her favourite doll outside to the backyard. She reached over the fence and extracted two apples from Hart's tree in the backyard. The apples were best left until late August, Hart always said, but they weren't all that bad now.

Sage came home in the middle of the afternoon, and he found Stacey in the woodshed, staring at the piles of wood as if they had a story to tell. He tried to talk to her. He tried to be reasonable in his tone and with what he had to say, but she ignored him.

What the hell is the matter with that kid? he demanded. She won't say a word.

She's not all that well, Della lied. She has a bad case of laryngitis and can barely talk. It's been an upsetting couple of days. School starts in a few days so let's hope she's over it by then. Sometimes in life we need time to heal. Can you imagine a kid in school who didn't say anything? Now that would require an understanding teacher, wouldn't it?

Sage shook his head in disbelief. He tried to remember why he'd come home so early on a Saturday. For the life of him he couldn't remember.

10

DELLA HAD BEEN DREADING Stacey's first day of school for weeks. She planned to walk her there in the morning, and Sage had permission, for the first few days of school, to pick her up and bring her home at noon. Della dressed her in a navy blue skirt and white top, which resulted in her looking like she was starting private school. Still, she looked neat and tidy and clean, and none of the teachers would have anything negative to say about her appearance. There *had* been a problem with underwear, however. Stacey was fond of pink and Della knew that, and she'd bought seven pairs of pink underwear to start school, only to have Stacey state she wasn't about to start school the following day, a Tuesday, unless she had two pairs of black underwear.

You like pink. You've always liked pink. So what's the problem?

Yes, I like pink, but I need two black pairs too. You can never have enough underwear. You said so yourself.

But why black all of a sudden?

Because I have to start school on a Tuesday. And after that a Wednesday. It's a very sad thing to be going to school on a Tuesday and a Wednesday. They're not like the other days.

What's different about them?

One has seven letters and the other nine. All the other days have either six or eight. I don't feel safe going to school in happy pink when I should be wearing sad black.

Della didn't bother with a coat because it was warm in the early morning and bound to get warmer. She offered to make anything Stacey could name for breakfast, but Stacey opted for cornflakes as usual. Stacey had given little thought to her first day in school; in fact, having talked to Tommy about it many times, she was sure there wasn't much to learn in kindergarten that she didn't already know. The way Della was acting, the night before and over breakfast, confused her. Had she been older, she might have thought of breakfast as her last meal before execution.

Della promised not to cry, and she kept her word until Stacey disappeared behind the main door to the school, then she blubbered her way back home, thinking what a brave soul her little girl was. How absolutely grown-up.

She only had Charlie to babysit, walking now, and previously referred to as Baby. Dropped off at 9:15, by mid-morning he sat in a high chair, making a ripe banana into playdough while Della worked at the sink, cleaning beets she planned to cook for supper. Charlie had the habit of babbling with a range of intonation that resembled speech but made no sense most of the time, so Della thought she was listening to that until she turned toward the high chair and saw Charlie had his mouth stuffed with banana. She walked into the living room and found Stacey sitting on the couch, TV on, holding Pippi Longstocking, who was absorbing more of her attention than the TV.

Stacey, what are you doing back home? Kindergarten goes until lunch time.

I didn't like it there.

What do you mean you didn't like it?

I didn't like it. You ask a question, and she tells you to wait a minute. She has too many kids to look after.

Della cleaned up Charlie and put him in the stroller. She

figured if Sage were home he'd get mad and march her back there right away, but she would not get mad. Going to school every day was like going to work. It was natural to not want to go. She sat on the couch beside Stacey and explained how school was a morning thing and that she couldn't just go for an hour and come home because the school and her mother had to know where she was. Stacey agreed to return but wanted to take Pippi with her. On their way down the street, they encountered Molly the Nose, out front and curious. Della explained and Molly said kids are just like dogs, and once she was fed snacks every day, everything would be just fine. When they got close to the school, Stacey handed her doll over because she knew Pippi wouldn't like it there anymore than she would.

Are you missing anything? Della asked when they found the kindergarten room.

Missing? the teacher asked.

Yes, missing. Stacey's been home for an hour. I thought you might have noticed.

Della couldn't remember the teacher's first name. Deerhome was her last name, and she was young. Her face turned crimson, and she tried to offer an explanation but had none.

Less than an hour later, when Della was back home tending to Charlie, Sage drove up and Stacey got out and went into the backyard. Della wanted her out of her good clothes but thought better than to press the issue. Sage did not understand what had gone on, so Della filled him in.

I can't believe she wandered off and came home. The teacher hadn't even noticed. Do you realize how dangerous that could have been?

The school is only eight blocks from home, Sage said. She knows her way.

I know that, but anything could have happened. She could have been abducted, and no one would have noticed.

At supper that night, Della tried to quiz Stacey about her partial day of kindergarten. We learned the rules and sang a song, Stacey said.

What else?

That was it, except she explained about the alphabet, and everyone got to colour a picture of the letter *A*.

What colour did you make yours?

I didn't. I found a Curious George book in the corner and read it instead. They let us outside for a few minutes, but we weren't allowed on the monkey bars, and a boy with cross-eyes peed his pants, and a girl cried because she got her dress dirty. Then Dad came and it was over.

Della looked at Sage, now laughing quietly. It's not funny, she said.

Well, I think it's damn funny, Sage said.

Della wanted to know if Stacey looked forward to going to school the next day but was afraid to ask.

Hart had sold life insurance for twenty-two years. To his credit, he never pestered Sage or Della, even though he must have guessed neither of them had insurance of any kind. He went to his office downtown for some part of every morning and made house calls in the afternoons and evenings, Molly the Nose said, but from what Sage and Della observed, Hart was not a man to stretch himself out of shape. He spent most of any free time he could gather inside the house, and they knew he was in there somewhere because they saw his car parked outside. He bought the *TV Guide* and circled in red pen any Western movies scheduled. Often the movies he wanted to watch aired on weekday afternoons and Saturdays, and his flexible schedule allowed him to view most of them. Molly the Nose, now that she babysat weekdays, went to bed earlier than in years past, which allowed Hart to take in, without contention, shows like *The Johnny Cash Show* on Wednesdays at nine. He took out of the library and read voraciously any books, both fiction and nonfiction, that dealt with the life and times of the Wild West. The way Hart saw it, once people had settled North America and cities harnessed their attention, something of spiritual value disappeared.

Every year both Hart and Molly went to Calgary the first week in July without exception. Molly mostly visited with her sister, and Hart went to the Calgary Stampede. Tie down roping, bull riding and chuck wagon races were his favourite events, but he also enjoyed things like sheep shearing and blacksmith competitions. Molly and her sister went with him for one day, and they liked the Musical Ride and petting the miniature donkeys. Hart always came back from his one week of holiday with a smile on his face and a few well-chosen artifacts, ones he suspected he'd paid too much for.

Since Stacey had started kindergarten, the weather had been bright and warm in the afternoons with just a hint of cool around the edges, weather that pulled you outside as if some force of nature suggested one ought to memorize the sun on the leaves of yellow and brown and red so they might be fondly remembered in the whiteout that would soon descend upon the valley. With kindergarten a morning affair only, Stacey could stay home and enjoy the afternoons that fall, and on one particular Monday, Sage stayed home too because he hadn't felt well enough in the morning to go to work.

There's a horse in Molly's backyard, Stacey exclaimed with such enthusiasm that both Della and Sage got up from the couch to investigate.

It can't be a horse, Sage said.

Dad, I know what a horse looks like.

It was a horse all right, a huge chestnut brown horse with a thick mane that matched a black saddle, glistening in the afternoon sun. Hart stood beside it, wearing a pair of cowboy boots, brushing the already shimmering hair and chatting with two police officers who kept their distance, more from the horse than from Hart. The three Howards made their way through the gate and onto Ferguson property without invitation. It wasn't every day a horse showed up in the neighbourhood.

So you don't claim to own the horse? one of the officers said.

No, of course not, Hart said. You asked me that already. I took the horse for a ride. Rode it in from Bull River.

You're trying to tell me you rode this horse all the way from Bull River?

That's what I'm trying to do.

It's almost an hour by car to Bull River from here.

By car it is, yes, officer. You've got that right. It took two and a half hours, but I took a shortcut through the mountains. That's what our forefathers had to do. Take the shortest route possible.

The two policemen exchanged glances. It was clear they didn't believe a word Hart was telling them.

Can I touch him? Stacey said.

Touch him? You can get up on him if you want. Come here, I'll give you a boost. Della was about to suggest it wasn't a good idea, but Sage shoved Stacey forward and Hart grabbed her and helped her up.

It's high up here, Stacey said, stroking the horse wherever she could reach.

They do rent horses in Bull Creek, one officer said to the other.

I know they do. But no one could make it through those mountains on a horse. It would take days to do such a thing.

Okay, Hart said. Maybe I exaggerated. It may have taken me a bit more than three hours to get here. I didn't have my watch with me.

Where's Molly? Della said.

She's in the house. She's afraid of horses.

Della turned and went inside. It would have been Molly the Nose who phoned the police when her husband showed up with a horse, and Della, as a fellow church-goer, felt the need to offer comfort.

And do the people who own the horse know where it is?

Probably not. I told them I was going on an extensive ride, but I didn't say where. I plan on phoning them and explaining that I won't have the horse back there until tomorrow. I've ridden horses before, but it's been some time. My butt's sore if that makes any sense. Hart kept brushing the horse while he talked. He helped Stacey down and undid the straps and removed the saddle, talking to the horse as he did so. He's got plenty to eat in the backyard for now, Hart said. I'll get him some water, and he'll be fine. It will be good to have a horse around the house for a change.

Sage watched the whole procedure without comment. Hart wasn't the sort he would likely engineer a connection with, and he wasn't sorry about it either. He wasn't feeling too perky, and just observing his obsessed neighbour wasn't improving his health any.

What's the horse called? Stacey said.

Murphy, Hart said. Well, it's Jesus Murphy, they said, but I call him Murphy. The horse is an important part of our history. If it weren't for the horse, none of us would be here right now.

Tommy wasn't being cared for after school by Della that day, and Stacey couldn't remember why. She was happy about it though. Tomorrow when she saw him at school, she would talk horses until he couldn't stand it anymore.

When they were back home, Stacey said, Can we get a horse like Hart's horse?

That's not Hart's horse. That man doesn't own a horse, and he doesn't have his wits about him. You can't own a horse in the city.

Hart's interesting though, Stacey said. He does interesting things. And he knows a lot of stuff.

Sage opened a women's magazine Della had borrowed from Molly the Nose. He lit up the biggest joint he'd ever rolled and thumbed his way through the pages. The ads appealed to him the most, and he wondered about the people in the ads. They all looked like nice people on the page, but he realized some of them were probably not nice at all. Not everything a person sees is what they think they see. Stacey might find someone like Hart interesting now, but over time he knew she'd grow out of it.

11

FOLLOW THE MAP AS FAR AS ARGENTA, then turn around and drive exactly five miles back, park at the side of the road and wait inside the car for thirty minutes and someone would come to fetch him. He wasn't to get out of the car, just sit tight, and if anyone came along and asked what he was doing there, he was to say he wanted to enjoy looking out over Kootenay Lake. Sage set out on his own, and the trip from Fernie took longer than he'd planned. Only once did he stop for gas and a chocolate bar, and it still took him almost six hours. He left early Saturday morning and told Della he was going fishing for Kokanee with a guy from work he refused to name. He hoped to be back late on Saturday, he told her, but if the fishing was good or there were problems, he might not be back until Sunday because his fishing partner had a two-man tent.

What's wrong with fishing in the river right here in town? Della asked, and Sage told her the river didn't have Kokanee and it was Kokanee he was after.

It was a clear fall day with a noticeable chill in the air, and Sage hoped to complete the trip in a single day. He wasn't keen on sleeping out on what would be a frosty night in the Kootenays. He had made a big deal about packing his fishing equipment the night before, and Della told him when he got back maybe he could put the same organizational skills to work in the back shed and workshop.

The lake, when he arrived, was beautiful. A slight breeze riffled the water, and it glistened like diamonds in the sun. Soon after he got there, a pickup truck passed his parked car, heading back to the north end of the lake, and then nothing broke the serenity. His eyes focused on the water, but something told him to look across the road and into the woods where darkness filled the spaces between the close pines. Loping along, parallel to the road, a grey wolf stopped every ten feet or so and looked out at Sage sitting in the car. There weren't many cars on the road, and maybe the animal had never seen a purple car before. Sage had been told to stay inside the car and wait. It seemed like a good idea.

About twenty minutes later, the pickup truck came back down the road and pulled up beside his car. Sage rolled down the window. Is anything wrong? the man asked.

No, Sage said, just enjoying looking out over the lake.

Perfect, the man said. Follow me. He turned on the gravel road and headed north, and Sage had to hurry to keep up. A few miles farther, the truck turned off onto a side road that led away from the lake but quickly turned into a dead end. The man pulled to the side and told Sage to drive to the end, then turned his pickup truck sideways, blocking any easy exit. The man lit a cigarette, then he got out of the truck and turned away from Sage and peed into the loose gravel.

You understand we don't deal in anything less than ten pounds? You won't get it any cheaper, I can tell you that much, and you got the cash on you or we don't go any further.

I got the money. A thousand bucks. I need to see the stuff.

Smoke some if you want, the man said. You may end up driving back on a slow road is all.

Sage had papers with him and rolled a small joint. When he lit up, the forest around him came alive, and the man in charge kept looking back into the woods. Sage figured someone was planted nearby, probably with a gun, in case he caused trouble. It doesn't feel like ten pounds, Sage said, lifting the huge black bag off the ground.

That's because we hung and dried it for close to a week. There was at least ten pounds in there when we picked it. Of course it weighs less now.

Sage knew how much a small bag would sell for in Fernie, and he knew people were hungry for it in Cranbrook. He wouldn't have a problem making money from his one-time investment. Sage reached into his pocket and pulled out the envelope that contained the thousand dollars. The man ripped it open and counted it twice, then looked back into the woods one more time.

All right, he said. The stash is yours. If you're stupid enough to get caught, you don't remember where you got it.

Don't worry, Sage said. I won't get caught. If this goes well, when can I come back for more?

We're almost done for this year, Bud. This time next year will be your best bet. You can check with your contact, and if we're still in business we'll do it again.

The man got in his truck and drove away. Sage lifted his gear out of the trunk, including the spare tire, and set the bag deep in the well and covered it up with the tire, the fishing equipment and his green sleeping bag. He needed gas and drove slowly back to the main road. He didn't want to drive so slow he drew anyone's attention, but he didn't want to burn up much gas either.

He drove around the end of the lake, then south until he got to Kaslo and filled up with gas. He'd never been to Kaslo and got out to walk around town, and down by the docks, he watched a man and his son pull their boat out of the water and unload their gear.

Looks like you were lucky out there today, Sage said. Is that two fish you got there?

It is, the man said. I didn't catch either one of them, can you believe it? My son caught both. First time we tried White Shoepeg Corn, and it worked like a hot damn. With a dodger, of course.

Of course, Sage said. I've never caught one of those. I told my wife I'd bring her back a Kokanee for our anniversary. I don't imagine you'd consider selling one of those, would you?

That's up to Brent, not me, the man said. He and Sage both looked at Brent who looked down at the two fish at the bottom of the boat.

I'm not selling the big one, Brent said.

I'll give you twenty bucks for the small one then.

Twenty-five bucks, Brent said. But Dad's gotta take a picture first.

Sage offered to take a picture of the two of them in front of their boat, then he handed over twenty-five dollars and accepted the fish in a plastic bag.

Are you going to tell your wife you caught it? the kid wanted to know.

I am, Sage said. But I'll tell her a young man named Brent taught me how to do it.

Sage had a sandwich and coffee at the local cafe. Pods of hippie types huddled on the sidewalks of town, wearing leather moccasins and baggy clothes. One group had a cat on a leash, and most of them looked stoned and paid little attention to the pedestrians who walked around them. These would not be his customers. They had little money, that much he knew, and they grew their own pot anyway. One man had his eyes closed and still played a clear tune on a hand-carved flute. Sage thought about returning to work at the mine on Monday, and he envied them.

He didn't plan to stop unless he had to, and even then he wouldn't be home until close to midnight, but having the fish in the trunk of the car left him elated. He doubted he would be stopped along the way, but a fisherman with a fish in the trunk provided a reasonable story, plus the trunk would smell like fish instead of weed. On his way home, Sage would have plenty to think about. His landlord, who lived in Vancouver, wanted to sell the house they were renting, and he'd told Sage if he didn't buy it before New Year's, he would put it on the market in the spring. The bank told Sage he would need five thousand to qualify for a mortgage, and he only had a little more than a thousand dollars saved up.

Della had fretted day and night since they'd found out. She didn't want to move, she said. She didn't want to start all over again now they were settled. He knew it was about Stacey more than anything. The town knew them as a family now, and she didn't want to change that. Sage told her not to worry. He would look after things. Rich people knew how to run their own business, and Sage was in business now.

Only five girls attended the morning kindergarten class of sixteen. The boys in the class wanted to run around and build with blocks, and whenever they got the chance to draw, they drew cars and coloured them red or blue. Stacey became fast friends with Amber. Amber tolerated her attendance as much as Stacey did, and the two of them, during free time, huddled in a corner and read books. For both, snack time was the best part of the morning. After snack time, when Amber read in their reading circle, Stacey never tired of staring at her face that had so many freckles they looked spray-painted in place. In the afternoons, Amber walked to her grandmother's house to eat tomato soup and a cheese sandwich, not toasted, and then she watched her grandmother knit while listening to the radio because her grandmother had no TV in the house. Stacey suggested Amber should come to her house in the afternoons, and about a week later, Della had another client to look after, thanks to Stacey's persistence.

For a short time, Tommy went home after school because he only had two hours before his dad came home from work, but he missed playing at Stacey's house, and soon the three of them were hanging around, deciding what they would get up to. Tommy got his way at the end of September when they reminded Hart that he'd promised to help them make a genuine bow and arrow. They piled into Hart's car and spent the afternoon down by the river where the leaves had begun to turn, and Hart showed them how to test the willow trees for suppleness, find a branch just the right thickness and about three feet long. They picked out a dozen smaller branches that he said would have to dry out for a few weeks but would do to make arrows. On the way home, they stopped at a turkey farm and got feathers for the arrows, and the adventure felt so exotic that Stacey and Amber enjoyed it as much as Tommy.

Just before Sage left on his fishing trip, Della told him that he ought to spend as much time and effort on straightening out the shed and garage as he did on his fishing trips. The following week, he did just that, as he needed an accessible place to hide his stash. Della then told him it was stupid to put so much effort into a place they would have to leave in a matter of months.

You told me you didn't want to move away from here, he said.

I don't want to. You know that. We can't afford to buy this place.

Della, stop that. I have a plan. We'll be just fine.

What kind of plan?

I can't tell you right now.

You've got a plan to find the money to buy this house, and you can't tell your wife?

It's complicated. And besides, I want it to be a surprise.

You're not thinking you'll catch enough Kokanee to raise the money, are you? That's the stupidest idea you've come up with since I met you.

Look, Della. We got off to a slow start. I plan on making up some ground. Just leave it to me and look after the kids. And I'll go fishing if I want to. It's no different than going to church on Sundays. At least at the end of the day I have something to show for it.

Sage's pronouncement sounded true even though, since he'd taken up fishing, he'd landed only one bull trout. Once he had enacted his plan and sold off his stash, he would have time to develop the art of fishing. He hated to ask Hart for anything, but he borrowed some of his tools and built cupboards in the back of the garage, a building awkward to get to that had never held a parked car. This took up one weekend, and the next Sunday when Della and Stacey went off to church, he busied himself packaging the weed into small bags he would sell for $25 each. He only needed one of the cupboards for his marijuana, but he put separate locks on all three cupboards, and he told Della he was keeping tools in there and didn't want the kids messing with them. Della never went into the dingy garage because she was afraid of spiders, and there were plenty of those.

Sage had three or four bags hidden in the trunk of the car at any given time. When he sold them, he replaced them so that when he was out and about he could always do business. He had a competitor selling in the valley, so he had to reduce his price to $20. He went along with it, then wrapped his bags smaller and smaller, and no one noticed. He always put a package of cigarette papers, Chanticleer, in the bag. Selling the stuff put him on edge, particularly when he sold to high school students. Still, they found the money, and they found him, and within a month, business was booming. Twice he went to Cranbrook and made a killing. He opened a second account at the bank and put extra money in their home account to give Della hope and keep her quiet, but almost all of it he socked away in a savings account.

His sales progressed as he had expected well into the month of November. One Saturday he was in the garage sorting out what he thought he might sell over the next week when Della appeared. The kitchen tap was leaking and squirting water all over the floor. She came up behind Sage and saw what he was up to.

You must be out of your mind.

This is just temporary, Della. We're going to get this house, you watch. Nobody's getting hurt.

You have a wife and daughter you're supposed to be supporting. What happens when they throw you in jail for six months? What am I supposed to do then? I don't know how to stop the kitchen taps from spraying water all over the house. There's a minor flood in there.

Sage tended to the pipes, glad to have something legal to do. He shut the water off under the sink and took the tap apart. He would need to rebuild the tap or just buy another. Right now he had Della to defuse.

Come with me, he said. He went to his sock drawer and pulled out the two bank books he owned. First he showed her the one she knew about but likely hadn't looked at for a while. Eight hundred dollars sat in their household account. Then he showed her his separate account with the total that stood out at the bottom: $2,916.55. I'm more than halfway there, he said. Nothing will go wrong. We'll be buying this house by February.

Della didn't know what to say. She thought she had things to say, but her voice felt trapped in her throat. Nothing could get past her scattered and conflicted thoughts. She gathered towels and mopped the kitchen floor. Sage said he would go to the hardware store to get parts. Still, Della said nothing. She kept mopping the floor as if the leak hadn't stopped and she would be mopping for the rest of her life.

Sage fixed the tap an hour later and went back to the garage to tidy things. He looked up to see Hart standing outside the garage. Just standing there, as if lost. He said he wanted to get weed to smoke, but he didn't want Molly to get wind of it or she would make him flush it down the toilet. Sage didn't want Hart to know where he kept the stuff, though by the way he studied his renovations and the three cupboards locked up, he had already guessed, but he went out to the car and came back with a bag which he sold to Hart for $25. Sage found him a small tin and told him he could keep it in there and showed him a good place to hide it in the woodshed. They each rolled a joint and sat down on two wood blocks and looked out at the houses and dilapidated fences that met up with the backyard. Sage and Della wondered why Hart always seemed to get by without working too hard at anything. They wondered if maybe they'd had an insurance policy on the boy they'd lost years ago and that was part of the reason. They didn't want to ask about a thing like that, but it was something to think about at least.

I don't drink anymore, Hart said. He filled his lungs with smoke and held it for a long time. I was drinking a fair bit when we lost Billy, he said. That's not why we lost him, but I've never cared to go back to it since.

Sage told him that this weed was more powerful than most and that sharing the one joint would be enough to even things out for the rest of the day. He said nothing about what his neighbour had mentioned. He didn't need to. The way Hart had spoken the words made it feel like the two of them had shared a lifetime of grief without knowing it, and the sharing had cemented a bond between them.

12

IN THE MIDDLE OF OCTOBER, Della read a sheet stapled to a drawing of a bow and arrow Stacey had done at school. The sheet announced a meet-the-teacher opportunity to take place in the afternoon the following week, and they invited parents at individual times, should they wish to have a one-on-one chat with the teacher. Otherwise, they were welcome to come for a visit in the evening. Miss Deerhome had specifically written a note on the side for Della and Sage, suggesting if it were at all possible she would like to meet them at the appointed time so they could discuss Stacey's deportment in the class. Della read it to Sage one night after supper.

She's touched in the head, Sage said. There's nothing wrong with her behaviour.

Stacey can be strong-willed, Della said.

There's nothing wrong with having a mind of your own. Her name's *Miss* Deerhome, and my guess is she's never married and never will. She has nothing better to think about.

Still, I guess I'll ask Molly to take over for an hour. I'd better go down there and see what's up.

The day of the meeting, Stacey came home in a downpour. Della didn't have the car so she dressed in boots and carried an umbrella and fought her way to the school. An afternoon kinder-garten class was in progress, but Miss Deerhome sat waiting for her in an office off to the side.

Thank you for coming, the teacher said. Your husband couldn't make it?

No, he's working. Is there a problem with Stacey? I can't imag-ine there being a big problem.

I don't intend to worry you, Mrs. Howard. There's no big problem at all. I thought it would be useful if we compared notes on Stacey's behaviour at school with what you see at home. I'm hoping that way I can get a handle on what your daughter is like. She's very smart, that's not in question here. Every year we have one or two arrive in kindergarten already reading, and she's quite accomplished in that regard.

Then what is the issue you're talking about?

Miss Deerhome got up and shut the door to her office. Della wasn't sure if it was for their privacy or to block the singing of "The Wheels on the Bus Go Round and Round" bouncing off the walls of the small classroom. Then she opened a file folder where she had scribbled a few notes since the beginning of the school year.

One thing we try to build in kindergarten is a sense of coop-eration and working with others. More often than not, Stacey refuses to join in with what we have organized.

I'm not sure what you mean?

Well, for example, you can hear the afternoon group working with our music teacher, which they get to do twice a week. If the teacher suggests it would be fun to learn a particular song, Stacey will often refuse to sing. Once when this happened and all the kids had finished the chorus, we could hear Stacey off in her own little world singing a Beatles song. I believe it was the Beatles. Sometimes we'll place the children in groups of four or five and ask them to use the building blocks and work together to build something specific, say a skyscraper. Stacey refuses to help at all because she says the colours don't match.

The colours don't match?

That's what she said. She said you never see a skyscraper made with different colours, so she refused to build one. We have a small nutritious snack served with hot chocolate in the middle of our morning. The kids love that. Stacey loves it too, which is great. But the cups are all the same, kind of wide so they're more stable, except for one cup that is more like a conventional cup.

And why is that? Della asked.

Well, most everyone wants the nice wide cups, but there is just the right number for the class, so someone must use the narrow cup. In other words, they have to learn to take turns.

You're saying Stacey refuses to take her turn?

No. She budges her way to the front during snack time and picks up the narrow cup for herself. None of the other children need to take a turn. You see what I'm saying?

Della wished that Sage was beside her. He would think of something to say to this nervous teacher, fluttering like a feather in the wind and flushed in the face already from the exertion of explanation. Della could bring up that Stacey had come home on her own the first day and no one had noticed, but she thought better of it. Well, Della said, trying to think like Sage, what I hear you saying is that Stacey saw a problem in the social organization around her and solved the problem before it got out of hand. I would think you should thank her rather than criticize her.

The teacher mentioned other examples of Stacey`s noncompliance, as if she owned a gun with anemic bullets and hoped that by employing spray and pray she might make an impression.

Do you see any of this behaviour at home? Miss Deerhome asked.

I wouldn't say so, no. She's asked to help with the housework on Saturday mornings, and she does so willingly. She's a real trooper and sometimes shames my husband into being neat and tidy. She keeps her room immaculate. No, I wouldn't say she acts anything like uncooperative.

Della could have told the teacher that Stacey only ate with two or three forks in the drawer because the tines were uneven on the rest, but she wasn't about to give her any lopsided information. The fifteen-minute meeting had stretched to half an hour, and a set of parents stood outside the door looking in. Miss Deerhome mentioned qualities she liked about Stacey as Della got up to leave. She knows a lot about the Wild West, she said, but Della didn't bother an explanation of any kind. She didn't know how to explain Hart in any case.

Della was wet and uncomfortable by the time she got back home. Molly the Nose wanted to know how the interview went, but Della told her everything went fine. Sage got home late because he was out doing business, and he'd forgotten about the meeting at school. Della waited until Stacey had fallen asleep before she filled him in.

I don't think she dislikes her, Della said. But she's not used to someone who thinks the way she does. She's always been that way. Remember? She wouldn't talk for the first two or three weeks when we got her. She refused to say a word. Not to mention her silent treatment after the bloody nose incident.

Sage said he remembered. He wasn't as worked up about what had gone on as Della thought he would be. He was thinking about the two boys he'd sold to after work. They were high school age, but he could tell they were dropouts. They kept asking questions about where he got his stash from, and Sage said, none of your business. Something about the whole transaction didn't feel right.

She offered the class a chance to paint anything they wanted one day, Della said, and Stacey painted a bow and arrow, and

Miss Deerhome said she'd never seen a girl paint a bow and arrow before. It's because Hart is helping them make their own bow and arrow, but what do you think about that?

Hart's helping them make a bow and arrow?

I told you that. Tommy and Amber are making one too. Sometimes I swear you never hear half of what I have to say.

Sage reckoned Della was right on that count. He was only half listening now. Being married to a woman like Della, who talked twice as much as she should, gave a man the right to only take in half of it. He almost had enough money for the down payment, and he didn't want anything to screw it up now.

After Sage decided to spend more than eight hundred dollars to rebuild the engine on his old friend the purple car, he told Della that they now owned a car that would last them for years to come, but then he changed his mind and drove to Cranbrook one Saturday and spent another six hundred dollars to trade his car in on a green Valiant owned by an old man who didn't drive much. When he drove up to the house in the car, Della looked intrigued. She looked into the glove compartment and saw nothing there but the registration and insurance papers and a plastic tool for scraping ice.

What did you do with our stuff in the other car?

What stuff?

I kept a St. Christopher's medal in there, and we never had an accident the whole time we owned that car. And Stacey had a little kewpie doll she liked to hold on long trips. You didn't throw them out, did you?

I didn't do anything with them.

Well, where are they?

Sage tried to explain that the slant-six engine in the new green car was an innovation, an engineering breakthrough. The car looked old, but it hadn't been driven much at all. A good deal, he said. Stacey saw the car and asked if he planned to paint it purple.

He didn't explain to Della that he'd become a marked man in the purple car. The day the cops had pulled him over was likely the only day for months he had none of his stash in the car. They asked him about it and searched the car briefly, and when they drove off, his hands were shaking so badly he had difficulty driving. By late November, he had sold most of the bags and had almost had enough money for the house. He rearranged the woodpile out back and moved what remained in the cupboards to under a haphazard pile of wood in case the cops showed up and wanted to carry out a search. He moved the tin Hart used to keep his weed stored, up to the sagging cap plate of the woodshed and put a block of wood underneath so Hart, who wasn't as tall as Sage, could reach. Why the cops were watching him, he wasn't sure. It might have been some of the kids he'd sold to. Kids blabber about what little they know, and it would be easy to describe how they got their stuff from a guy with a purple car. For a time, he wondered if Hart might be the problem, but once a week, usually on Sunday nights, Hart drifted over in the late evening, and the two of them sat out back and shared a soft conversation. This happened less and less now that the weather was turning mean, and Sage had put out of his mind the fleeting suspicion.

December brought a Christmas Sage would never forget no matter how hard he tried. He negotiated with his landlord in Vancouver, and they agreed the title to the house would exchange hands on January 2nd. Della, overwhelmed with relief, told him she wanted nothing else for Christmas: the chance to own their own house was more than enough. But he bought her a few gifts anyway, things he knew she wanted, like a new dress she could wear to church and some fuzzy slippers for around the house. Santa organized a new bike for Stacey, racing red, a bike without training wheels, and he purchased a St. Christopher's medal and a kewpie doll for the new car. Della orchestrated the weeks leading up to Christmas Day. She read excerpts from Dickens' *A Christmas Carol* to the family each night before Stacey went to bed. It wasn't always easy to gather the family together for the event, and as they got close to Christmas, with time running out, she had to leave out some middle parts to reach the end by Christmas Eve. The ending felt lacking somehow, as if it hadn't earned its way into the book without the middle parts.

I'm going to lie down on the couch, Stacey said.

Della said, It's the middle of the afternoon. Are you not feeling well?

I feel fine. I just need a nap.

You must be excited about Christmas. It can take a lot out of you.

Yeah, Stacey said. That's what it is.

But really she wanted to have a nap in the afternoon to bank sleep in the daytime and stay awake late enough when Santa came. Tommy told her once that there was no such thing as Santa. Yet each year he ate the cookies they left out for him, or partly ate them, and this year she wanted to get Santa's autograph so she could shut Tommy up once and for all, but that wasn't her entire quest. She wanted to know if Santa took his boots off when he walked through the house. She thought he must or her mother would have noticed.

It snowed on Christmas Eve, a snowfall that continued for two days straight, and because he had four days off in a row, Sage didn't bother to shovel the snow out front. The whole neighbourhood stayed huddled in snow-bound houses, and Della immersed herself in the Eudora Welty novel, *The Optimist's Daughter*, that Stacey had bought her on the bookstore's recommendation. Everything had worked out as well as could be expected. Everyone in the Howard household deserved to sit back and reflect on all they had.

But Sage found it difficult to sit back at any time. His life, over the last several months, had been chaotic and stressful, but exciting and new. On Boxing Day, he poured himself a rum and coke and reread last week's newspaper. He met up with Hart, and the two of them sat in the woodshed and smoked and watched the snowflakes continue to pile up while Hart went on and on about the three pairs of argyle socks he got for Christmas. Later Sage lay on the couch, and Stacey sprawled out beside him and read him the middle chapters of a Bobbsey Twins novel until he fell asleep, but Stacey didn't notice and kept on reading until suppertime, then they ate turkey sandwiches from the leftovers. The scene could have been one portrayed in a Norman Rockwell painting, a different print from the one that featured a boy and his dog fishing that now hung in the living room, a present to Sage from Della at Christmas.

The clock made the only sound in the house past midnight. Sage put his coat and toque and boots on and slid out of the silence into falling snow, a frenzied and hectic spectacle that tricked the mind into believing in an even deeper silence. He walked to town, a town that had most of the roads ploughed but in the middle of the night, two days after Christmas, looked and felt like a place abandoned by humanity. He walked up and down the streets several times, as if lost or deranged, someone with no destination in mind. The walkway that ran along the back of the bar had been shovelled during the day but was filling with snow once again. Sage put a gloved hand into his coat pocket and confirmed that the small box he had wrapped earlier in the week remained there. He hadn't added a bow or card of any kind, but the box contained an expensive pearl necklace. He'd thought about Selma often for months now and of her being alone in her apartment with no family around over Christmas. It was a gesture, he told himself, something he would drop off with well wishes and then be on his way.

From where he stood on the landing, he couldn't determine if Selma was home. He listened at the door and thought he heard something, but maybe not. He knocked lightly, and when he didn't get a response, he pushed his shoulder against the door and entered a room with one small light on behind the couch. In front of it stood Selma, naked, tending to a young man Sage had never seen before. The man had an unbuttoned shirt on but nothing else, and Selma turned away from her kissing when the door flew open. What the fuck? the man said, but Selma turned his head back toward her and continued with her lovemaking.

When Sage stepped outside and closed the door behind him, he didn't move at first, just stood there on the landing, processing as best he could what had happened. He walked down the snow-littered steps and spilled onto the soft snow of the sidewalks, walked through town and down to the river and stood on the bank for a long time before he reached into his pocket for the small box that he threw with all his might into the cold and indifferent river, a river that didn't care, one way or another, that Christmas had come and gone.

13

DAILY, SOMETIMES TWICE A DAY, Della wrote in her journal with a medium-tipped pen, slowly, so that the carving of every letter felt like a revelation. Sage had garnered more than his fair share of attention in her writing, and sometimes she reread what she'd written in an attempt to see the shape of her life. *September 15. Sage has been acting funny lately. Always out of the house for some reason or other. He always has a reason. Today I found out what it is. He's into selling again. He was selling when we first got together, and I told him to stop. Now he's at it again, and he says it's to earn enough money to buy the house. Every night when he gets home, I look out on the street, and if there are no cops tailing him, I say to myself, that's one more day gone by. If he gets caught, he'll lose his job, and who would bring their kids to be babysat at a druggie house? He's not afraid to make things happen, I guess that's one thing I can say. Not the kind of man my dad was.*

She'd been doing that a lot lately: comparing her life with what she remembered growing up. She liked the way Sage always had a bike of some sort for Stacey to learn on. Della had learned to ride her friends' bikes and didn't get her own until after her thirteenth birthday. Her dad had been a low-level civil servant who earned one promotion in thirty years, one who enjoyed licking envelopes and keeping files of important information, most of which he didn't take the trouble to understand. For years they didn't own a car, and when they finally got one, her dad wouldn't use it except to buy groceries. Della's mother finally got her driver's licence, and once a month, she packed Della and her younger sister, Sadie, into the back seat, and they tootled around the country and stopped for a picnic lunch. Sometimes their dad would come, and when he did, he sat in the front seat and looked out the window wistfully, thinking the few thoughts that tended to occur to him, like about his small stamp collection that he stared at for hours on end. Some people don't say much most of the time, and when they do, what they say is worth noting, but Della's father had rarely said anything anyone could remember.

Della's mother had been flighty on occasion. Della remembered a few times when she was fall-down drunk, but most of the time, she sipped on stashes of gin she kept in her dresser and in the kitchen and down in the bowels of the basement, a place no one went to except to do laundry. Her mother would sometimes go for a walk in the middle of the day and forget to come back in time to make supper. She would arrive and explain how her feet were sore and swollen, while Della's dad warmed something sprinkled with Hamburger Helper on the stove for them to eat. She would do exciting things, like dress up even more extravagantly than Della or Sadie did on Halloween. She painted the inside of the house at least once a year. She'd come into Della's yellow room and ask her if she was tired of yellow yet; did she want to consider a pink room because she'd read in a magazine that pink helped your imagination, though it could raise your blood pressure at the same time. Little kids don't need to worry about high blood pressure, she said, so if you want a pink room now's the time to get it.

If Della's dad was like the ancient fir tree that stood rooted in the backyard, her mother was like a dandelion weed that popped up where you least expected it.

In grade six, Della and her friend Marcy read the Nancy Drew series and decided they should open up their own investigation bureau because no one suspected kids of being detectives and because of this they could get away with things that others could not. For several weeks one summer, they spied on their parents, mostly when they took turns sleeping over. They pretended to fall asleep, keeping their talk to a whisper, then waited until their parents went to bed and crouched down by the door to listen to what they were saying. Marcy's parents would talk for at least an hour before falling asleep, and they talked about things they'd heard on the news or some rumour about someone in town, topics they might have discussed in broad daylight. One night a gem surfaced when Marcy's father mentioned that Bert Turnbull had been charged with manslaughter and released on bail. They both knew Rachael Turnbull, who was a year behind them in school, and they set out a plan to start playing with Rachael and get inside the house to see if they could unearth evidence that might be useful in the court case. If they could do that, they would have a detective agency people would know about, and they could start charging for their services and not have to worry about having enough money when the next book in the series came to the bookstore. They tried spying on Della's mother and father too, but soon after the girls retired to bed, Stacey's mother would busy herself reading a magazine and her father would only snore rhythmically.

They took turns asking if Rachael could sleep over, thinking the offer might be reciprocated, but with events in her house as they were, Rachael wasn't allowed to go anywhere.

When Della thought about those years, so filled with adventure, she often wondered if Stacey hid behind their door listening for gems of her own. Likely not, but Della refused to talk about Sage's business when in the bedroom just in case.

As the eldest, Della had tried to do the right thing. She didn't notice at the time, but looking back, she had always tried to tame her younger sister who, the older she became, patterned herself after her mother. Although nearly two years younger than Della, by the time Della had graduated to drive-in movies and sharing popcorn and a few fond kisses with Cody Renton, Sadie wanted to stay up long into the night describing what a hassle it was to help a guy put a safe on in the dark in the back seat of a car, or how important it was to have a couple of towels handy the first time. But it was worth it in the end, she said. Sadie often dated two or three boys at any given time, and it wasn't until years later that Della contemplated the destination of her mother when she wandered off in the middle of an afternoon.

It would be ideal if Stacey had a sister of her own, even a problem sister. Della was content to have at least one daughter to raise, though she had mentioned to Sage the idea of adopting a second child. The question was a mistake. In his stay-at-home-drinking mode the night she asked, and depressed for some reason, she thought the question might spark some new direction, but instead Sage said if she thought he was going to drive back to the town of Hope and scour the fairgrounds for another kid she had something wrong with her. Della started to cry and went to bed early. They had a happy family, and they were giving Stacey a good life, so it hurt that Sage would bring up a history she worked so hard on a daily basis to forget.

In town all the snow had turned to water, and like every year hope was in the air. Sage wanted to fish in his spare time. He went out with Bart Sanderson a few times and picked up some pointers, but he preferred to fish on his own. When he spent the day with his office manager, all conversations eventually led back to Bart Sanderson: the fish he'd caught, the things he'd done, the people he knew. Everything Bart said to him felt exaggerated, like a fishing tale. When he claimed to have shaken the hand of John Wayne on a movie set in Wyoming, Sage was tempted to ask him how this happened, but chances were Bart would have to make up an even larger tale to make it seem real. The little time Sage spent with the man convinced him that if someone like Bart could be part of the management team, there was no good reason he couldn't do the same, so despite his yearning to spend time on the river alone, once a month he agreed to go with Bart Sanderson so he could pick up a few ideas about how he might get promoted.

Fishing felt like an extravagance since they had officially bought the house. The house had suited Della to a T when they were renting, but now that they owned it, she regularly found issues that needed tending to, and if Sage didn't know about them, Della was quick to inform him.

The first week of his vacation, he replaced the roof. Emery helped him for one day, but the rest he did on his own. Sage said he planned to go fishing for a few days, but Della insisted it was time they had a family vacation instead, so they ended up camping at Whiteswan Lake where Stacey and Della tried to keep a fire going and Sage went off by himself to fish. They slept in an old army tent borrowed from Molly and Hart. By the end of the first day, Stacey had all their supplies organized inside and outside. She saw only a few kids at the campsite to play with, but she tried hard to like camping. Dirt everywhere was hard to get used to, and Sage insisted they keep all their food locked in the trunk of the car at night because of bears. Stacey felt certain her dad was kidding, but on the third night of their wilderness vacation, they woke in the middle of the night to the clanging of pots and pans from somewhere down the lake. A few minutes later, thanks to the silhouette provided by a three-quarter moon, they could see and hear and smell a bear investigating their side of the campground. Stacey started to cry, and Della held her close to her chest to muffle any sound that might draw attention. Eventually, the bear moved on, but Stacey couldn't sleep for the rest of the night.

The water was cool for swimming, though Stacey didn't mind it. Some fellow campers told them about Lussier Hot Springs, so Della and Stacey drove there for the day and stayed until dusk. They wore their bathing suits and watched people coming and going until eventually they had the pools to themselves and skinny dipped until the stars came out. They invited Sage the second night, but he said he wasn't interested in sitting in hot water unless it was in a bathtub and said he'd prefer to stay behind and drink beer. Their last night at Whiteswan, the moon shone close to full, and Della and Stacey returned from their nightly spa feeling carefree with their towels draped over their shoulders.

I don't want to go to bed yet, do you?

No, Stacey said. I'm still too hot.

Della spread both towels on top of the picnic table. Here, she said. Climb up and we'll lie under the moonlight until we cool off. The moon glowed, so far out in the wilderness, and its powerful cone of light glistened across the still lake.

It feels good not to wear clothes, Stacey said.

It does doesn't it. It's difficult to get away with this in the city. My sister and I used to swim naked all the time growing up. That wasn't all we did naked. I remember those times like it was yesterday.

How did you get to do that?

Well, for a few years my parents belonged to a nudist colony. You wouldn't think so if you knew my dad, but it was his idea. My sister was young then, but I remember we stayed for a whole weekend sometimes.

And *everyone* was naked?

Absolutely naked. You'd feel out of place if you weren't. Some adults just wanted to sit around in the sun, but the kids were always playing something. I liked the pool the best.

Why did you stop going?

I'm not sure. My mom didn't like it at first, and then she wanted to go any chance we got, and it might have been my dad that resigned. I'm not sure what happened. I was pretty young then.

So why don't we belong to one of them?

Well, they aren't around every corner for one thing. In a place like Fernie, you need to go off in the woods and find a place like what we have here. I thought back in the days we lived in Vancouver that your dad might like that, but he wouldn't discuss it.

How long would it take to get a tan from the moon? Stacey asked.

Well, it might take a long time. I think the key is to lie still and close your eyes and let the light soak into your skin. Della thought about the good times she had growing up. Her mother didn't know how to swim, and her dad said he could, but she'd never seen him swim once. Most of the time, she and Sadie went off alone, inventing their own fun. She wasn't sure if she should regret that or embrace it.

Della fell asleep lying there, and when she woke, she saw Stacey asleep with what looked like a smile on her face. She didn't want to wake her to hobble twenty feet to the tent, so she woke Sage instead.

Stacey is fast asleep on the picnic table, she said. I need you to help me get her to bed without waking her. Sage didn't know how long he'd been asleep or what time it was. He remembered hearing their voices outside the tent, and then he'd started dreaming. He wandered to the side of the campsite and peed at the base of a tree, then returned to see Stacey bathed in mellow light, her skin radiant. He slid his arms under the towel and picked her

up. It had been a while since he had carried her, and he couldn't
believe how heavy an eight-year-old weighed. He crouched at the
entrance of the tent and slid her beside Della under the blanket
they used to cover the large double sleeping bag. Stacey stirred
but stayed asleep, and she turned toward Sage and wrapped
herself around him. Della laughed but Sage didn't say anything.
She thinks you're me, Della said. Don't move for a while. You'll
wake her up if you do.

14

HART TOOK DOWN THE SMALL REPLICA of a fort he had built in his backyard and moved the teeter-totter to the Howards' backyard. Hart had bigger plans, he told Sage one night when they sat in the woodshed, sharing a smoke. He planned to construct a much larger building, a replica of Fort Whoop-Up near Lethbridge, Alberta. The house Hart and Molly owned had a double lot, with no garage or shed in the back like Sage had. Such a building would easily fit, though it would have to be smaller than the real Fort Whoop-Up that Hart said he'd visited twice over the years.

You should see the artifacts they have there, Hart said. Guns, trading supplies, a blacksmith shop and a bar. Everything like it was in the old days. I spent an entire day there last time, and if I could live there and still sell insurance, I would have never come back home. I'll set it up like a small museum of the West. I have quite a few items already, and once I get the building finished, I plan to buy more. Picture this, Hart said. Right above the fireplace, a full-spread buffalo hide.

Sage listened to all Hart knew about the place, which was plenty. He looked at the sketch of the four-room version of the fort Hart envisioned, a complicated endeavor, and to Hart's credit, he had thought through many of the details. Already he had a small delivery of logs in the backyard, but he said he would hold off on construction until he dug a well.

Are you allowed to dig your own well in the city? Sage asked.

We'll find out, I guess.

And don't you need a permit to build?

Oh, probably they'd want you to ask for one, but asking comes with the risk of them saying no. By the time I have it finished, they'll be so impressed, they won't have an argument that makes sense. Back in those days, they didn't have building codes anyway. They had survival codes.

Fort Whoop-Up, Sage said. You've got yourself an idea there, I'll say that much.

I might just call it Fort Whoop, Hart said. It'll be smaller, and I don't want to come off as some kind of competition.

What does Molly say, Sage asked. Is she okay with all that?

The older that woman gets, the more ornery she becomes, Hart said, passing back the last of the smoke. If there's nothing bothering her, she'll turn rocks over until she finds something. She's good at it.

Sage felt certain Hart's project was designed to get him out of the house and away from Molly's relentless scrutiny. Hart said once he finished, if she went through two or three days of mean and nasty, it would give him a place to hunker down. For the rest of the summer and well into the fall, Sage didn't go fishing or work on his own house so he could help Hart with the fort, but only after watching him toil for a week by himself with the well. Hart dug and kept on digging until he had a square with walls three and a half feet that went down into the earth seven feet or so. Hart had taught himself the art of witching for water using a forked piece of willow. In the back corner of his yard, the willow bobbed fifteen times once and twenty times on the second try, which he said meant there would be water twenty feet down, maybe less. After he got the square dug down over his head, he had trouble getting the dirt out of the hole. Sage considered lending a hand then, but he wasn't enthralled with the project yet, so he held off. Next, Hart built an auger bit and attached it to PVC pipe that had wings on it so he could twist the contraption and dig a narrow hole below the seven feet he'd dug by hand. He spent three days doing this, and eventually water came bubbling to the surface. His tenacity impressed Sage, who went over to help him fit a cement casing into the water flowing into the cavity. Hart then built a wooden frame for the top and found an ancient hand pump from a salvage depot, and sure enough, with a little effort, he could get a pail of water when he needed to.

I'll take a few gallons out every day for a while, he said. That way things will settle down and the water will run clear.

The effort of it had tuckered Hart out. He sat down and mulled over the plans he had for the fort. Sage said, It seems like a lot of effort you've put in when you've got running water in the house. Why, you could have run a hose out from the house for water.

I know, Hart said. I could have done plenty of things. But I want this fort to be an exhibit. I want it to be true to life—a place where a man can spit on the ground. Few things are true to life these days. There's a word for what I'm looking for. Bucolic. Right here in the middle of the city, I'm going to capture some bucolic.

So Sage said he would help him on weekends. He ended up helping in the evenings as well, and by late September, the two of them had logs in place and mortared and floor boards set down in two of the four rooms. This turned out to be a long-term project, but Sage was committed. There would be no electricity in the fort; Hart wouldn't hear of it. Instead, he had three kerosene lanterns that allowed him to putter away after dark in the winter. Sometimes, past midnight, Sage wandered out into the backyard and saw the lanterns still burning, with Hart out there roughing it, secure and away from the venom he wished to avoid, much like the pioneers he so revered.

Della had no idea if Stacey had been baptized as a child and didn't want to involve Molly the Nose in her solution. A revival meeting and baptism had been planned by the Pentecostal Church down at the river in mid-July, and Della wanted Stacey to be saved, to give her being over to the grace of God. Della had been baptized as a young girl, and would do it again with Stacey, if she agreed. She didn't.

In September Stacey would begin grade five. She was a good student, her teachers had said at the end of grade four, and could have straight As if only she weren't so stubborn about some things. Spelling was a strength, they said, but Stacey refused to represent her class in the district spelling bee because she hated having to spell words that didn't have an even number of letters like her own name. The compositions she started in class she finished at home because she favoured words that didn't have an odd number number of letters, making the process laborious. When she had to use "a" or "the" she wrote "an" and "they" and drew a line through the last letter when she finished. When given a math problem that challenged her to determine the cost of seven people to ride the bus when two people were senior citizens and one was a child and the total came out to $23, she answered, then put in brackets: (+1 = $24). She told her teacher odd numbers felt lonely, but when they got together with other odd numbers, they became happy because they were finally even. Her last teacher set up an appointment with the district psychologist and informed Sage and Della after the fact. Sage had stormed the school and told them to call off the dogs or they could expect a bucket full of trouble.

Stacey gave Della a hopeless look when she mentioned the

baptism. I'm not exactly falling off a cliff, she said, so I don't see why I need to be saved from anything.

It's not that kind of saving, Della said. You know better than that. It's to assure your redemption once your life on Earth comes to an end. It's publicly stating your faith in Jesus Christ.

I'm not convinced about the whole Jesus Christ, God thing anyway. I've never met him, and I haven't met anyone who has. If there was a god out there looking after us, then John Lennon would still be alive today.

John Lennon had been shot on a Monday, and Stacey had refused to go to school for the rest of the week. John had been her favourite Beatle, and she told everyone that when she grew up, she would visit John Lennon in New York and they would record a song together. Sage threatened to destroy all their Beatles music if she didn't return to school. The hollow threat seemed to work, though Stacey went back because Della had insisted she stay in her room to brood during the week if she felt too sick to go to school. Because she missed her friend Amber, she had agreed to return.

Well then, why do you even go to church if that's how you feel? You come almost every Sunday, and you sing along with everyone like you mean it.

I like the singing, okay? There's nothing wrong with singing. I sing at home too, but that doesn't mean I'll come through the back door forever. It's a great story, though.

What story? What do you mean?

The whole Adam and Eve thing. Adam was born so Eve was created, and that should have been the end of it, but there was a problem. Adam and Eve got bored with each other and started picking fruit they weren't supposed to. I think Eve wasn't very good-looking. How could they be so bored they wanted to steal fruit?

Where did you hear such a tale?

I didn't hear it anywhere. I made it up. It's what I think.

Della could do nothing to sort out her daughter's mind once it got wound up in a knot. The following Sunday, Stacey declared that she would go to the river; she would take a break from church and go fishing with her dad and Tommy and Amber on Sunday.

And why the sudden interest in fishing? You've always said no when your dad asked if you wanted to learn.

Nature's like a church. That's what Dad says. He also says it's up to people like us to catch enough fish to feed the Catholics on Fridays.

Why are you always so stubborn? I'm going to consider this conversation closed.

Closed works for me. If you ever want to open it up again, I'll be down by the river.

Della went to church with Molly as usual. It didn't feel the same, and Molly had to ask why Stacey wasn't coming. Molly's advice rarely offered comfort, and it wasn't much different on this occasion. She said an ideal solution would be if they all attended church as a family, like the Pierrynowski and Smith family. They entered the house of God as a family, Molly said, and left as a family, cohesive and blessed. Della wanted more than anything to remind Molly the Nose that Hart didn't attend church as part of his family, but that would be a futile argument because the way Hart saw it he attended church every Sunday: the one he had created himself in the backyard.

Della had toured Fort Whoop on two occasions, both times because Sage wanted her to see what had been created over the years. The help he'd offered went on longer than he had imagined, and he took pride in what they accomplished. The fort had four rooms according to its original design and a centerpiece river rock fireplace in one room with a bison pelt Hart bought from a farmer in Saskatchewan. The fireplace took him most of one winter to construct, and he made a point of cooking supper there once a month, although Molly wasn't interested and made herself a sandwich and a pot of tea on the nights he did so. They tested the water from the well, and it was safe to drink, though hard and full of minerals, which Hart said were good for you, nature's fortification against disease and an important part of our ancestors' diet. Hart had an outhouse in the backyard, albeit a compromise, a chemical toilet, as he didn't have enough land at his disposal and he didn't want to compromise his water supply. The largest room was the living quarters, with two beds against the wall on one side and a small piano and rustic bar on the other. A room at the back Hart kept as a workshop and forge, though the forge wasn't yet functional, and on the side of this room, he had a counter with supplies, a diminutive version of the Indian room found at the original Fort Whoop-Up. On the walls in various rooms, he displayed his burgeoning collection of artifacts from the Wild West, including two new guns and an original whisky jug he had paid too much for at a secondhand store in Medicine Hat. Stacey brought all her friends to see Fort Whoop whenever she could, and she always pointed out the bow and arrow that hung on the wall, as Hart had helped her make it in the original style a few years earlier. Stacey never laid claim to having made the bow and arrow because Hart always passed it off as a genuine article and that was sufficient commendation. Framed signs in various places inside the fort explained the function and purpose of what he had so those who visited Fort Whoop could make better sense of it. Originally, the plan had been to charge admission, but Hart thought it best to let people enjoy the facility for free, and he placed a donation box on the way out. A surprising number of people found their way to Fort Whoop, and any money collected he put back into building his collection.

Sage never said so, but it impressed him that Hart's vision had come to fruition. Hart was a different man in or around Fort Whoop. Unless it was ungodly hot, he wore his light brown leather jacket, fringe-styled like he'd seen in his photo archives. In his car and doing his insurance rounds, he looked like a well-kept puppy, but when he wore his jacket and toured the fort, he had a more confident air about him.

Molly the Nose had let anyone who would listen know she didn't think the fort or museum or whatever it was would ever get done. Her at first vociferous commitment to her husband's impending failure only petered out like a seasonal creek near the end. She told Della the one good thing about the building was how it provided a place for Hart to store the ugly saddle chair that had taken up room in their master bedroom for too many years.

15

STACEY LEARNED TO SWIM. Not proficiently, but she could do the dog paddle and tread water, and that satisfied Molly the Nose who knew better than most the importance of such a skill. Learning had less to do with her next-door neighbour than it did with Amber's parents who went to Surveyors Lake every summer, and the summer before grade eight, she came home with severe sunburn and had to spend most of a week in the shade of the backyard with a tube of aloe vera cream, which didn't bother her much because she was reading the *Flowers in the Attic* series by V.C. Andrews. Amber was reading them too, and they spent hours of impassioned discussion on events that carried them through the summer. The books contained all sorts of family troubles, including the main character, Cathy Dollanganger, falling in love with her brother after he rapes her.

I don't see how that could happen, Amber said. My brother is two years older than me, and I can't stand him. Cathy must have had a mental problem.

They all have mental problems, Stacey said. I guess I can imagine it happening if the conditions were right. I mean, look at the house they're living in. The family is nuts. Besides, it's what's called a broken family, and that means the people in it are broken.

Reading about the Dollangangers made most of what Stacey had to put up with tolerable. Sage fabricated a reason to be miserable and foul-tempered every few weeks, and she held more hope of changing the Fernie weather patterns than of adjusting his tirades. It was Amber's family Stacey idolized. They had two parents and two children, and that seemed right. When she went somewhere with Amber and her older brother wasn't there, she pretended to be Amber's sister, living in a normal family. Amber's father referred to them as "you girls," and Stacey thought that a father with two daughters would say that. He would lump them together as part of the puzzle, inseparable.

Most of the time, Stacey's mother and father got along, but once a month, as if it were an event marked on the calendar, they would fight about something that resulted in either Della taking refuge in her bedroom or Sage heading out late at night to the pub, sometimes both. The next day, everything would be back to normal, and Stacey could forget the battle had ensued, but as the conflicts repeated themselves, over time she developed an air of wariness, an expectation that at any time Sage could run mad. A couple of years earlier, when she had just started grade six, her father came home late from work and had stopped off at the pub with Emery first. Della and Stacey had finished their dinner, as Della for several years had stopped waiting for him if he didn't come through the door by six, and Sage sat at the kitchen table, eating alone. When he finished, he joined them in the living room and watched Della get her weekly fix of *Dallas*, with Stacey keeping her company.

Sage wasn't interested in the show because he said it wasn't realistic. He waited until an ad came on, then said, Have you two had the talk yet?

What talk? Della said. What are *you* talking about?

The talk. You know. The birds and the bees. Emery says they teach them everything they need to know in grade six. I wondered if you'd filled her in yet.

Well, we talk all the time, Stacey and I. I'm sure she'll be prepared.

Big changes are coming, Sage said. He turned away from his wife and focused on Stacey. You'll menstruate before you get to junior high, that's a given. Your breasts will grow, and before you know it, you'll have to hold them up with a bra. Then what will happen—

That's enough, Della said. Stacey knows what's in front of her. You don't need to make it sound vulgar. She'll become a woman in her own time. A beautiful woman I might add.

Stacey sat inert, staring at her mother and regarding her dad skeptically in her peripheral vision. She thought about the hefty episode that would make its way into Della's journal later that night.

That's what I'm saying. She'll be beautiful, and that's when the action starts.

Stacey took the book she had been half reading, went to her bedroom and closed the door.

What was that all about? Della had said. We were having a perfectly relaxed evening watching TV, and you come and spoil everything.

Excuse me for asking a question. I guess you've thought of everything. There's no need for me to think anymore.

Since that night, Stacey had felt a new separation between her and her father. Every room in the house felt one way when he was in it and another way when he was not. If she had a point of view about something, he would enter the room and her idea would vanish. It felt eerie to her that, just as Sage had predicted, she had her first period before grade eight began, as if he had willed it to happen, and that part felt abnormal. Many of her friends, including Amber, had been complaining about their plight for almost a year, and where they once held ties as children, they were now bound in the mysterious journey of adolescence, through more than physical changes. Stacey and Amber now wove their way through the world with knowledge of something new and startling, and although it didn't have a label, they had become members of a vulnerable species. Teachers looked at them differently, or so it seemed. They did look at them differently, didn't they? This they discussed over and over, and boys, particularly older boys they had known for years who had tried to avoid contact at all cost, now suggested games like tag football that would be fun to play together. The grade nines had three sock hops a year, and the grades eights were invited to the last one of the year, in June. Most of the girls and some boys couldn't wait. Stacey wasn't so sure. She thought about what Sage had said about this being when the action started. Sage did so much that was infuriating, but while he acted like a dumb ass most of the time, he might be smarter than she thought.

Unless she could come up with a good excuse not to, Stacey was responsible for cooking on Monday nights, and Della said this was good preparation because when *she* left home, she knew how to boil water and scramble eggs and not much more. Stacey often fried sausages because it was the one meal Sage never complained about, but sometimes she would cook fish if he came home with any on the weekend. Della encouraged Stacey when she could and reiterated that learning to cook was an important part of becoming an adult. When Sage joined in the discussion, he talked about the real world and how Stacey had no clue what a chore life would be.

On sausage night, no fish in sight, Della had taken the two kids she was babysitting to the park for exercise and a Popsicle on the way home. A year earlier, Stacey might have joined them if she had nothing going on, but now she yearned for time alone, and one way to accomplish being alone was to announce she wanted a bath. Today she had the house to herself, and with no announcement needed, she shed every stitch of clothing and put them in the hamper, then laid out a comfortable pair of shorts and a top for when she finished. She started the water running and stood in front of the bathroom mirror. The contents of the bathroom cabinet had changed over the years. She now used Wild Madagascar Vanilla body wash and Grapefruit Scented Dead Sea bath salts on alternate days in her bath water, and she always coated her skin with ultra shea body lotion when she got out. Her breasts had changed but were still not much more than bloated nipples. She liked to examine their progress before her bath and again after, convinced they got puffier after every bath, and some days she thought the one on her right side had gotten a head start. She owned a training bra she wore with certain outfits, but the training consisted mostly of learning how to put it on and take it off. Amber owned two bras and was lucky enough to need them.

A solid hour in which to submerge herself in warm, soapy water and finish *If There Be Thorns* felt like such luxury that making dinner and doing the dishes after would be easy.

Stacey had slept in so she had forgotten that her dad had taken one week of his holidays and had gone off fishing early in the morning. She knew he had entered the house because no one else made that much noise. Della? he yelled, but Della wasn't home to answer. He assumed she was off with the kids somewhere and opened a beer from the fridge, plunked it down on the kitchen table and stormed his way into the bathroom.

Hey, Stacey yelled, trying her best to use her paperback as a shield.

I didn't know you were in here, he said.

Well, I am, so please leave.

Sage stared at his daughter squirming in a foot of water, book in hand. It looked as though he were about to explain something, or apologize for the circumstance, but he stood there and said nothing, and the six or eight seconds that followed felt like hours to Stacey.

I'll take a piss in the backyard then, he said, and turned to leave. If you don't want this to happen, you should lock the door next time.

She pulled herself from the bathtub and locked the door. Unsure whether she could dry herself off in time to make it to the bedroom, she climbed back into the tub. She didn't feel like reading anymore. She would wait. If she dried herself off and wrapped herself in her bath towel, then made her way to the bedroom, she would pass the kitchen where Sage would be sitting at the table drinking a beer and reading the newspaper. He may be waiting for her to do just that, but she would hold on. Her mother would make her way home, and she would bring her clothes to the bathroom. It felt like he'd taken everything in while he stood there pretending to be stunned, but maybe he only saw her book and her face, her knees above water. She would cook sausages for supper as usual, and he would have nothing but good things to say about that.

Molly the Nose had stopped babysitting after three years. Della always had more kids to look after than she did, and after a while, it felt like the effort wasn't worth it anymore. She had enjoyed the extra money, but it left so little time in the day for doing things she wanted to do. After she stopped, they had about the same amount of money because once Sage's Mary Jane stash ran out, he told Hart about the business proposition, and since then the two of them took a one-day business trip to Argenta every September. Sage said he didn't want to run around dealing like he had in the past (he knew it would be an ongoing battle with Della if he did), so in exchange for a personal year's supply, he passed the bundle on to Hart who now had plenty of storage in Fort Whoop. Anyone in town interested in buying dropped by in the afternoon and asked for a tour of the fort, and in the small version of the fort's original Indian room, the dealings took place. Not much had changed from the early days of Fort Whoop-Up, except that they traded in weed instead of whiskey.

Not once did Molly the Nose question how they had enough money to get by. She had an idea that Hart was up to something, with so many people eager to visit the fort in the backyard, but if a more detailed explanation existed, she didn't want to know. Besides, she made her own financial contribution with petit point, a tedious and exacting fine needle art form that sometimes took months to complete. She finished a rural scene titled Glade Creek Grist Mill first. She liked it because the scene could be viewed around Fernie. She kept this picture framed and mounted on the feature wall of their living room. Hart didn't say much, only that it looked good. In her first year, she finished three similar pictures and took them to a gallery and sold them for four hundred dollars each. She still preferred to work on scene projects, but petit point designs that adorned purses sold better, and they took less than half the time.

For the first few years after the Howards moved to Fernie, it was Molly who poked her nose around the neighbourhood, while Hart sold insurance or hunkered down inside the house watching movies. Now, Molly didn't get much sun, and as if they'd traded places, Hart was always outside working on something to do with his fort. Some logs had settled over the years, and the caulking kept him busy, plus one window had cracked due to the shifting logs and needed replacing. Every Wednesday Della hosted a bible study group, and Sage and Hart held a meeting of their own at Fort Whoop.

Hart loved country music, but he couldn't play a single tune on the guitar he'd owned for a decade. Sage had been in a rock band that did a lot of Crosby, Stills, Nash and Young, so with Hart's persuasion he would play, and the two of them would sing a few songs badly. Hart loved "I Walk the Line," and Sage learned it, though the song felt like a lie. He much preferred "Oh Lonesome Me" and "King of the Road."

If I don't get a management job soon, I'm going to quit, Sage said. The two of them had finished smoking, and now Sage cracked open one of the two beers he had brought with him. When he wasn't drinking, he set the bottle down on top of the Bible that Molly insisted Hart keep in the fort because, historically, forts housed an ongoing battle between the word of God and a thirst for whiskey. Sage thought it worked fine as a coaster.

What would you do then?

Don't have a clue. This is the longest I've worked anywhere. I hate staying in one place.

Not many good paying jobs in this town, Hart said.

I know. There are other towns, though.

If I could do one thing over, Hart said, I would have bought property outside of town. Something near the river maybe, so I could expand my fort. I can't make it any bigger the way it is now. I feel trapped with what I got.

When the two of them sat together, long periods of silence punctuated their conversation, and this was one of them. They often thought about what had been said or what to say next, but sometimes they simply enjoyed the opportunity to think without someone in the house wondering why they weren't talking. Hart sported a long mustache, wild at the sides, that he'd grown after completing the fort, and it occupied the ends of his fingers.

At least you've got your daughter to raise, Hart said. That's something at least.

Sage said nothing back. He knew his thinking about that, and he knew what Hart was thinking, and they shared the same thought. Sage knew he and Della wouldn't be raising her much longer. Stacey was growing up fast. Too fast.

16

MOST SUNDAYS, STACEY STILL ATTENDED CHURCH with Della, though more for the music than anything, and she liked some of the stories, in particular the parables the minister favoured. On Bible study nights, she and Amber and a few others made sure they had something to do and somewhere to go. Amber had a boyfriend now, named Morgan, and because he played the piano, they called him Morgan the Organ. Stacey didn't mind Morgan, but she thought Amber was wasting her time because they mostly play-wrestled while the three of them watched a movie, which meant that Stacey couldn't concentrate, or they'd argue about things that didn't matter to anyone but them. Morgan's dad was a scientist and often travelled around consulting for companies. Stacey didn't think Morgan had the brains to do that, but when she and Amber began grade nine, he started up an Environmental Club, and Amber and Stacey and a handful of others followed his lead. They started a paper-recycling program at school. Morgan took Stacey and Amber along for support when he outlined for the teachers his plans for a new way of doing things around the school. Morgan said if it takes eighty to a hundred years for a tree to grow, then we ought to use the tree more than once. His speech reminded Stacey of the previous week's church service about the faggot of sticks. Alone the sticks could be easily broken, but together as a bundle, no one could break them. Working together, the task could be accomplished. Morgan got most of his ideas from his dad, but where he got them from didn't matter. He found places that would take cans and another that would take glass. With recycling new to everyone, Morgan was astute enough to convince the school they could brag about their program to other schools. The members of the Environmental Club also became a menace to many because they monitored what went into the regular garbage at lunchtime. Every Friday they stayed behind to bundle the paper and sort through the cans and bottles. Once Della understood her daughter's vision, she wanted to help any way she could. Her father wasn't as keen.

You know what happens to a can, don't you? You leave it out in the dump, and a year later, it rusts away to nothing. Two years maybe.

Stacey waited until he stopped talking. She knew from experience to wait until he'd expelled any negativity before saying anything. This time it didn't take him long. Her practice worked well until Sage was drinking. Then she knew to wait until morning.

That's exactly what happens, she said. Iron oxides filling the dump where there were no oxides before, rain pushing it into the drinking water nearby and polluting rivers where the fish you like to catch need to live. New cans can come from old cans. There's only so much of everything in the world. It's finite. Morgan says the only things that should make it to the garbage dump are things that will rot back to earth in a friendly manner.

Morgan, Morgan, Morgan. Who is this Morgan? The second coming of Christ?

Della listened to the debate, supportive, but as usual she wouldn't say much. Stacey wanted to suggest Morgan might be the second coming of Christ but didn't want to lose her mother as an ally.

It took almost a month before Sage tired of resisting his daughter's recycling ideas. The newspapers went in a large cardboard box and the cans and bottles in separate plastic pails. Once a month, Morgan and his dad drove by and picked up everything. The first time Morgan and his dad came, Sage said, they're putting garbage men out of work is what they're doing. Morgan stared at Stacey when he heard that. He looked at her like he'd just realized what she might be up against.

He wasn't her boyfriend, just a boy in the Environmental Club named Hugh, a year older than Stacey and in grade eleven. One Saturday, after sorting the recycling in Morgan's garage, Morgan invited Amber and Stacey to watch *The Kung Fu Emperor* at his house. His dad was away for a few days, his mother was out shopping, and it was pouring rain. Stacey couldn't think of a good reason not to. She found the movie boring, but the boys liked it, and the storm howling outside made it almost night-time dark in the living room. Amber and Morgan snuggled together, sometimes tickling one another, sometimes kissing. Hugh took this as a signal and wrapped his arm over Stacey's shoulder, and she didn't mind that part. For the longest time, nothing else happened, and then Hugh whispered something in her ear she didn't catch, and next thing she knew, he moved in and kissed her on the lips. Stacey had never kissed a boy before and surprised herself, not only because she didn't resist but kissed him back for almost a minute. Hugh sat upright after that and seemed satisfied with what he'd accomplished. By Monday morning, Stacey felt so sick she couldn't get out of bed let alone go to school.

Della got her to the doctor's office to see Dr. Mesmer, a man much younger than the doctor who had examined Stacey's rash years before. Della took this as a good sign. She thought a younger doctor had to be on top of the newest medical discoveries.

Stacey had a fever and a sore, swollen throat. Dr. Mesmer

took a swab from inside her mouth and said he would send it to the lab for testing to be sure, but it appeared she had a severe case of strep throat. Since Della and Sage were not at all sick, the doctor said to keep it that way Stacey should drink from her own cup, and they should wash all the dishes immediately after she used them, at least for the first couple of days. He said strep throat could be acquired from airborne particles and discouraged any close contact. She should stay home and rest and drink plenty of liquids and make a return visit on Friday. She would miss a whole week of school, maybe more, while the penicillin went to work.

Amber dropped homework off every day after school, and she wrote Stacey notes telling her anything of interest she missed. Hugh was sick too, one note said. So sick he wanted to die.

Stacey didn't want to die, but she didn't feel like doing much of anything. She spent an hour each evening doing her homework and watched TV during the day. Despite being a first aid man, or perhaps because of it, Sage excused himself from the dinner table and ate in front of the TV news, which suited Stacey because it gave her a chance to have a discussion with her mother without Sage around to edit everyone's thoughts. Della said she remembered having the chicken pox when she was younger than Stacey, how she had a fever most of the time and felt itchy in places people told her not to scratch. She had a bath twice a day and wore calamine lotion for a week. When the ordeal ended she gladly returned to school.

Stacey wanted to be at school too. She didn't mind most of her teachers for some reason, and she liked being part of the Environmental Club. One of the assignments she'd passed on to Amber to take to school concerned the annual poetry contest that their teacher, Miss Carlson, was gung ho about. Before the week ended, Amber brought the news that Stacey's poem had won first prize and would be published in the annual. She'd gotten lost for most of an afternoon completing her poem because she would only write it her way. She called it "Even Then."

Even Then
gang dogs wild on snow hill
lonely as wanted dreams
segregated soulmate with
need of town folk who'd
feed this desire
in ones or twos
bitter or harsh
with nuzzle hazard maws
feet high in mica or quartz
left yips then yaps at
brazen doorstep unkind
to lonely canine hackled
friendship coated gold

Della read the poem twice and said she didn't understand it. She passed it to Sage, and he said the poem seemed straightforward but didn't elaborate. Stacey didn't care one way or another. If Miss Carlson chose it as the winner, it was good enough for her.

She was glad she had kissed Hugh, even though doing it had made her sick. She didn't want to kiss him again, though, and she had her mind made up to pull him aside and tell him that. He liked doing jars, and she liked doing cans, and that wasn't the only difference between them.

How old were you when you and Dad got married?

We were older than most, twenty-nine and thirty-one. I was married briefly before your father and I got together, but I told you that already.

Tell me again.

I could help you with your homework. You have homework, don't you?

You're just stalling, Mom. I want to know about Willy.

Well, it's what happens to young girls when they get too serious about boys at a young age. I thought I was ready to marry, and I thought Willy Hofner was ready too, but he wasn't. Five days after he married me, he went to work on a freighter. Your dad went with him. Willy never came back, and no one has seen him since.

This Willy sounds like an idiot, Stacey said. Who would marry someone and then run away?

Willy Hofner would. Some people aren't meant to get married. I can see that now.

Was Willy Hofner handsome or kind to people? Stacey meant was he better-looking than Sage or more understanding and even-keeled, and she hoped her mother wouldn't catch the angle of her question.

Willy looked too striking for his own good, I think. A good-looking person carries a burden most people don't understand. He thought about himself a lot.

So you thought Dad suited you better. Is that it? Is that why you married him?

What happens is you get used to things. Once and a while, you see two people and think how well-suited they are. People mention it when it happens. Most of the time, you see people together and you think: How did that happen? *They* probably think the same thing too, but that's just life. The world has more Willy Hoffners than it knows what to do with.

Sage came into the kitchen and left his dinner dishes beside the sink. What's all this serious talk going on here? Solving the world's problems, are we? *Who* thought a lot about himself?

Willy Hofner, Della said. Stacey wanted to know what he was like.

A complete asshole, Sage said. He grabbed a beer from the

fridge and went out the back door to see if Hart was in Fort Whoop yet. If he wasn't there, it didn't matter because he always left the door open. He would start a fire in the fireplace and sit by himself watching the hungry flames.

What is it with Dad? Stacey said.

I don't know. He means well, and he's not happy at work, I know that. He feels trapped sometimes. You might feel that way some day. It doesn't seem to matter where your father is in life, he thinks there's somewhere better. He's always been that way, and suggesting he change is like asking water to give up on running downhill.

He makes little things look big, Stacey said. Only big things are big.

You're right about that, Della said. I think when he was young, he learned to think of big things as little, so now when he makes little things bigger than they should be, it makes big things from the past not so important.

What kind of big things?

Your dad has an older brother, Danny. He told me one night that his brother used to get away with murder. He never explained any of this until a year after we got married. Your dad had been drinking more than usual one night, and that's when he told me everything. Their family lived in Vancouver at the bottom of a steep hill. Danny was about seven or eight, so your dad might have been five. They had this wagon they used to pull each other around on, and sometimes they would pull it to the top of the hill and tie the handle in the middle and send the wagon down the hill. There weren't many cars on their street, but when they came down the hill, they came fast. If anything made it out on the road, which sometimes happened, the cars would slam on their brakes and leave strips of rubber on the road, and Danny thought that was fun. One night, just as it was getting dark, they tied a large teddy bear into the wagon and hid behind some bushes at the side of the driveway. Their driveway sloped toward the main road, and Danny told your dad to wait until a car was halfway down the hill and push the wagon onto the road. The person driving would think a kid sat in the wagon and slam on their brakes, hard. Your dad didn't want to do it because he didn't want a car to run over his teddy bear. Every time a car came down the hill, your dad refused to push the wagon, then after a time, a small car came down the hill, and Danny lined the wagon up and pushed it onto the street. The old man driving the car didn't see the wagon or the bear at first, and at the last minute, as he hit the brakes, he tried to swerve out of the way and ran into a telephone pole and died instantly.

That's his big thing? Stacey asked.

It is. It's haunted him ever since. After, he thought maybe if he had pushed the wagon like his brother asked, it wouldn't have happened. It was Danny's fault, that much is obvious, at least as far as the stupid things kids get up to can be faulted, but when you're little, you don't see things clearly. Danny didn't treat your dad well after that. Who's to say why he would be mean to him, but he was. When Danny turned thirteen, he got into a squabble with his dad and ran away, and no one saw him after that. Thirteen is young to run away. Your dad thought his brother running away was his fault too, and your dad left home at sixteen, and he's been running ever since. He's talked about moving again. You don't need to worry, though. I told him there's no way we're going anywhere, at least until you graduate. I like living in Fernie. Don't you?

Why does he want to move? What's wrong with Fernie?

There's nothing wrong with Fernie. I shouldn't have mentioned it. You have nothing to worry about. He means well. You need to know that. He wants the best for us all.

Stacey knew her father's habits. She knew he would be next door with Hart, smoking pot and bitching about life. Amber once described Sage as a stoner, and Stacey could think of nothing to refute it.

Why does he get stoned all the time?

It's your father's way of putting the day behind him. He's in a better mood when he smokes than when he's drinking. I like it better.

Morgan the Organ smokes dope sometimes, Stacey said. Amber and I tried it, but I don't see the point. Once you start smoking pot, you think everything in the world is amazing when really it's not.

17

SHE HAD BEEN THINKING ABOUT IT all day Friday. And since her mom and dad rarely went out of the house together, she would suggest they go to town for dinner and a movie or whatever else they could drum up, and she would have the house to herself for a few hours, have a few friends over for the evening. She wouldn't call it a party because that would set off alarm bells and lead to a definitive no. She came home early from school so she could try the idea on her mom first, otherwise she had no hope. As soon as Stacey walked in the door, she knew it would not happen.

I'm going to ask a huge favour, Della said. You can say no if you want to, but if you agree, it will make things much easier. Your Aunt Sadie is coming to stay, and I'm hoping we can offer her your bedroom.

I have an Aunt Sadie?

You know you do; I've mentioned her many times. She just hasn't been around for twenty years. God only knows what made her surface now.

Whenever Della had mentioned having a sister, she had talked of her in the past tense, describing how the two of them grew up and what they did to pass the time. Never had there been any mention of meeting up with Sadie, and as far as Stacey knew, her mother and her aunt never even wrote each other.

How did she find us? Stacey asked.

I can't imagine how. I'm afraid to find out, if you want to know the truth. She's like a stranger to me now.

And so Stacey got busy on the phone and told her friends not only that the party at her place wasn't going to happen but also that if it happened somewhere else, she couldn't go. With her missing aunt coming to town, she had to stay home to find her.

The babysitting kids had been picked up by the time Sage got home, and Della made the declaration all over again. Stacey went into her bedroom to arrange a few things for her aunt's arrival. If she weren't in the same room as her mom and dad, the conversations got more interesting to listen to.

So, Sage said, she's not around for your first wedding, she's not around when your parents died, and she was nowhere in sight when we got together, and now out of the blue, she shows up. She must need something.

I wouldn't be so harsh about it. She's family. I'll bet she's getting along just fine and wants to reconnect with her only sister.

Sadie had insisted that Della shouldn't worry about dinner. She would catch a bus into town and would arrive at six-thirty. She didn't mind walking, she said, but since she didn't know the layout of the town, maybe someone could pick her up.

After several slanderous statements pulled out of thin air, Sage appeared almost upbeat about Della's sister. Sadie's arrival provided something new, and he liked that. Because Stacey and Della were busy changing sheets and tidying things after dinner, Sage washed and dried the dishes by himself, whistling a tune the whole time.

Buses are often late, Sage said. I'll be over visiting Hart for a while. Give me a shout when she arrives.

The bus arrived fifteen minutes late, and Della and Stacey stood at the side of the depot waiting and watching the three people who disembarked. Sadie stepped off last by a considerable measure, and even after twenty years, Della recognized her immediately. Stacey stood back while her mom wrapped her arms around her long-lost relative. The two looked somewhat like sisters, but Sadie wore her hair long and straight, and she was the thinner of the two.

Sadie, this is Stacey. She's in grade ten already.

Stacey said hello, but that wasn't enough for Sadie. She gave her a hug, just not as long as the hug she'd given her sister. Sadie pointed to the large suitcase so the driver could extricate it from the bowels of the bus.

You have such a nice smile, Stacey, Sadie said. You must have to beat them away with a stick.

They drove around town. Sadie had never been to Fernie before. She said she'd never even heard of it. When they got to the house, Sage wasn't home yet, but Molly the Nose stood at her front window taking everything in. Stacey went to Fort Whoop to fetch Sage, but he wouldn't respond right away when she got there because he and Hart were arm wrestling.

So this is my long-lost sister-in-law. Sage stuck out his hand. He didn't hug often. Certainly not people he'd never met.

Pleased to meet you, Sage. I've heard a lot about you.

Della, you must have talked her ear off from the bus depot home.

Your wife hasn't said much about you, Sadie said. Willy Hofner gave me the lowdown.

You know Willy Hofner? Sage said it, and Della thought it.

I do. We met on a holiday cruise a few years ago. That's how I knew how to find you. He told me you'd moved to Fernie.

That miserable son of a bitch, Sage said. Where is he now?

I have no idea. He had an American wife when we met. Her name was Izzie, and I think they might have lived in Montana, but don't quote me on that. Anyway, I remember Izzie telling me they were moving back to New York. Her family lives there.

Sage went to the fridge for beer and offered Sadie one. She said she had a bottle of rum in her suitcase, if they had a glass and some ice. Della said she'd join her, and after everyone had their drinks and went into the living room, Stacey opened a bottle of beer for herself and poured the contents into a plastic cup.

A cruise? What kind of cruise?

Well, it was in Mexico. It was my first time in Mexico, and that's where we met. After he'd had a few drinks, Willy told me everything.

How does he know where we live? Della asked.

That part he didn't explain. He said he didn't think you'd want to meet up with him again. That's what he said.

I'll bet he did, Sage said. Is his wife one of those rich upstate New Yorkers? The bastard owes me money.

I couldn't say for sure. Izzie had beautiful nails, that much I remember.

Stacey listened to the conversation that bounced off the walls, and after everyone else helped themselves to a second and third drink, she went to the fridge and poured herself another beer. Her Aunt Sadie had done many different jobs, her favourite as a hostess on a cruise ship. She said she had the time of her life, and the way she said it, everyone understood she'd seen a thing or two in the men department. When she did finally marry, it was to a man named Marvin, kind but useless, and only after he died did she realize he owned a shopping mall in San Jose, which became hers. When Della asked how Marvin died, Sadie said old age, and Sage laughed so hard he fell off the couch.

After nine-thirty, Amber knocked on the door to see if Stacey could join her and Morgan and a few friends crammed into the back seat. Sage saw her at the door and invited them all in, despite Della's objection. Morgan brought a bag into the house with some beer, and Sage rolled joints for those who wanted one. Everyone loved Aunt Sadie, but no one more than Stacey. She told Amber that when she grew up, she wanted to be that kind of woman.

Stacey's friends left just after one in the morning, and soon after, Della and Stacey felt too tired to stay up. Della showed Sadie the bedroom where she would sleep and where to find clean towels for the morning, then she went to bed, which was what Stacey wanted to do, but she was assigned to the couch in the living room, and Sage and Sadie said they wanted a night-cap because life was too short. For a time, they sat on separate chairs in the living room, and Stacey lay down on the couch with her eyes closed. Finally, they turned the lamp in the living room off and went to the kitchen table to play Rummy. Stacey heard her Aunt Sadie say the jokers needed to be part of the deck and considered wild cards and Sage saying he'd never heard of jokers being included before. Stacey hated cards and didn't know what they were talking about.

She dozed off and woke again to hear Sage insisting Aunt Sadie dance with him. Come on, Sadie Pooh, dance with me. One quick dance before we go to bed.

You're being silly. There's no music. We can't wake Della up.

No, no. That's not how it works. You think up a song in your head, and we'll dance to it, and I'll try and guess what the song is. Then we'll be psychically connected. It's all on the count of four.

I'm going to bed now. Good night, Sage.

Fine. Go to bed for all I care. Leave poor old Sage in the kitchen to dance by himself.

Stacey heard him open another beer. She heard him shuffling his feet and banging into the kitchen chairs. She lay on her side, facing the doorway, and could see Sage come and look in on where she pretended to sleep. It occurred to her he might try to get her up to dance with him, but he just stood against the door frame, leaning, as if thinking were tiresome. He then fumbled into the bathroom. She heard him vomit and flush the toilet twice. He left the kitchen light on and made it into his bedroom. Stacey thought about getting up and turning the light off to save energy. She turned over on the couch, ignored the light from the kitchen, and listened to the blessing of silence.

Saturday morning, Stacey woke with a headache. She heard things being moved around in the kitchen and knew it would be her mother. Despite being a Saturday, their usual cleaning frenzy couldn't happen while Sadie was getting her beauty sleep. Stacey closed her eyes against the light streaming through the window, tried to imagine herself being in her Aunt Sadie's shoes, standing on the deck of a large passenger ship, staring at a horizon with no end in sight, but each time she did, a violent red light, that wasn't anything like a romantic sunset, clouded her vision.

They didn't finish breakfast until after ten, and Della knew if she didn't take Sadie over to visit Molly the Nose, that her neighbour would end up on her doorstep insisting on an introduction. Sadie got a brief tour of Molly's latest petit point project, and then Hart took over and coerced Della into yet another visit to Fort Whoop. When they got back to the house, Sadie said she'd love to see the downtown. They dropped Sage off at the river with his fishing gear and took the car because Sadie wanted to see everything there was to see. Stacey stayed home, thankful for some peace and quiet and a chance to take aspirin and have a hot bath. When she went back to bed to read, she wished she had gone with her mother and her aunt. It wasn't everyday someone like Sadie came to town, and Sadie saw the world as a startling place. Stacey thought about how, until now, she hadn't seen the world as ready and waiting to serve her needs. Aunt Sadie said you can only accomplish the things you can imagine, and Stacey couldn't stop her mind turning in circles.

In the middle of the afternoon, Della and Sadie returned,

and Sadie asked if she could borrow the car and take Stacey to a restaurant for a coke so they could have time to get to know each other. Great idea, Della said, but it took her a minute to say so. First she thought about how she'd be sending Stacey off with her younger sister who wasn't as much like her as she remembered. Aunt Sadie sprayed perfume on her index finger then dabbed it around her neckline. She told Stacey to hold out her index finger and accept a dab of her favourite perfume.

If you smell good, there's always a chance you look good, her aunt said. Farrah Fawcett wears this stuff, so they say.

Stacey followed her aunt's lead applying makeup and lipstick. After several minutes of scrutiny, Aunt Sadie said, There now, doesn't that look better? What? You don't think we both look like secret weapons heading out on the town?

I guess so, Stacey said. I sometimes wonder what life would be like if there were no mirrors in the world. If no one actually knew what they looked like. Have you ever thought of that?

No, Aunt Sadie said. I never have.

Stacey could still feel the effects of the party the night before and wasn't hungry, but Sadie insisted they go somewhere nice and found a place that served mussels they could share.

I've never eaten mussels in my life. Never even heard of them.

I'm not surprised, Sadie said. I'd never had mussels when I was your age. Someday I'll take you out to eat escargot. Have you had escargot before?

No. Aren't those French slugs?

Snails, actually. They come in many nationalities. I know they sound weird, but they're yummy. I think you'd like them. Most people won't give them a try. That's what holds people back from a lot of things.

So how long are you staying?

It won't be for long. Your house is small, and I'm putting you out of your bedroom.

I don't mind. You should stay longer.

Your mom wouldn't like that. I'm happy I tracked everyone down, and I'm especially happy to get to know you. I hear you're good at school. What else do you do?

Stacey explained her life in Fernie. It didn't feel like much in the telling, but Sadie listened like it was the most enthralling tale invented. She told her about her close friends, the Environment Club and the play she was in last year that was okay but not something she would do again because unless you're one of the main characters, you were just hanging around, making everyone else look good. By the look on her aunt's face, she was meant to continue describing her life, but it didn't take long to run out of things to say.

Do you go on dates?

I wouldn't say dates, exactly. I hang out with the Environmental Club a lot, and sometimes we do things after. Like watch movies or go swimming.

That's smart, Sadie said. You don't want to get tied down too early. Even in high school. Best to be good friends with lots of people. Every person you know gives you a new perspective on the world. It makes sense, don't you think?

I do. Everything you say makes sense, compared to most of the people in this town.

Well, I think that's a little over the top but sweet of you to say.

Stacey didn't like the look of them, but she ate one mussel just to be polite. She liked them, and after eating several more, Sadie noticed her counting how many were left, and she told her to eat all she wanted. When only one remained, Aunt Sadie said to finish things off, but Stacey said she'd already had eight, and if she could avoid it, she didn't like to eat an odd number of anything.

The thing is, Aunt Sadie said, eventually it all comes down to boys. You may be lucky and favour girls, but chances are it will be boys. They think we've got what they want, which we do, but actually it's the other way around. A girl as good-looking as you are will be in the heat of the action soon enough, and the thing about boys is you can't trust them because they come at you blind. They own their manhood like they own their car, and any boy with a car doesn't leave it parked in the driveway for long. You don't want to have anything to do with raising kids unless you're older and want to own one. If you have a good mother like you do, then you might want to try it yourself. Me, I decided long ago not to bother. The thing is you've got to take control of your life.

I haven't thought about having kids, Stacey said. My friend Amber has. She has a hope chest and everything. I want to be more like you and travel around. You've been everywhere.

I've been a few places, that's for sure. But one thing I've learned after all these years is that you don't need to go places. If you stay in one place and keep an open mind, the world will come to you.

The waitress came by and asked if everything was okay. Aunt Sadie said it was and ordered two more cokes. She stood up from the table and told Stacey to follow her.

The women's washroom had three cubicles, and Aunt Sadie fussed with her makeup until all three emptied. Follow me, she said, and inside one of the cubicles, she locked the door. Have you seen one of these before?

No.

I would imagine not. It's called a diaphragm, and if you know how to use it properly, you'll never be afraid of boys again. This is nothing to worry about or get embarrassed by. This is important and will change your life.

Aunt Sadie lifted her skirt and slid off her panties and stuffed them into her purse, then pulled out a tube of spermicide and used her index finger to cover the diaphragm with the jelly substance, put one leg up on the toilet seat and demonstrated

how to fold it in half and safely insert the contraption inside.
You've got to make sure it goes all the way inside your good lady
until it stops, she said. This protects your cervix and keeps the
sperm away from your precious egg. Think you could do that?

I guess.

Great. Look what I bought you when I was downtown. Now
you have your own, but you need to buy your own spermicide
once this is all used up. Here, change places with me and try it
out. Stacey giggled but saw the insistence on her aunt's face and
did as she was told. Just stuff your panties in your purse to get
them out of the way. That's it. Make sure you put a little around
the rim before you insert it. All the way back. Does it feel all the
way back? You're a real pro. The sensation is a bit odd at first, but
within an hour, you will forget all about it, which is the whole
purpose. You won't get pregnant, and you don't have to think
about it anymore. The beauty of this is you can put it in before
you hit the road, or keep it in your purse for when you might
need it. Just be sure you leave it in for six hours or more after. Just
leaving it in overnight is the easiest. Now you're ready to live your
life without fear or worry. The boy doesn't feel the difference,
and you feel everything.

Thank you, Stacey said. You call it your good lady?

That was our mother. *I'm afraid my good lady is bleeding*, she
would say, often in front of our friends. God help us. You might
as well leave it in for now. When we get home, you can take it out
and wash it in the sink and find a safe place to let it dry. Leave
your panties in your purse for now. It makes you feel free as a
bird.

18

DELLA AND SAGE SELDOM DISCUSSED POLITICS and instead favoured discussions about the weather. Sage had strong views on the news, which he watched religiously, and Della wasn't interested in most of what went on in the world if it took place outside their house and yard. Hart had an opinion on most things, so Sage kept his sparring tongue in shape around the hearth at Fort Whoop, but he and Della had an unspoken pact, the foundation of which was silence.

Not long into Sadie's first day in Fernie, Sage realized an unending source of debate had taken up residence in his house. The following day, he agreed they could drive Sadie up into the mountains because she wanted to see mountains, and he offered to drive because he enjoyed the company of his sister-in-law. Stacey agreed to go because she wanted to hang around her aunt.

The capitalists of the world need to slow down, Sage said. Most of what he said he repeated from what he'd heard in the news or at work, but this statement, possibly just worded differently, might have been original. Everyone is too greedy, he added. Last year there was a big Expo on in B.C. showing off the latest and greatest of everything we have, and soon after, there's a stock market crash that left millions out in the cold. And who's to blame?

There may have been a miscalculation on the pace of growth, Sadie said. It's hard to pin the blame for something like that on anyone in particular.

There's a beautiful lake coming up just around the corner, Della said. It's so pretty this time of year.

I'll tell you who's to blame. You've got Mulroney running this country, and you can't tell that man anything he doesn't want to hear, you've got a woman running things in Britain, enough said, and the Americans call an actor who eats jelly beans and falls asleep in meetings their leader.

President Reagan eats jelly beans? Stacey said. I like black jelly beans.

Della kept her focus on the vista passing by out the window.

It's important to consider where you put your money, Sadie said, her tone of voice informative, as if aimed at reaching out to someone who understood what she meant and might be open to refining his strategy. Sage hung on her every word even though he'd never had money to invest in anything and his only assets were a small house in Fernie and a ten-year-old car.

Marvin used to say people always buy staples and scandal.

Why would people need to buy staples? Della asked.

Staples as in basics, Sadie said. Bread and milk and chocolate keep on selling. And anything that will take people's minds off their troubles: movies, sports, magazines. When hard times come, the liquor stores hardly notice a difference.

Here it is, Della said. This is the little lake I was telling you about. Pull over, Sage. We can get some fresh air.

The four of them got out and walked around the edge of Maiden Lake. At one point, Sadie asked that they sit down on a park bench and listen to the silence. They drove on through the mountains, and Sage showed everyone his favourite fishing spots along the river. They took a short hike to Fairy Creek Falls, but it took a while because Della didn't bring hiking shoes. There was a lot to show people who weren't used to mountains, and Stacey absorbed the beauty through her aunt's eyes.

Della wasn't keen on discussing the Jimmy Baker scandal, but Sage wanted to. Jimmy Baker had given religious enthusiasts a bad name, and it was one of the year's events even Della *had* heard about.

Everyone blames Jessica Hahn, Sadie said. She wasn't the only one, and his wife was sniffing out territory of her own. What paved his way to prison was ripping people off for investing in something that didn't exist. I mean, have you ever watched that show they had? Tears and emotion and crass begging. How could anyone fall for such a thing?

It surprised Sage to find a topic where Sadie's views matched his own. I couldn't have said it better, he said.

There are bad people everywhere if you look hard enough, Della said. Our minister isn't like that at all, and I plan on attending church service tomorrow morning the same way I do every week, and anyone's welcome to join me. Our minister knits in his spare time.

I didn't know Reverend Munson knits, Stacey said. What does he knit?

I have no idea what he knits. Ask Molly. She'd know.

They got back home, and Della said she felt tired. Sage said he wanted to discuss something with Hart, and Sadie said she'd join him. Sadie insisted she take them out for dinner later to thank them for showing her around. Della tried to protest out of a sense of politeness, and Sage came to her rescue and said it would be a great idea. Della sometimes didn't mind that her husband smoked dope. It made him easier to deal with than when he drank. When stoned, he forgot some of his objections about life. She lay down on the bed to read and fell asleep thinking of Tammy Baker. Stacey rode her bike over to Morgan's house. She felt bad that she had missed most of the

Environmental Club meeting, but Aunt Sadie was only in town for a while.

They went to the New Diamond Grill for dinner, and Hart and Molly the Nose tagged along. Stacey and her Aunt Sadie took forever getting ready, delayed by a lesson on subtle makeup application. For a reason Della couldn't fathom, Sadie found Hart worth talking to. Over dinner, Sage, pale from having drunk himself under the table the night before, and who knew nothing about actuary tables, had to work at poking his views into the conversation while Della sat back and took everything in. Her sister was older now, but not much had changed. Della had never acquired Sadie's ability to act so easily around people she barely knew, but Sadie knew just when to laugh, sometimes a laugh of approval, other times more as if she were laughing off what had been said to steer the conversation in a direction that suited her needs. If she didn't find the conversation engrossing, she would stare off into the corners of the restaurant, whether or not any artwork decorated the walls. She had complete mastery over the inevitable and predictable ebb and flow of conversations across the table, conversations of which she knew the choreography as if she'd planned it out ahead of time. Sadie had always liked having people around, the more the merrier. It seemed natural, now Della thought about it, that she had moved on to live the life of a social convener in a series of cruise ships.

You came by bus, Molly the Nose said. She wasn't the only one trying to figure out how a woman who arrived in town on a milk-run bus had the money to foot the bill.

I did. It's a scenic drive, and I met some fine people on the bus. I met a man from Oshawa who's been married four times in four different countries. If you want to meet people, hop on a bus that takes a long time to get where you're going. That's the ticket.

Does that mean you don't drive?

Oh, I drive back home all the time. My car is getting a paint job this week, so what better time to get out of town and track down my long-lost sister?

It must be a special car to get it repainted, Sage said. Did you have an accident?

No, thank god. It was Marvin's favourite car, a Mercedes convertible. Before he died, he made me promise not to sell it, but I figure he wouldn't have minded my painting it. It's a somber blue now, and when I get back it will be racing-car red.

I wish you had it with you, Stacey said. I've never ridden in a convertible before.

Well, maybe you can come down to San Jose and visit your aunt next summer. Maybe we can plan on doing just that. What do you say, Della? Let the girl see another part of the world?

When they had eaten dinner and were waiting for the bill, Hart said he knew how to bend a spoon using only his mind. He balanced a spoon on top of his wrist and closed his eyes and waited. Everyone else at the table waited too, for several minutes, but the waiter arrived with the bill, and the spoon had done nothing but offer a nervous wobble. Molly the Nose never laughed out loud, at least in public, and she wasn't laughing now, but her serene smirk resonated with satisfaction. This spoon's not made with real silver, Hart said, and dinner officially ended.

Sunday they all lazed about, with no concrete plan in place. Sadie phoned the bus depot to ask about the bus schedule. She planned to bus her way to Vancouver then fly home from there. She didn't mention when she might leave, and Della didn't want to ask. Despite her happiness that Sadie had shown up, Della wanted her to leave—or maybe she just expected her to leave because of their history growing up, when Sadie rarely stayed round the house and left as soon as she could.

An odd sense of expectation could be felt not only in the

house but in the valley. A chill permeated the air even in the slanted sunlight, but with snow still a few weeks away, they enjoyed this intermittent season that required something between short-sleeved shirts and winter coats, a wardrobe many stocked sparingly. Most of the migrating birds had left, but others hung around for the last few reasonable days before following their natural instincts to a world in which they belonged. Stacey hung around the house and contemplated starting an important assignment for school, and Della decided to make a pie. Sage asked Sadie if she wanted to go fishing. Stacey hoped she'd say no, but she said yes, and since Sage only owned two rods, that meant she would be left out of the picture. She had been looking for a good reason not to tackle her school project, and now she didn't have one.

Della was glad to have Sadie out of the house. She could get housework done and make a nice Sunday dinner without having to listen to an analysis of everything wrong with the world. Something odd was going on with her sister, and she couldn't figure out what it was. When Sadie described her life in California, it sounded extravagant, almost beyond anything Della could imagine, and yet she seemed tentative about leaving. Sage had asked Della to go fishing a few years back, and she'd said no. Maybe, in his desperation to share his fishing passion with someone, anyone, experienced or not, he would show Sadie a good time.

Around two, just as Della was about to consider what she'd cook for dinner, Sage and Sadie returned with two cutthroat trout, one huge one and a smaller one that Sadie had landed. Sadie wanted to eat them, and Sage said the two fish would be enough for four people if he ran out and bought buns to go with it. Sadie suggested the four of them play a game of poker, a phantom game of high stakes, with coins from Della's penny jar worth a hundred dollars and the buttons from her sewing hamper worth five hundred dollars. Stacey didn't have a clue how to play but desperately wanted to be included, so they gave her a brief lesson and a cheat sheet of the most powerful poker hands. Sadie and Sage claimed to be experienced players. Della imagined that Sage had played some poker over the years, but no one had played cards much around her house growing up. The stakes were that the two with the least money by four o'clock would cook dinner and clean up afterwards. Della thought this reasonable since she'd already baked a Saskatoon berry pie. Because Stacey was new to the game, no one ever believed she held a strong hand, and Della instinctively bluffed well, so by the time four o'clock rolled around, Della and Stacey sat in the living room watching a movie and Sadie and Sage had some decisions to make.

What do you want us to cook with the fish? Sage asked.

Doesn't matter to us, Della said. It will be good whatever you decide.

Dinner turned out burnt but delicious, and after everyone escaped to the living room, the world felt sad. Sage enjoyed having someone new in the house, and Stacey kept pleading with her aunt to reconsider and stay a few more days, until Sadie said she'd give it some thought. Della wondered if, once she left, she'd ever see her maverick sister again. Della's spirits lifted when she thought about a plan she wouldn't mention to anyone for now, one that would see Stacey go to San Jose to visit her aunt, with Della along for the experience, while Sage stayed home to fish for a week. She wondered if people walked over the Golden Gate Bridge or only drove over. She wanted to ask but couldn't, or Sage would catch wind of her thoughts.

At bedtime Sage wasn't tired and went for a walk. He didn't go far, just walked around and around the block for an hour, restless. When he got home, he sat at the kitchen table and had a beer. He heard an owl in a tree in the backyard. The house was still, everyone asleep, he thought, Stacey on the couch and Sadie in Stacey's bedroom.

But Della lay awake, on her back, staring at the ceiling. She heard Sage get up from the table and open the door to Stacey's bedroom. His opening and closing of the door was deft and confidential and different from the sounds she heard after she turned over and buried her head in her pillow.

Everyone went back to their routines the next morning, except Sadie who didn't seem to have a routine of any kind, but she said she would stay one more night. Stacey looked happy and said she'd get home from school as soon as possible. She wanted to get Sadie alone somewhere and hear what she had to say about going to the nudist colony as a kid. Sage said he had a big day of planning at the mine, and since he was posturing himself as a candidate for the management team, they expected him to attend meetings all day long and into the night if necessary.

The sound of three young kids running around soon filled the house. To avoid looking her sister in the eyes, Sadie stood with a cup of coffee in her hands, staring out the window at the impending death that comes with fall.

I'm sorry, Sadie said. I'm sorry about—

Nothing much has changed, Della said, not looking up from folding laundry. You are who you are, and that's all there is to say about it.

Sadie looked around for something she could help with, and finding nothing, she said she would go for a walk. Less than an hour later, she returned and packed her suitcase, then called a cab. If I catch the bus that leaves in an hour, it will be quicker, she said. If I wait until tomorrow, the bus doesn't leave until ten at night. I should have brought you something from California. I'll send you something in the mail when I get home, she said.

Where's Aunt Sadie?

What are you doing home so early?

Last class was meetings about school spirit. I wasn't in the mood. Where is she?

She left you a note. She took a taxi to the bus depot. I'm sorry Stacey, but that's the way it is with your aunt. She's restless and doesn't stay in one place too long. You could never rely on her growing up, and that part hasn't changed one bit. She isn't one for dwelling on goodbyes.

But she said she would stay one more night.

I know. I heard her. I tried to convince her, but it's hard to convince your aunt of anything. No one knows better than me. Your aunt Sadie always knows when it's time to leave. At least you got your bedroom back.

I'll miss her, Stacey said. She was fun to be around. Maybe I can go visit her next year. She said I was welcome.

We'll see. It might be nice. Things can change in a year.

Stacey turned on the TV and found the note wrapped in a half-bottle of Giorgio perfume. She read her aunt's note. It was short. *No one can live your life but you. Keep your chin up, kiddo!*

19

DELLA COOKED SUPPER FOR TWO. Sage could make it home for dinner, but she knew he wouldn't. Even if the business meetings ended early he wouldn't be home. Stacey walked to the library and got out the only book they had on San Francisco, which was close to San Jose, where Sadie lived. It had plenty of pictures, and she started a list of things she wanted to see: Chinatown, Pier 39, Alcatraz, the cable cars. She planned to write her aunt with a suggested list and ask her if she'd missed anything. There had to be plenty of nightlife in San Jose, and her aunt would know all about it. They would travel around in her Mercedes with the top down. Maybe, if she could find a job, she could stay there the whole summer.

The kids under Della's safekeeping didn't receive the mothering care she usually provided that day; in fact, she knew she had been impatient with all three of them.

After supper she wasn't in the mood to sit around watching TV and went for a walk to the river, something Sage did often. The cold weather compelled her to keep moving. It had only recently become her practice to smoke outside the house, why she wasn't sure because no one cared these days, but she chain-smoked as she walked. At a corner store on the way home, she bought two

Sweet Marie chocolate bars, one for herself and one for Stacey. She worried about Stacey. She was growing up fast and resisting her mother more and more. Della feared that she would think all men acted like her father, and all women, or at least the most alluring role models, acted like Sadie. What did Stacey see when she looked at her mother? Was it too much to ask that she might find her mother's life worth aiming for? These were questions Della was willing to ask but not keen to answer.

Della went to change the bedding after supper, but Stacey told her not to bother. She wanted to sleep in the bed just as Sadie had left it, the closest she would get to her aunt for eight long months.

He looked the part dressed up in his navy blue sports jacket and red tie, but his lack of sleep festered under his chipper exterior. The office manager in charge of personnel had retired. Sage was the preferred candidate, and his bosses clarified they wanted things done differently because, assuming that nothing alarming happened, once an employee took hold, the company was stuck with them. The new hiring process would be much more onerous, designed to hire only those who could manage the jobs available, often jobs with little excitement or creativity, but jobs that needed reliable candidates. Kaiser Resources had been bought out, and procedures needed to change. The model the company adopted came from other industries in an age where people expected more out of employment than just wages. The process involved a battery of tests to identify aptitudes, acquired skills, health history and expectations. Those with a passion for life outside of work looked promising, on the premise that some of the mundane jobs available didn't need to provide life-fulfilling gratification. He would give a seminar-style presentation to six or eight applicants, even if the company had only one or two jobs available, followed by one-on-one interviews. Sage needed to ask certain questions to expose applicants that might not fit the company profile a few months down the road. The meeting room had an air of excitement and an electricity Sage embraced. The plentiful information about the new model flooded his mind, forcing him to stay alert and proactive. He drank coffee all day, laughed when everyone else laughed and responded to everything presented as if it were a strategy long overdue. The company favoured married men and considered them more stable as a rule, but it occurred to Sage that were he to apply to the company under the suggested regimen he wouldn't stand a chance.

The company meeting moved to a restaurant for supper and a back room afterwards before they settled their business close to nine o'clock. Sage didn't want to go home right away, and with Hart likely home in bed already, he couldn't go to Fort Whoop. He stopped in at his favourite pub, and a new waitress, much older than Selma, served him. The waitress, dressed as if she were about to duck under a car and do an oil change, was efficient at her job.

What happened to Selma? Sage asked.

Her husband showed up two weeks ago and took her away. Funny thing was she left with wages owing and no forwarding address. You don't know where she might have gone, do you?

I don't have a clue, Sage said. Was she happy her husband showed up?

She didn't look happy or sad. She looked like she didn't have a choice in the matter.

He didn't want to get drunk. He nursed a third beer and left. The neighbourhood was quiet and somber, and he found himself in the back of his woodshed where he smoked to even things out. He thought about what the waitress had said. He didn't believe it. There were always choices.

Stacey had fallen asleep with her San Francisco compendium open to a picture of the Walt Disney Family Museum. She was dreaming of a summer in her future when she stayed with Aunt Sadie. She knew her aunt had more money than her family, and going by the pictures of apartments she found in the book, she imagined her aunt living in an upper-level apartment with one bedroom and fantastic views looking out over the Golden Gate Bridge. She could sleep on the couch if she wanted, but Aunt Sadie suggested she might want to take up half of her queen-size bed, so when she woke in the morning, she would see the city coming alive. That's what she waited for in the dream: the city to come alive. Her aunt had told her she could stay as long as she wanted. She had nothing to worry about.

She felt the tips of fingers tracing the roundness of her shoulders, and she remembered her mother doing the same thing when she worried as a child and couldn't sleep. Then she felt the silky sensation of lips on the back of her neck that forced her into an altered state in her dream, not the thinking a pleasurable dream demanded. The dream ended in a sudden wakefulness, and she turned around and screamed. Sage fell off the bed and hit his head on a table on his way to the floor. Stacey screamed again, and then Della stood at the door and the overhead light revealed everything.

What the hell are you doing in here?

Sage knew his wife had asked him an important question, but Stacey at first thought her mother was yelling at her.

Get the hell out of here. Get out of this house. You bastard. You sorry-looking bastard.

Stacey heard the back door slam. She fell into her mother's arms, crying hopelessly. It's okay, baby. It's okay. Everything will be all right. Della rubbed her hand over Stacey's head, hard, as if to rub her reassuring words into a safe place. Stacey spasmed in her mother's arms for a long time and finally got control of her breathing. Della brought her a glass of water and told her again that everything would be fine. Della knew they should both get up and move around. Drink some hot chocolate maybe. But she didn't want to move, she only wanted to hold her daughter in her arms. Stacey didn't say anything for a long time, and Della didn't expect her to.

When she spoke, she barely whispered: I didn't do anything wrong.

He shouldn't have done many things, but the last one he shouldn't have done was leave the house. He left and got in the car and drove down to the river, only a few blocks away, and shivered in the dark. He could have got a motel room, but in a small town, there would be questions, and he didn't feel like driving an hour out of town for the few warm hours of sleep it would provide. He couldn't afford to miss work, not now, with his being under a microscope for the management position he'd worked so hard to qualify for. He wasn't sure he was the ideal specimen they were seeking, but it was now or never. Soon after the sun filtered through the tree line, he ate breakfast at BJ's, a place popular with truckers who came through town. He had bacon and eggs and three cups of coffee, tried to ignore the boisterous comments of his fellow patrons, then headed to a garage convenience store and bought a razor and shaved in the washroom. He looked like hell and felt like hell, and he wore the same clothes as the day before. If anyone mentioned it, he would say he was superstitious and the previous day had gone so well he didn't want to risk changing things up.

He would get through the day somehow, and when it ended, he would return to the house and explain to Della that he had been sleepwalking and half drunk and half stoned and hadn't known what he was doing. All night he'd replayed what had happened and how he had climbed into Stacey's bed to find Stacey asleep instead of Sadie and how he hadn't noticed the difference. At the time, everything had felt exactly the same. Even with his daughter lying there, the bed had smelled exactly the same.

Sage felt the burden of the unreasonable power he held over his wife. Without her having to say so, he knew that if they were rich she would have taken Stacey and left him years earlier, but they weren't rich, and her mothering instincts would not be tampered with. Della would do anything to stay in the house and raise her daughter because the way she saw it, this was her purpose in life. She constantly wrote in her journal about their life, paltry as it was, and when he asked her what she was writing, she told him, and he didn't care enough to worry about whether she told the truth. Once she was writing about her vision of Stacy's graduation; another time she had imagined Stacey getting married in Hart and Molly's backyard, in the summer, with Fort Whoop as a backdrop. There was nothing extravagant about the life they lived, but it was enough for Della.

When he got home, there would be a battle, but he would weather the storm, and things would be close to normal again. They would because his wife wouldn't have it any other way.

Della lay awake most of the night, but Stacey finally fell into a deep sleep, the two of them lying side by side. In the morning, Della suggested Stacey stay home from school and she would write a note claiming illness. Stacey kept shaking her head and didn't want to discuss what might happen during the day or in the evening when Sage returned, as they both knew he would. She packed her own lunch as usual and walked out the door without acknowledging her mother, only she didn't walk all the way to school but walked down to the river and sat by herself, listening to the water that raced its way south toward Lake Koocanusa. She welcomed the cold air coming from the river, even when the ends of her fingers and toes felt numb. By the time the morning disappeared and hunger kicked in, she had decided what to do.

She went around to the back of the house and knocked on the door, but no one answered. She knocked again, and Hart showed himself.

Stacey, what are you doing here? Don't you have school today?

She had prepared exactly what she would say and planned on a rational explanation that might make sense, and at all costs she would not get emotional. Despite her planning, she cried before she could formulate any words.

Why don't you come inside, Hart said. I was about to make a pot of tea, and I'll make enough for both of us.

Hart plugged in the kettle and handed her a box of Kleenex. He busied himself at the sink with the teapot and two cups and looked in the cookie jar but found it empty. Things aren't going too well for you today, he said.

No, they're not. I can't tell you what happened, but I can't live there anymore. I just can't. I was wondering if I can stay at Fort Whoop for a while. Until I can figure things out.

Hart filled the teapot and brought it and two cups to the table. He wished Molly were home. She would know what to do.

I don't mind if you stay there. Molly's out right now, but as far as I'm concerned, you can stay. Do your mom and dad know where you are?

Mom thinks I'm at school. Dad left in the middle of the night, but he doesn't care where I am or what happens to me. He'll come back again, and I can't be there when he does.

Were you planning to stay for just a few hours?

No. I need a safe place to sleep. I don't want to quit school. I want to graduate and move to San Jose.

Tell me about it, Hart said. Tell me why you want to move to San Jose. He hoped if he got the girl talking, it would pull her away from her misery. If she talked long enough, Molly might come home. Stacey gave him some of her reasons, but there weren't that many. Hart looked at his watch.

I've got two appointments this afternoon, and I've got to skedaddle. I'll leave Molly a note and get you settled. Do you know how to make a fire? You know how to make a fire, don't you? Come on. We'll get you comfortable. Are you hungry?

I've got my lunch. I'll eat that.

Hart showed her where he kept the newspaper, kindling and firewood and pointed to the matches. It took a while, but she got a fire roaring in the fireplace that soon made the main room of Fort Whoop comfortable. Cocooned within the logs and mortar, a picture of reclusion with no sounds or distractions, she ate half her lunch and lay down on the cot in the corner and fell asleep.

When she opened her eyes, the fireplace had filled with a healthy flame, and she thought she had dozed only briefly. She turned over onto her back and saw Molly the Nose sitting in a roughly hewn wooden chair, staring at her.

You probably feel better after sleeping, she said. Stacey nodded and sat up on the small cot. I heard some of what happened, and I've talked to your mother. She knows you're here. She understands how you feel, but she wants you to come back home.

I'm not going back there. I won't. I'll figure something out.

Your mother said you'd say that. It's okay if you want to stay here. Your mother said if you insisted, it would be okay. It's not much, what Hart built here. But if it will do for now, and you're welcome to it.

Thank you, Stacey said. That's what I need. I need to be alone.

I'll have supper ready in about an hour. You can come to the house then and eat with us. The door isn't locked.

I'll stay here if that's okay with you.

Molly pulled her hands to her face and massaged, as if trying to rid herself of something deep below the surface. She looked at

Stacey who stared into the flames.

Very well. I'll have Hart bring your supper over if that's what you want. I'll pack you a lunch for tomorrow. You plan to go to school tomorrow, don't you?

Yes. I'm going.

Good. Your mother insisted on that. You can come into the house in the morning and shower before school. It will make you feel better.

That's okay. I can shower at school. They have showers there.

Well, I'll leave you be. You can change your mind any time. Hart and I often play a game of crib after supper. We can play three-handed crib. See how you feel.

From anything Stacey had observed over the years, Molly was not an affectionate woman, but she got up and walked over and put her hand on Stacey's shoulder before she left, and when she left, Stacey cried all over again.

20

SAGE SPENT THE MORNING consulting and going over the new model of recruitment that made up the personnel manager's portfolio. Sage wasn't sure why this was necessary. He thought maybe they wanted to test him or trick him into not knowing what he knew. Because he was tired, Sage felt he successfully bluffed his way through the day, and then two things happened in the middle of the afternoon that made no sense. They invited him into the manager's office, and he sat down on a comfortable chair (a chair that said this comfort might someday be yours) and looked out the large picture window at the steely grey sky that hinted at the first snow of the year. It wasn't yet cold enough to snow, but when he looked outside, it felt like it could happen any minute.

The manager said that his interim status was over and Sage was now officially a member of the management team, and the manager reviewed the company's expectations, not only the expectations of the newly designed job description but the company's faith that Sage would fit the role impeccably. He heard the words that described his appointment as unusual, in that the company had brought him up through the ranks of construction and first aid attendant and how the move would offer inspiration to company employees across the board: if they worked hard and showed initiative, they too could ascend the hierarchy. But while Sage listened to the manager's guarded welcome and what it would mean in terms of wages and benefits and holidays moving forward, he had a strange sense of not being in the room participating. His ears rang, and it demanded his full attention to comprehend the sentences floating about. He stared at the manager as he spoke and tried to smile, but he wasn't sure he was smiling, and once or twice, while speaking, the manager looked at him as if maybe the pace of his verbal barrage needed to slow down. Sage's right eye wanted to close, and for a minute it felt like he was staring at his superior with one eye only, and he reached up nonchalantly with his fingers to pry his right eye open.

Thank you, Sage said. Thank you for all of this. The words didn't sound like they came out of his mouth, and his ears continued to ring.

I can see this is an emotional time for you, the manager said. You've had a lot to take in over the last week. I'll just get you to sign on here. The document lists all we have agreed to, and you will get a copy by tomorrow. The office you used last week is your office now. We ordered a nameplate, but it's not up yet, and your business cards should be here in a few days. You can take the rest of the afternoon to organize your files and so on. Make things the way you want them. Once you've done that, you can make your way home to share the news with your wife.

Sage took the pen and leaned over the paperwork. The words looked fuzzy, and he wasn't about to read through it all now. His arm and fingers tingled, and he scrawled something close to his signature at the bottom. The manager reached across the desk to shake his hand, and Sage complied, with fingers so numb it didn't feel like a handshake.

Once Sage sat down in his own chair in his own office and looked out the window, a much smaller window than the one in the manager's office, he felt better about things. His vision cleared up considerably, and he could endure the headache that felt thick in the back of his skull. The office secretary knocked on his door, congratulated him and asked if he wanted a coffee before they cleaned up the office pantry for the night. Sage said that would be a good idea. A strong coffee might temper his headache if nothing else.

He did his best to organize his files and focus on the details of his new job starting the next day. He had no idea when he'd taken refuge in his office or how long he'd been staring at the piece of paper in his hands.

Keeping that wife of yours in suspense a little longer, are we? The manager beamed at his office door, and Sage thought it was because he still sat at his desk, working. Everybody's abandoned ship, the manager said. The janitorial crew don't come until much later, so be sure to lock the front door on your way out.

I will, Sage said. He lifted his hand in a mock wave and turned back to the document he was concentrating on. He sat there waiting for something good to happen. His head ached more painfully than ever. Pulsating in the back of his head. His arm tingled again, and he stood, holding onto his desk, and stared out the window. The sky looked the same. No snow. No rain. A ceiling of threat. He got up and put on his coat, so dizzy that he traced the walls with his right hand as he headed to the men's washroom at the end of the hall.

The world felt uneven to Della all day long. She wavered from being so angry that if Sage had walked into the house, she could have scratched his eyes out, to feeling empty and foolish and unable to put the dishes in the cupboard where they belonged. Her daughter was a few hundred feet away and didn't want to talk to anyone. Della thought what Stacey was going through made complete sense, and yet she knew a resolution must be found at some point, and it had to start with her husband. Shortly after they'd moved to Fernie, and relentlessly ever since, she had been part of a United Church community, and her weekly communion had given her faith not only in God but in life. Every time Sage concocted another obscene behaviour, it had been her heartfelt belief he could change. She only needed to remain steadfast and be the wife and mother any man would want to revere. Now she was not so sure. Not much had been given to Molly the Nose in way of explanation, but she knew her neighbour had likely connected the dots on this latest incident. She saw, as Della did, how Sadie became an ornament in the presence of strangers and how Sage and Hart both were cast under her spell. Rarely forthcoming in sensitive matters, Stacey had likely not filled her in on how she had been affected, but here too Molly may have come to conclusions of her own. Della considered Molly a friend but not a woman she would ever be close to. When she had come over before suppertime to explain that she was harbouring Stacey on her property, she did so emphatically and yet with an element of grim satisfaction in every understanding observation she made.

Della expected Sage to return home with a lame explanation, expecting supper, thinking of life as a timeline to be followed regardless of the events recorded there. He didn't return at six or seven or eight or nine. If he came home late, he would be drunk, and there would be no valid resolution to pursue because he wouldn't know what he was saying, let alone remember it the next day. She didn't bother with supper. Stacey wasn't home to eat, and if he came home now, she would tell him to prepare his own damn meal. But he didn't come. Spending most of the day preparing for battle exhausted her, and as a last gesture, leaning toward closure, she walked out to the shed in case he had come home but was wary about entering a house he had violated the night before. She took a flashlight and saw that it was snowing.

She didn't believe it at first, this snow. It wouldn't last, as the thick wet flakes melted everywhere but on the grass. Sage was not in the woodshed. Sage would not be coming home tonight.

She made herself a cup of hot chocolate and went to bed with her journal. If Sage weren't man enough to return to the scene of the crime, she would write all the things she planned to say to him. She meant the writing to be cathartic, but the more she wrote, the worse she felt, knowing he was such a pathetic human being. Had Sage lingered near the front door or the back door just after eleven o'clock, he wouldn't have dared to enter after Della let out a scream of anguish heard in the neighbourhood several doors down in any direction.

At seven in the morning, the phone rang. At first the phone rang only in her dream, but then Della realized it was ringing on the wall of her kitchen. She wasn't about to bounce out of bed to answer it. There had been several crank calls over the last few weeks. Kids phoning and letting the phone ring twice then hanging up. Or calls that, once answered, offered a deep and creepy breathing on the other end of the line. The phone rang and rang and wouldn't stop. They didn't have an answering machine because Sage didn't like them. Still, the phone continued to ring. When Della got out of bed to answer it, she imagined it would be a repentant Sage somewhere outside a bar in Castlegar, depressed and sick and with a car he'd smashed into a telephone pole, wondering if Hart could come to pick him up, but despite all of her well-formulated predictions, the female speaking on the phone, notwithstanding her exasperation for the delay, explained as concisely as she could that Sage Howard was in serious but stable condition in the hospital with what doctors were calling a stroke, and because they were continuing to run tests, it wouldn't be worth visiting until later in the morning, after ten preferably, and even then only close family would be allowed.

In the small cot on the wall opposite the fireplace, Stacey felt sedated through the night. The small bed had room for one person and one person only. That gave her comfort, and she'd woken refreshed and used the outhouse and brought water in from the well to wash her face. Hart brought her a bowl of cereal and a lunch Molly had prepared and said he needed to get an early start, but if Stacey wanted anything, Molly would be home. On her way back from the outhouse, she saw her mother in a panic walking between the two houses to the Ferguson's front door. She slipped into the backyard and made her way to the street through the Brown's cluttered property. She felt stronger than she had the day before, and nothing her mother had to say would interest her.

Della arrived in a state of panic. She wasn't seeking her daughter but needed Molly to take over her babysitting for the morning. In return for her help, Molly only required the reason for the sudden request, and she agreed to be at the front door to greet her clients when they arrived. An emergency of any kind delighted Molly the Nose.

It would take less than a half hour to walk to the hospital, and Della left before any of her kiddies arrived at the door. She took a circuitous route there and stopped for coffee on the way. She didn't know much about strokes. Her father had a stroke when she was young, but it didn't seem like a stroke at the time because he'd been bedridden when it happened and he did make a full recovery. Sage was younger than her father had been at the time, and Sage was full of piss and vinegar, one of her mother's favourite phrases, and she imagined him lying in the hospital, cursing the nurses and threatening to get up and walk home in his hospital gown. When she got there, the head nurse suggested she take a seat in the hall and wait for the doctor who would offer a full account of her husband's status. She picked up a magazine to give her hands something to do. Sage would see himself as a victim after the stroke, and she knew he had a right to that, but she wasn't about to let the circumstance of his health be confused with compassion from any other quarter.

The doctor sat down in a chair beside her and spoke softly as if they were planning a surprise party. His gentle manner confused her: did it mean there was nothing serious about the situation? Or was he preparing her for devastating news? She didn't know which would be more welcome.

Mrs. Howard, your husband has suffered a thrombotic stroke. At this point in time, the right-hand side of his body is dysfunctional. He is unable to see out of his right eye, and he can't move his right arm; it has impacted his right leg as well. He cannot stand on his own. His speech is slurred, and the best avenue for communication at this point is asking yes or no questions so he can nod or shake his head. It's difficult to determine the precise state of his confusion. He may remember what happened to him, or he may not. A janitor at his office found him passed out, lying beside the toilet, and his head took a severe whack on his way down. There is no way of knowing how long he lay there. Time is an important element with the body's ability to recover from a stroke. We've run a CT scan, and there has been brain damage. How much can be recovered is something we will learn over the next few weeks and months.

Della listened intently but said nothing. When the doctor finished his explanation, she heard a Dr. Harris being paged over the intercom and the man beside her stood up. Do you have any questions? he asked. Della said she didn't think so. You can go in and visit him now. He's drugged and sleepy. He's suffering, so best not to stay too long. I'm sure he'll be relieved to see you.

Dr. Harris was halfway down the hall before Della stood up. She entered the doorway the doctor had pointed to and saw four beds in the room. One other man lay opposite Sage, and she was thankful that she wasn't alone with her husband. Half of Sage's face was purple and yellow from the fall. Della ignored the chair by the bed and stood beside her husband. He had an intravenous in his arm and a breathing contraption stuck in his nose. Sage turned his head and looked at her with his one good eye. His lips quivered, but no sound came out of his mouth. She turned and saw the man in the bed opposite watching, waiting for her to say something.

The doctor says there's a chance you'll recover from all of this. He doesn't know yet. She turned around again and noted that the other patient, his leg raised and in a cast, was reading a magazine upside down. Someone had brought flowers, and they sat on the table beside the man along with a small radio with headphones. The doctor says you need to rest. I'll come back tomorrow and see how you're doing.

Della felt tired suddenly. She wasn't ready to return home and take charge of the three kids with Molly. She sat down on a seat in the waiting room at the entrance to the hospital and tried to sort through her thoughts, to focus on only the most important things spinning in her mind. A receptionist came up to her and asked if she was waiting to see a doctor. Della said no, she had seen a doctor already.

Della got home close to lunchtime. Molly the Nose was her usual concerned self, and Della told her what she knew. What she knew about her current situation, she managed to wrap her mind around; it was the unknown, stretching out into the future, she feared.

Hart's older brother had a stroke a few years back, Molly said. Did he recover?

He didn't get the chance. He was dead when they found him. The doctor told the family it's a blessing sometimes, when that happens. Can you imagine a doctor saying something like that?

Yes, Della said. I can.

Stacey spent the afternoon with Amber, planning. Amber said she could ask her parents if Stacey could stay with them. The two of them could sleep in the same bedroom and could make Stacey's stay seem more feasible by cooking supper for the family twice a week. And they could do the vacuuming and dusting on weekends. Amber said her parents liked Stacey a lot, and once they heard even a little of what was happening at the Howards' house, they would agree. When the two girls parted, it was up to Stacey to tell her mother that this was what she wanted to do. Both girls realized that if Della didn't want it to happen, it wouldn't.

It was almost dark by the time Stacey returned to her living quarters at Fort Whoop. Molly the Nose had left a note on her bed. *Your father is very sick and in the hospital. Your mother needs you.*

Stacey walked in through the back door, Della hugged her until it hurt and cried for the first time since finding out about the stroke. He had a stroke at work, she said. It must have been late in the day because they didn't find him until close to midnight. It's serious, the doctor says. He can't stand up. He can't even talk.

Oh my god. How did this happen?

No one knows for sure. It might have been the life your dad lived off and on for years, but sometimes healthy people get a stroke. Hart's brother died from a stroke, and he was only fifty-six. Della watched something stiffen inside of Stacey then. It was the dying. She shouldn't have mentioned it. Don't worry, she said. Your dad's not likely to die because of it. The doctor says he might recover most of his faculties. Sometimes they do, and sometimes they don't. One thing is certain, he'll be in the hospital for a while. There's no chance of him walking in that door, and I want you back home where you belong. If anything changes, I promise I'll let you know.

Will you tell Molly and Hart?

I will. It's been a rough day for all of us, and I haven't even thought about supper. I'll go next door, and you can phone that pizza place you like. I washed the sheets on your bed by the way.

We can afford pizza?

Della pulled a ten dollar bill from her purse and left it on the kitchen table. She took her purse with her. Stacey must have eaten food over there. The least she could do was offer to pay them something.

21

TWO WEEKS HAD GONE BY since Stacey had moved back home, and she was actively participating in the Environmental Club again. With her dad being sick and hospitalized, she found it easier to be with them because she had less to explain. As her best friend and confidant, Amber knew some of what had gone on, but empathetic glances from any of her other friends were based on her father's health. She liked having a close-knit family of friends because each of them knew they could say things they might not say to others, take tenuous positions on issues or things or people, and no one in the group would offer anything more severe than a ridicule-flavoured teasing. Everyone looked up to Morgan as leader of their group, especially Amber, who had told Stacey that, once upon a time, young women organized their future by building a hope chest. Stacey had never heard of such a thing, but Amber said the custom came from a previous era and deserved a second chance. In the basement, she discovered a large cedar chest with fancy carvings on the outside, which used to belong to her grandmother, and Amber made it her hope chest, with her own private lock to keep it that way. Stacey saw the chest one day, but it contained only a fancy tablecloth and two candleholders sitting in the bottom.

You're planning your marriage. Is this what it means? Please tell me you're not planning to marry Morgan. You're only in grade ten.

Morgan knows I have a hope chest. He doesn't think it's stupid. And he's in grade twelve already. Besides, a hope chest is just for hope. It doesn't mean you have to marry anyone in particular.

Stacey could imagine what her Aunt Sadie would have to say about such an idea, but Stacey admired whatever Amber favoured, she did so unequivocally. Stacey had learned to qualify her acceptance of most things and some people. Every time they did something with the Environmental Club or went somewhere as a group, Hugh was always there, and he often sidled up to Stacey as if they had been together for years. One night he asked her if she wanted a shoulder massage, and she told him she didn't, then sitting there on the floor against the couch watching a movie, her shoulders felt tight and uncomfortable, and she wished she had accepted, but she didn't want to ask him for a massage. She wanted to keep Hugh at a distance.

There wasn't much distance between Amber and Morgan, and everyone understood that. They were subtly affectionate when with the group, but sometimes they disappeared and everyone knew they were together. One night when Stacey stayed over at Amber's house, the nature and rhythm of their relationship became clear.

During the era of the hope chest, Amber explained, couples saved everything they could experience until the night of their wedding. My mom was like that if you believe what she says, and I do. These days people breed like rabbits. If you're a boy rabbit, people think you're a stud, but if you're a girl, you're called a slut. Morgan and I decided several months back we didn't like either of these extremes. Morgan is methodical that way.

So what did you decide?

We do it during the first week of every month. His parents

are usually away or my parents are busy, and if not there's always his uncle's cabin up at the lake. One special day each month to look forward to.

So you do it once a month, and that's it?

I said one day a month. It doesn't always mean just once.

What would happen if you got pregnant?

We won't. Morgan is very scientific about it. We use a condom to begin with and only do it on the days I'm not ovulating. It's hilarious at our house at the beginning of every month. My mom and dad get paid, and I have something to look forward to. Everyone is in a good mood.

Have you ever considered a diaphragm?

I thought about it. I think my mom uses one now. But Morgan was the one who suggested a condom, so it's one less thing I have to worry about.

Stacey thought of mentioning the diaphragm she'd received from her Aunt Sadie, and she would tell Amber about it one day, but not until she got around to using it.

The weeks that followed Sage's stroke felt like purgatory at the Howard household, a time complicated due to the uncertainty of its tenure. Stacey had been nervous at first, not believing her mother's description of Sage's condition, thinking the hospital might release him at any time to live at home again. Stacey refused to visit her dad, and even though he lay in a hospital bed blocks away, Della agreed to have Hart come over and install a lock on Stacey's bedroom door. Della visited daily at first, then every second day and eventually twice a week. The doctors expressed concern that many of the effects of the stroke showed no sign of improvement. With the help of a physiotherapist, he walked up the hall and back every second day, leaning on a walker the whole time, but left on his own, his instability yielded to gravity. Hart and Molly stopped in to visit Sage, and Hart went back a week later. He couldn't do much but stand by the bed and tell Sage what little news there was in the neighbourhood and assume he could take in what they were saying.

Della never visited more than twenty minutes at a time. Once when she arrived and found him asleep, she pulled up a chair and watched him breathing, trying to figure out what had gone wrong. When they met, Sage had felt like a man who would provide a good time for everyone around him, a rascal waiting for an audience. She had been charmed by him, no doubt about it, but they had known each other the second time around for only three days before they married in Las Vegas. The man she thought she had married still existed and always had, but so did the man he had become.

For the first few weeks, she fretted over what would happen when he made his way home. What was best for everyone had a thousand story lines, and Della reminded Stacey daily she would be protected however it all played out, but the doctors failed to recognize any progress, and Della revised the scenarios that might see him at home again. The company employed Sage now, not the union, and documentation had arrived by mail suggesting that Sage had been placed on long-term disability that provided a monthly stipend less than his full wage but enough that they could get by on it.

He looked defeated lying there, as if each breath he worked on could be his last. She tried to imagine what thoughts he had. The doctor had suggested he might not remember anything about the incident itself, but since then, the nurses encouraged Della to talk to him, saying he could understand and it gave him something to think about. Some days Della had plenty to say to him if only she could have got him in a private place, but the circumstance never presented itself, and she wouldn't have felt right if he couldn't defend himself. Most of the words he uttered were reverberations that left her guessing.

As the weeks passed, the routines Della and Stacey adopted became more intentioned. Stacey was more like herself again and doing well in school, and the parents of the kids Della looked after had stopped asking after Sage's recovery. There had never been a family Christmas without all three of them present, and were it not for the focus on Christmas Day and Christmas dinner and expectations for gifts, their ship might have sailed on with little interruption, but Della, for the first time in months, felt her husband's absence. He always had ideas about what to buy at Christmas and how to celebrate the season. He was the one who guided them off into the woods to pick out a Christmas tree, the one who held Stacey, when she was younger, up high so she could put the blue angel on top. It was the season when all the barbs that had snagged evidence of Sage Howard living in the house became most evident.

To avoid the inexorable depression she could see coming with Christmas Day, Della rented a small hotel room in Banff for her and Stacey for three days. The day before Christmas, Stacey, for the first time, accompanied her mother on a visit to the hospital. They had wrapped a small ghetto blaster and headphones so Sage could listen to the world if he wanted to. Stacey didn't stay long, but she showed the attending nurse how the functions all worked. Della had coerced Stacey into coming by suggesting that the visit would be a short one. Stacey made sure that was the case by leaving to wait for her mother in the car.

With the roads ploughed and no snow in the forecast, they agreed three days away from Fernie would be their Christmas present, except for one book each. Stacey got *Firestarter* by Stephen King, and Della got the book she'd been dropping hints about for weeks, *The Handmaid's Tale* by Margaret Atwood. Despite a reduced price because most families wanted to be home for Christmas Day and Boxing Day, Della had to work hard at rationalizing the cost of the excursion. The two of them needed something filled with hope.

The first day they walked around town, swam in the pool and then alternated between reading and snoozing in their room. Della gave their holiday one full day of whatever happens happens, but once day two turned the page, she insisted they have a heart-to-heart talk about all that had happened. Stacey wasn't one to embrace conflict, and Della supposed she wasn't either, and yet Della understood the time had come to clear the air.

The doctor said there's a chance your dad might come home after the new year.

How's that supposed to happen? He can't even look after himself.

Well, I guess all the details will be worked out. They mentioned a nurse coming by twice a week to give him a bath and a massage and to monitor him. That's all I've heard so far.

Let's go swimming, Stacey said. It's freezing out there, and swimming inside feels luxurious.

We can go swimming. But first we need to talk about what happened. I wish we didn't have to talk about this, but we do.

You know what happened. I don't see why we have to talk about what we already know. He came into my bedroom and climbed into my bed and started rubbing my back and kissing me. It's disgusting. I hate him. No one should have to go through that kind of crap. I hate his guts. Amber said I can live with her family. If he comes back, that's what I'm going to do.

Stacey went to one of the two chairs in the room and positioned it to face the window. She sat down with her back to her mother.

It was disgusting what he did, Stacey. There's no forgiveness for any of it. But there's something you need to know. Something I should have told you right after it happened.

What? That I have a dad who believes in incest?

Your dad was out all night. He thought Aunt Sadie was in your bed. She said she was staying an extra night, remember? He was half drunk. Not that that's any excuse.

What makes you think he'd be after Aunt Sadie?

He went into your room the night before. He came home late that night, and I heard him come in, and he stayed in there for an hour. Then he left again. I heard everything.

Stacey stood up and faced her mother. Her mother had started crying, but that only made her look more pathetic. Why didn't you say anything? Why didn't you throw him out right then?

I know that's what I should have done. I know that now, and I hate him for doing it… but… I didn't want…

You didn't want what?

I want us to stay together as a family. That's what I want. At least until you're finished school. The way he acts scares me the most because he wants it to end, and he wants me to think that way too.

How could you think like that? He's a disgusting man, and it's just a matter of time before he tries to rape me. He tries to catch me when I'm naked, like the time he came into the bathroom when I was having a bath and he refused to leave. He just stood there taking everything in. He's always barging into my room when he thinks I'm changing. Does he do it when you're in the house? Not a chance. And he leaves chocolate hearts tucked into my underwear drawer. He wants me to say something, but I won't give him the satisfaction. Haven't you noticed? I'm never alone in the house with him anymore. If you go out, I go out too, even if I have nowhere to go.

Why didn't you tell me all this?

I told you about the time he watched me in the bathtub, and you said he was just a dad admiring how his daughter was growing up. You didn't say anything to him. You should have told him to fuck off, but you didn't say a word.

Della tried to hug Stacey, but she shrugged her off and headed for the closet. I'm going out for a walk. Out where it's freezing cold. But don't worry about me. I'm used to it. I do it all the time.

Della sat in the chair where Stacey previously sat and looked out at the view, knowing she was partly to blame for all that had happened. She saw no sign of her daughter; she must have gone out a back door of the hotel because she didn't want anyone to see her, including her mother. The doctor that attended to Hart's brother said sometimes death because of a stroke was a blessing. There was more than one reason for this to be true, and it was possible that Sage thought so too.

The holiday getaway that had begun with such promise felt more like a bruise waiting to heal once it ended. Stacey didn't want to go swimming again even when her mother suggested they go together. They both finished reading their novels, and when Della turned on the TV, Stacey went to the lobby to read magazines. The two of them didn't converse more than necessary, both of them busy assessing the circumstance they lived in, contemplating what came next.

On the ride back, Della took advantage of a captive audience and said it could be months before Sage returned home and possibly he never would. She asked Stacey to keep an open mind about what might happen next and said never again would there be compromise because she would never let it happen. To shut her mother up, Stacey said she would think about it, and because Stacey had softened her position, when they stopped for coffee in Skookumchuck, Della drove the car onto a side street and let Stacey drive around the block twice.

Once they were home and unpacked, Stacey said Amber had invited her to stay overnight and go skiing with her family early the next day. Della tried not to look hurt. When she looked at her daughter, what she saw was what everyone deserved at her age: a face full of hope.

You'll be back on Tuesday then?

I'll be back on Tuesday. It might be late, but I'll be back. Stacey wanted to tell her mother not to worry, that the two of them needed to stick together now more than ever, but she didn't. Instead, she walked up behind her mother where she sat at the kitchen table and wrapped her arms around her, hoping to convey the same message.

Della went to the hospital the next day more conflicted than ever. Sage looked much the same except that they had his bed propped up and he had a clipboard and paper and pen on his left side. The nurse explained that speech was still an issue but that using his left hand he could communicate his needs. Della looked at what he had scrawled there: water, bathroom, radio, light off, yes, no. She had a few things she wanted to get off her chest, but the other three beds in the room had filled and it wasn't the time.

So, they've got you writing things down I see.

Sage took the pen and pointed to the word yes. Then at the bottom of the page, he worked his pen ponderously until she could make out the word Stacey.

She's upset. What's happened has pushed her over the edge. She's skiing with Amber today, which is good. It will take her mind off things. She'll never be the same, and there's no room for forgiveness here. You need to know that.

Della wanted to choose more pointed words, but everything she said in the room would form a riddle for the other patients and the nurse to solve. She wanted to say: *You fucked up big time. You're a sleazebag, a lowlife, a man who deserves nothing but contempt. Your daughter doesn't want you around, and I don't want to be around you either. You've burnt the last of your bridges, and no one feels sorry for you.* Della stared at him as the words she so wanted to say formulated in her mind. She could see Sage picking up on her thoughts, and that made the visit feel worthwhile. I'll talk to the doctor before I go. Is there anything you need?

Sage took the pen and pointed to no, a satisfactory response. If he'd wanted something, she wasn't in the mood to get it for him anyway. She should find the doctor and see if anything concrete had been decided, but she didn't feel like doing that either.

They needed groceries. She usually went to the grocery store armed with a list of what they needed, but with Christmas and the days away, they needed almost everything. She would buy a whole chicken, she decided. They'd missed out on a turkey this year, and with just the two of them, it wasn't something she wanted to contend with. And Stacey still had another week of holidays, so next Friday or Saturday she would tell Stacey to invite Amber to sleep overnight. Maybe the three of them could go bowling, though the more she thought about it, the less likely it seemed that two teenage girls would want to visit a bowling alley with a mother. A movie maybe. She would let the girls choose, even if it meant driving to Cranbrook. Sage never wanted to go to a movie downtown. They could watch plenty of movies on TV he said and they didn't cost a dime. Even better, the three of them could stay home for the night and dye their hair. Stacey had mentioned dyeing her hair red, and Della had told her it would be a mistake, but what the hell. Molly dyed her hair all the time even though she wouldn't admit it. She would have to check with Amber's mother, of course. Della's hair didn't look awful, though it was thick and tight and hard to manage. There were streaks of grey coming on strong so maybe she would dye her hair a silver grey, invite the inevitable and embrace growing older.

When she pulled into the grocery store, she noticed the sticker in the corner of the windshield, a reminder to get the oil changed. She would see to it next week. Sage had always fussed over things like that, but now it would be her job and she looked forward to it.

22

ON TUESDAY DELLA PREPARED SUPPER even though she knew Stacey might get home from the ski hill late. She might have stopped for dinner with Amber's family, or they might have done something else, but she wanted her to return to the house and sit down to asparagus and eggs and baking powder biscuits, one of her favourite meals. While she prepared supper, the winter air filled with the wail of fire trucks so close that at one point Della stood on the front porch to listen. She saw smoke feeding the sky several blocks away. The asparagus and the baking powder biscuits were ready, but she would wait to cook the eggs until her daughter arrived. She turned on the local radio station while she waited, and the news report made her heart feel heavy in her chest. A retired couple living on 9th Street had been asphyxiated in their beds in a house fire possibly started by an old oil heater. The firefighters could not salvage the house, most of which had burnt to the ground.

Stacey arrived hungry. I've cooked one of your favourites, and I'm so glad you're home, Della said. They ate and Stacey gave a full report on the skiing experience. She had only skied once before, but she liked it, she said. Della thought Stacey liked it because she wanted to keep up with Amber, but she didn't say so.

Instead she summarized what she had heard on the radio. She said when something like that happened, it made you want to cherish every given day.

Where did they live? Stacey asked.

A few of the houses at the end of 9th Street are older. I don't know which one it would have been.

The uncertainty of it all and the compulsion to earn a stake in anything catastrophic provided reason enough to put on toques and scarves and boots and walk in that general direction with the same curiosity that made boys on bicycles race after fire trucks whenever they had the chance. It was late by the time they walked down 9th Street, and cars drove by and slowed toward the end of the road. The fire had been extinguished earlier, and now smoke curled out of the carnage. Della and Stacey stood at the side of the road, taking in the tragedy and the yard cordoned off with yellow luminescent tape that framed the disaster like a dystopian masterpiece. Two cars drove by, and they could hear muffled voices inside the cars, no doubt voicing thoughts similar to theirs. At the side of the yard, lit up by the streetlights, a tree had been scorched by the flames, and toward the back of the yard, a similar tree had gone unscathed. Stacey looked at the two trees, so close together and with such different fates. Underneath the second tree, she thought she saw something move, and she took a few steps toward the side yard.

You can't go in there, Della said. They've probably roped it off because they have to investigate more in the daylight.

Something's alive over there, Stacey said. She moved ahead and stepped over the yellow tape, and even though Della knew better, she followed. A black dog with a smattering of white on its chest and on the tip of its tail sat in the dark. The dog lay in front of a doghouse but had its head raised, pointing to the charcoaled remains.

Oh my, Della said. This must have been their dog. He's

waiting for them to come out. He doesn't understand what's happened.

The dog allowed Stacey to squat beside it and rub her hand over the top of its head. He looked up at her once and whined, then turned his focus once again on the house. We can't just leave the poor thing, she said. We should take it home for the night where it will be warm and safe. It's okay, boy. We'll look after you. She wrapped her fingers around his collar and coaxed the dog to his feet. The dog didn't object, but he limped. He's hurt, Stacey said. In the hint of light available, they confirmed that the dog's right front paw was burned.

We can't carry him, Della said. It's too far. You wait here with him, and I'll get the car.

As soon as Della left, the dog lay down again. He licked at his paw and then turned toward the house. Stacey rubbed her hand along his back and told him everything would be fine, until her mother pulled up and opened the back door. We should carry him, Stacey said, so he doesn't step on something sharp. Why Della had her purse with her, she did not understand. She slung it over her neck, and between the two of them, they carted the dog to the back seat of the car. On the way home, they stopped at a corner store and bought three cans of dog food and a small bottle of peroxide.

We should call him Lucky, Stacey said from the back seat where the dog lay with his muzzle on her leg.

He's not our dog, Della said. There could be relatives that want to claim him.

Well, if there are relatives, they have no right. They should have thought of the dog out there by himself in the middle of winter. He's lucky we found him.

They brought the dog into the house and laid him on a rug in the living room. Della opened a can of dog food and got a small dish and filled it with water. Lucky got up and hobbled toward the kitchen. The dog ate nothing, but he looked thankful for the opportunity to lap away at the water.

Let's get him back to the rug, Della said. I'll need you to talk to him and distract him while I soak his paw in a peroxide solution. He won't like it.

The dog, to their surprise, didn't flinch while Della attended to his paw, as if he understood someone had to help with his recovery and these people were as good as any. After his paw had a good soak in the peroxide, they rinsed it off, patted it dry with paper towels and wrapped it with one of Sage's dress socks and masking tape. Stacey took the extra blanket from her bed and put it on the floor. The dog walked over, looked up at her once, then circled himself into his bed, his curious face toward the doorway. Della talked to him while Stacey got ready for bed, and when she settled facedown, she left one arm slung over the side of the bed so she could comfort him on their way to sleep.

On the third consecutive snowy day in early February, Della sat watching a storm that had made everyone in town aware of their vulnerable human existence. The school wasn't closed, but Stacey had stayed home anyway and Della didn't blame her. Lucky stayed with Della every day, but the dog had bonded with Stacey. As the snow continued to mount in the yard and on the roads, Stacey spent most of the day outside playing with the dog, the two of them burrowing tunnels in the snow, and short, high-pitched yelps and raucous laughter filled the yard. Two of Della's clients made it to the house that morning, but she stood at the window off and on and watched her daughter frolicking with the dog, and it reminded her of when Stacey had been very young and spent the warmer winter days in the yard playing by herself. Della had documented everything significant in their lives since they'd arrived in Fernie, and now she looked out at her daughter who would graduate in two years. It felt like all she had recorded had happened in a matter of minutes. It was late afternoon before dog and child made it back inside the house. Despite his physical exertion most of the day, Lucky pranced on his paws around the house as if he wanted to tell Della about the wonderful day he'd just experienced. Della waited until those in her charge were picked up before she shared with Stacey what she'd known for most of a week.

The doctors want to try your dad living at home. If it doesn't work out, they will find somewhere else for him, but that will cost money. If he stays here, a nurse will pop in three days a week to check on things and help your dad out. That's what they've decided.

Stacey was lying on the fake Persian rug in the living room, scratching Lucky's belly with one hand. If she stopped for a minute, the dog would poke her with his paw until the scratching resumed. For the last two months, the dynamic of the household had changed significantly. Stacey felt much closer to her mother, closer than she could remember, and now with Lucky also part of the family, their way of living suited her. She had been mean, at times, to her mother, and she realized, only after Sage was out of the picture, that she had lumped her mother in with the rejection of family, a poison she needed to purge. Her mother wanted the best for her and most of the time would do whatever she could to see she was happy. Twice, since they'd returned from their short Christmas getaway, Della had taken her on short driving stints and promised they would do more in the spring once the roads had cleared. Stacey had the driving licence manual memorized in anticipation. She spent as much time with her friend Amber as always, but now Amber wanted to come to her house. She liked Stacey's mother, she said, because Della differed from most of the moms in town. They got together one night for a hair dyeing session, and all three of them had their hair treated. Stacey and Amber convinced Della she was too young to go with silver, so she opted for a light blonde that suited her, just as the girls said it would. Stacey had dyed her hair red like she wanted, a startling red, and now she wore her toque as much as possible. Amber's hair looked the most spectacular: Della and Stacey had worked hard at separating strands of her hair which, streaked in blue, gave her the look of someone with attitude who'd had moved to Fernie from Haight-Ashbury.

Della carried on as if she had memorized a speech. He'll sit in a wheelchair most of the day. I'll need to keep an eye on him and help him to the washroom and help him get in and out of bed, but that's about all we can do for him. The nurse is trained to handle helpless people and will bathe him when she comes. He's unable to talk in any way we can understand, but we can talk to him. You don't have to if you don't want to, but he'd like it if you did.

How are you supposed to do all that and look after three kids?

I'm not sure yet, but I'll manage. Like I said, this will be a trial period. If it doesn't work out, we'll explore other options.

Stacey tried to imagine the scenario. She wanted things as they were now. She couldn't imagine Amber wanting to come over with a zombie sitting in the middle of the living room. If she talked to her dad while he sat in his wheelchair, it would be when her mom was out of the house, and he would not like what she had to say.

Before spring comes, Della said, Hart has agreed to build a ramp out the back. I'll wheel him out into the yard when the weather is good. I know what you're thinking. It's not the way you wanted it to work out. I can't say I wanted this either, but for now there's no other choice. There will be a different dynamic around here starting next week, and I know you've talked about getting a part-time job, but I'd like you to focus on school, so I'm going to double your allowance so you'll have more freedom to do the things you like.

We can afford it?

We'll afford whatever it takes to keep this family together.

Sage wasn't the man he had been. You could see the fear in his one good eye and hear it in his slurred speech that rose and fell, loaded with incomprehensible emotion. With no ramp to the house, the nurse and Della situated the wheelchair on the front porch, then maneuvered Sage up the steps to the main floor, as if he were an injured football player heading to the sidelines. It soon became obvious that Belle was a no-nonsense woman, serious about her profession. Della tried her best to reassure Sage, but when she did, Belle overlapped her words with her own, suggesting that this was Sage's life now and he would have to get used to it. Della had been worried about this day but had given little thought to where Sage would find himself once inside. Belle took command immediately, leaving Sage and his wheelchair by the door while she moved a chair off to the side and moved a lamp toward the corner of the living room. Then she backed the wheelchair into the newly designated spot.

From there, Belle said, he can see what's going on in the living room, and there will be nothing going on behind his back, so to speak. He can see the TV if you turn it on for him, and if you want to have him in the kitchen with you when you're cooking and cleaning, you can wheel it there. If there's nothing on TV and you have the drapes opened, he can look out on the street from here and watch the kids trying hard to grow up. I think this might work out after all.

Belle inspected the bathroom and then demonstrated the proper procedure for helping Sage use the facilities. Sage squealed in a manner that suggested he didn't want to go to the bathroom right now, but Belle ignored him, grabbed the handles on the wheelchair and told Della to follow her. His left hand is somewhat serviceable and getting stronger day by day, so he'll help you by balancing himself while he's still standing. Sage, grab hold of the counter there. That's it. Now he won't topple over, and you can down his trousers like so. He's wearing a large diaper as you can see, but that's just like a pair of underwear. If nothing goes wrong, he can wear them all week if he wants to, but if things go sideways, this will make cleanup more manageable. Once you get them in, the best thing to do is plunk them down and then leave them be for five minutes. He sits just like so whether it's number one or number two. That's important.

Belle signalled for Della to leave with her, and they pushed the bathroom door almost closed for privacy. Leaving it open a tad allows you to hear him if he's having trouble. Or he'll mumble grumble when he's finished.

Maybe he's done now, Della said. He shook his head when you took him in there.

I know, I know. Best to leave them for a few minutes. They think they don't need to go, but once they get seated, things happen. I wish your tub wasn't so low, but we'll manage.

The nurse volunteered to take an unguided tour of the rest of the house. She looked out onto the backyard, and Della explained where the ramp would be installed. Unless Belle was issuing instructions, she didn't say much. She said *h-m-m-m* as if most of what she saw was workable but not ideal.

Will the dog be a problem? Della asked.

Not unless he doesn't like dogs. Dogs always add more than they take away.

Belle retrieved Sage from the washroom and wheeled him back to his new place in the world. She said she didn't normally work Saturdays, this was an exception. She would arrive in the morning every Monday, Wednesday and Friday, and she left her card and a card belonging to the call service if something urgent came up on the off days. She pointed to a seven-digit number on the back of both cards, which referred to Sage Howard and no one else. If everything worked out like she hoped it would, a month from now, an appointment would be arranged with Dr. Harris for a reassessment. That's the kind of doctor he is. He likes to know how his patients are making out.

Belle left and Della sank into a kitchen chair, exhausted. Stacey had left early in the morning for an Environmental Club meeting, and Della was glad she hadn't been home when Sage arrived. She would have felt like Della did now, that this whole thing was more than she could manage. She lit a cigarette. Smoking in front of Sage might make him antsy for the chance to smoke dope, and he had enough to cope with for now. When she returned to the living room, Sage sat like a mime who had perfected his job.

Well, you're home after all this time. I'll turn the TV on if you like. There might be a movie starting at one.

She turned on the TV, and someone knocked at the door. Molly the Nose had flowers in hand as an excuse to get the lowdown. Della thanked her and went to fetch a vase.

Well, look who's home and looking bright-eyed and bushy-tailed. Sage looked up and moved his head in circles, a compromise between yes and no by the look of it. I brought you some flowers. Carnations. They don't give off much pollen, and they last two weeks if you keep them wet. Hart said hi. He'll be over tonight for a visit.

Sage didn't move his head up and down, sideways or in circles at Molly's announcement. Della figured he must be tired, and it was too much to take in.

Della made tea and served her guest in the kitchen. She made a small pot so Molly wouldn't have an excuse to stay long.

How will you cope with all of this? Molly said.

I don't know. I'll try. That's all I can do.

Della didn't want to explain that she pretty much had to make it work. If Sage went into assisted living, it would take all the money he had coming in from his disability to fund it, and it would be impossible for Della and Stacey to carry on. It wouldn't do to have Sage knowing the situation, though it was possible, she realized, that he'd already figured that out.

Molly left and Della checked on Sage, then lay down on her bed. She drifted off to sleep and woke because Stacey had climbed into bed and wrapped an arm over her shoulder. Stacey had seen her dad sitting there, seen how age had cast a shadow over his face. I'm scared, Stacey said.

I know, Della said. I'm scared too.

23

STACEY WASN'T ABLE to put into words the reason she felt compelled to earn high marks in school. Her Aunt Sadie hadn't gone past high school, technically hadn't graduated, and she seemed to find a life full of adventure and excitement. But Amber planned to go on to university somewhere and, in her mother's words, make something of herself. A social worker maybe. Stacey couldn't easily keep pace with Amber because everything she did had to be perfect, and sometimes Amber would dash off an assignment in one evening while Stacey would hone her work over an entire week. Rarely did either one of them miss a class. If a session bored them, they knew to get a head start on homework from their other courses, so they kept busy most of the time and socialized during Environmental Club meetings and sometimes on a weekend.

Amber and Stacey liked to carve out a few hours for themselves and pretend they didn't have a care in the world. One Saturday they hiked all the way to Coal Creek and back just to see the remnants of what had once been a bustling coal town; another time they hitchhiked to Cranbrook to buy clothes. They spent most of their time together in the town of Fernie, sauntering down the railroad tracks until a train forced them off or hanging out at a coffee shop. Such days, flirting with an imbecile world, felt liberating.

One Saturday night, they saw *Back to the Future* at the theater, where they sat six rows behind Hugh, who was sharing popcorn with the girl beside him. Amber said it was his cousin from Revelstoke, and Stacey had no reason to believe it wasn't true. Cousin or not, she had no problem earning Hugh's attention.

Most nights after a movie, they went somewhere to talk, and they had plenty to discuss after *Back to the Future*, but Amber had promised her mother she'd be home early because the family was driving to Calgary first thing in the morning. Stacey didn't feel like going straight home. She watched Hugh and the girl that might have been his cousin heading down 2nd Avenue, so she walked the other way, then turned down 5th Street toward the highway. In the dark, a train ripped through town then faded into the wilderness. Shortly after, she had a sense she was being followed. She turned toward the Elk River, walking faster than she wanted, and every time she glanced over her shoulder, she could see a man following in the shadows. Realizing that there would be little light by the river, she turned back toward downtown. The last place she wanted a man to follow her was into the woods where there would be no one else this time of night. She went down 2nd Avenue and wedged herself between brick buildings at the side of The Grand Central Hotel, crouched down and waited. It wasn't long before Angus Bland loped past her hiding spot. There was something not quite right about Angus Bland. Almost forty, he lived with his mother in the oldest part of Fernie, a stretch of houses that had miraculously avoided the fire of 1908 that vanquished the town to smoldering ashes in a few hours. Angus's aberrant behaviour was well-known in town, and a court order allowed him out in public only under the supervision of his mother in the daytime. Angus favoured children and girls. He would walk up close to people chatting on the street and watch them without saying a word. Often he urinated in public, if his mother wasn't beside him, with picket fences and privet hedges his favourite targets. Some in town saw him as a harmless cretin to be ignored, but some with children battled the authorities, eager that something be done. Angus's aging mother did the best she could, and rarely did Angus appear about town without her, but she often fell asleep at odd times, and when that happened, Angus took advantage of his freedom.

Stacey waited until he went a ways down the street, then watched from her brick hiding place and saw him head for 5th Street, the street she had been on earlier, no doubt thinking she might have followed the same route as before. She wondered if he knew where she lived. Probably not, but she didn't want him to find out. She crossed 2nd Avenue toward the railway tracks then walked north toward the old railway station. She sat on a bench and listened to the frenzy of patrons drinking at the Fernie Hotel who spilled onto the sidewalk. She imagined Angus following the same route he had before, and that he might follow this route two or three times before he would give up and go home.

An elderly man walked south from the Fernie Hotel, and the way he walked, he'd been inside drinking most of the night. Morning Missy, he said and sat at the opposite end of the bench. His hands fumbled inside his coat pockets and extracted a pouch of tobacco and some papers. It took several minutes to roll a cigarette, and then he couldn't find his matches, which had fallen under the bench when he'd searched for his tobacco. Stacey picked up the matches and offered to help light his cigarette, and the man accepted. It looks like it will be a beautiful day, he said, then stood up unsteadily and made his way across the tracks to home.

Stacey waited by herself until she calculated it had been the better part of an hour since she'd seen Angus Bland. Her mother would expect her to phone from Amber's house unless she got home soon. She wandered down the main street, but few people were about and it was quiet. She stopped in an alcove to focus on some artwork on display in the window, and in the reflection of the glass, she saw someone standing behind her. Angus Bland, standing on the sidewalk, three feet from where she was cornered, his hands fishing inside his open fly. Hi, he said with confidence, as if they were acquaintances familiar with meeting under such circumstances. Stacey moved to the left to walk out onto the street, and Angus moved to block her. She tried moving the other way, but Angus was not about to let her get away until he was ready. I'll scream if you don't get out of my way, Stacey said, and Angus, with the hand that wasn't busy fishing in his pants, raised a finger to his lips and said, Shush. Angus found what he was looking for and pulled his penis out into the cool air for her to see. Stacey screamed, and soon Hugh appeared in the alcove. He shoved Angus out of the way, and the man cowered against the door and whimpered.

You okay? Hugh asked.

I am now.

Angus is nuts, Hugh said. He doesn't know what he's doing. Do you want me to walk you home?

No. I'll be fine. Thanks for being here.

I saw you walking down from the station. I wanted to catch up to you. If I had, none of this would have happened.

Well, thanks anyway. I have to get home now. They're expecting me.

Fair enough. Every town has an Angus. I'll take him home before the police do.

Hart didn't show up the first night like he promised. Della figured Molly had told him Sage was too tired. He showed up the next night about seven and checked his watch as he walked in, as if he had an appointment and was determined to be punctual. Molly had told him to check the carnations had water, so he did that.

Potholes, Hart said. Life is filled with them, but I've yet to find a road riddled with potholes I couldn't travel down. What do you say I wheel you over to Fort Whoop for an hour? Change of scenery. Sage said nothing, but his left eye looked interested. Very well, then. Sound good to you, Della?

If he wants to go.

Oh, he wants to go. I know what this guy wants.

Before they left, Della explained about the clipboard and pen and told him to take it along to make things easier. Hart looked at what she had and tucked it under his arm.

Be careful, Della said. There's no ramp out there.

I know, I'll get on that tomorrow.

And there's a lot of snow.

I've already shovelled a path to Fort Whoop. We've got everything covered.

Hart showing up like the good fairy caused Della and Stacey to look at one another like they'd just discovered a mountain of gold in the living room. Della could use the time to clean up and put her thoughts in order after a hectic day, and Stacey could watch any of the TV shows she liked without Sage sitting in the corner like an overseer. Della had told Stacey she could pick out one or two shows she wanted to watch every week and they would tell Sage that's the way things worked, but now she didn't need her mother to negotiate on her behalf. They both knew Hart wouldn't have Sage back in an hour. The two of them would soon be mellow and oblivious to time.

When Sage had first arrived home, Della had insisted that Stacey at least go into the living room and say hello to her dad, so she did. Now she spent most of her time in the kitchen or her bedroom or somewhere other than the house. When she had reason to enter the living room, she did so expediently and didn't look him in the eye. She no longer worried that Sage would say or do something hurtful, but his one good eye was still omnipotent. With each sojourn into the space her dad occupied, she felt braver and almost giddy, like the time years earlier when she and Tommy roamed the backyard during a warm summer rain, free to dance in muddy patches on the lawn, wearing only their underwear. He watched her, she knew, and listened too. Sometimes she'd say things out loud to herself while passing by. *Tonight is going to be fun. I think I'll take a long, luxurious bath. Yeah, only one week until the dance.*

She hadn't committed to attending the dance. Amber and Morgan were going. Hugh had asked her, and she'd told him if she did it would be a last-minute decision, but if she showed up, she'd dance with him once if he wanted.

She pulled her favourite chair up close to the TV but not so close that her mother would make her move back from the invisible rays she'd read about. She turned on the TV and passed over *Married With Children* because it apparently wasn't suitable and settled in to watch *Murder She Wrote*. She put a glass of milk and two chocolate Peek Frean cookies on top of the TV and said a silent prayer in honour of Hart next door.

Inside Fort Whoop, Hart had a fire roaring and two joints rolled and ready to go. He lit one and handed it to Sage, who had to work hard at inhaling enough to fill his lungs with magic, but he managed. Hart talked to him because it was easier that way. He told him about some changes he'd made to the fort and how he was thinking of offering it as a bed and breakfast for people who wanted to step into the past. Molly thought it was a stupid idea, so if he went with it, he would have to organize the breakfast part himself, which he didn't see as a problem because it would just be beans and bacon chunks and a bread he had painstakingly learned to cook in the fireplace in his portable oven. After his vivid description, he wanted to know what Sage thought, but the clipboard was hard for Sage to balance on the arm of the wheelchair and his legs, sitting there, were jittery and uneven. Hart took the clipboard and went to the small shop portion of Fort Whoop and soon had it cut in half lengthwise. He ripped the paper in half and then taped the contraption (using duct tape because he didn't have thin wire handy) to the arm of the wheelchair. Then he attached the ballpoint pen to the clipboard with a string, so if Sage lost control, he could start again. He looked at the rumpled and dirty copy of desires someone had written, and he started again with a clean copy. At the bottom, he added *smoke* and *home,* and Sage was set, coming or going.

Hart wanted to delve into stories of the Wild West with Sage. He knew most of the American tales of Butch Cassidy and the Sundance Kid, Wyatt Earp, Calamity Jane and Billy the Kid. These bandits were renowned because they were American and Americans excelled at talking about themselves. Physical reminders of every shape and size spread like smallpox across the skin of America everywhere you went. They call them heritage sites these days, Hart said. What thrilled him most, though, was the knowledge he'd accumulated about Canadian stories like Boone Helm, an American, true, but one flushed into British Columbia who enjoyed eating those he killed. He knew about the exploits of the McLean brothers, the horse stealing duo of Gaddy and Racette and his favourite, Bill Miner the Gentleman Bandit. These and other tales Hart never tired of reciting, so he did his best to limit himself to one a night. Most of the tales of the Wild West Hart had likely already told to Sage when they'd spent Sunday evenings in the woodshed, but good stories, Hart figured, can hold up to retelling in the same way as *The Three Little Pigs* which every kid had heard dozens of times growing up. And besides that, Sage, in this state in front of the fire, was a different person than before, a person who might not remember the stories that ran through Hart's veins like thin blood. One a night. That's what he'd decided. Then he'd move onto something going on in the world, something eating away at their tax dollars.

So that Mulroney as prime minister is a piece of work. Would you give him a thumbs-up or thumbs-down? Hart waited until Sage pushed out his left arm and pointed his thumb downward. That's what I thought. Before he got elected, he was against free trade, and now he says we've got to have it. I wonder how much money he made with that deal. Our coal sold just fine without it. Say, did I tell you a Muslim family moved to town? They came into my office because someone told them they had to have insurance to live in this country. Imagine that. I straightened them out on that one. They pray five times a day and face east every single time. They live on south 11th Ave. That must mean from their house they pray toward the small valley between Fernie Ridge and Morrissey Ridge. That's a good plan, I'd say. It's about the only place a prayer could squeak out of this valley.

Hart wanted to know what had gone on next door before Sage had his stroke. Molly had offered a dozen possible scenarios, and she counted on him uncovering a few gritty details she could mull over. But Hart abandoned the idea on that first night, glad to have Sage back, sitting in the comfortable environ of Fort Whoop, the two of them able to ponder anything in the world without repercussion. If Hart had learned anything in life, it was that archeologists dug up the past and he wasn't one of those, he was an insurance agent who believed in term insurance with a conversion privilege. He'd have nothing to keep him busy if people didn't believe in the future, so he'd stick to that. The past had sucked for Sage, and his present wasn't too rosy either. He knew without asking that his neighbour wanted things to operate this way too.

24

HAVING SAGE HOME required reconfiguring the rhythm of life Della and Stacey had grown accustomed to. The spectacle of a man sitting in a wheelchair in the corner of the living room watching *Sesame Street* every morning bothered all three of her clients. Matty, the two-and-a-half-year-old, cried the first three days whenever she looked at him. After a while, Sage blended in with the furniture as far as the kids were concerned, though Matty turned around when something funny happened on TV, as if unsure whether laughter was allowed. Sage never laughed. He sat there like a sentinel.

Patient and tractable when he had to be, Lucky nevertheless liked kids less than Della did. The dog had been owned by two elderly people for years, and he wasn't used to poking and prodding. Della left him outside for most of the day and brought him in for his afternoon snack. The kids got to pet him for a minute, and then Della parked him in Stacey's room for the rest of the day.

Most nights Hart wheeled Sage to Fort Whoop, and Stacey felt the most comfortable then. In the mornings or after school or during the odd evening that Sage remained at his post, Stacey slid from room to room pretending that he wasn't sitting anywhere in the house. She had become a big fan of nurse Belle because she scoured the tub with bleach after every session with her dad, but she was never home when the nurse arrived to deal with him. Listening to Della's description of what went on—his bath, his limited exercise routine and the military treatment that came his way with nurse Belle in attendance—was more than she wanted to consider. Fantasizing that he no longer existed allowed her to cope. When Della left the house, she took a different approach.

Every year when the first hint of spring entered the valley, Della liked to get outside, and she preferred to walk by herself, meditatively, with a cigarette. Stacey agreed this would be okay even if Hart didn't come to pick up Sage. Trapped indoors with three kids and an invalid all day, her mother needed the break. Once or twice a week, Stacey loved to take a book and sit in the bathtub until her toes wrinkled. With her mother out for an hour and Sage watching TV, her behaviour changed. She would pull herself out of the tub, dry off and saunter to her room wrapped only in a towel, having left her change of clothes in the bedroom. The first time she did this, she didn't look his way, but the second time, she walked even more slowly and kept an eye on him watching her.

Every week or ten days, Hart didn't come to fetch Sage, and these were nights she looked forward to. If it were raining and Della hesitated about going for her walk, Stacey encouraged her to take the car out and have a coffee somewhere to break up the routine. With each passing episode, she revealed more. She would wrap a towel around her midsection and walk into the living room ostensibly to consider the offerings on the bookshelf. She wasn't a big fan of hair dryers because Morgan said they emitted too many positive ions into the air and made you lose energy, so for two years, it had been her habit to dry her hair with a towel and let evaporation do the rest. One night while she stood in a tentative pose in front of the bookshelf, Lucky, who followed her everywhere, wanted to play tug-a-war and grabbed a corner of her towel in his mouth and pulled until the towel sat like a puddle around her feet. She retrieved the towel and vigorously dried her hair, leaving the rest of her anatomy open for inspection. She did so nonchalantly at first, as if Sage were not sitting there, but after a time, she looked at him looking at her and turned around so that nothing was left to his imagination. His sibilant nose-breathing grew louder than usual. She wanted to tell him if this was what he'd been after all these years, well now was his chance. But Stacey didn't say a word. She didn't need to. She had for months imagined herself as Greta Garbo in a silent movie, and she would carry out her role to perfection.

One night, Amber came over to work on a history project with Stacey while Amber's mother hosted a Tupperware party. Stacey said she could come but warned her that her dad would be sitting in a wheelchair, his one glazed eye taking everything in. Amber knew all Stacey had been through, and Stacey worried her bias would prevent her from just coming over like in the old days, but if Amber held a grudge of any kind on behalf of her best friend, she hid it.

Hello, Mr. Howard. Do you remember me? Amber? I'm working on school stuff with Stacey, and we'll be working in the kitchen. Do you need anything before we get started? Sage took his pen and pointed to the word water. Amber got him a glass then met Stacey at the kitchen table.

Imagine having to sit in one place all day long, Amber said. Reliant on people to bring you a glass of water. I don't know if I'd want to live if I had to live like that. Do you have to help him to the bathroom?

Hell no. My mom and the nurse do that. I changed the channel for him once. As if to prove this were true, Stacey went into the living room and changed the channel to *Miami Vice*, which was just about to start.

Amber was big on lip gloss, maybe from all the kissing she did. They had both stopped using lipstick because Morgan said most lipstick contains barium, which contributes to breast cancer. She got a tube of gloss out of her purse and coated her lips, still not ready to start their project. I guess as long as your mind is working, she said, you've got a reason to keep on living. If your mind went blank but your body stayed good, then you wouldn't know the difference if you were living or not. Or maybe you would. Maybe you would be like a chicken, able to walk around and live your life but never burdened with history reports, but then when it came time someone grabbed your feet and put your head on the chopping block, it *would* matter to you. I'm guessing there are all kinds of ways we want to keep going. What do you think?

Stacey had everything ready to begin. She had two pens and two pencils for Amber and two of each for herself. Two clipboards filled with loose-leaf paper for them to make notes. That way they would both have a copy of what took place.

I think he still gets something out of life, Stacey said. Imagine if you were in solitary confinement in prison, stuck in a small, dark room all day with nothing to do, and then someone gave you a break and let you watch a half hour of TV once a day. You'd look forward to that, maybe because it reminded you of your life before you were in solitary confinement, and it would give you plenty to think about for the next twenty-three and a half hours. He's way better off than that. He gets to see all kinds of things during the day, and people talk to him and bring him water. Just what he sees around him with his one good eye gives him more than enough to think about.

She not only went to the school dance, she stayed until it ended and a little bit more. The Environmental Club had offered to clean up and recycle the refuse, and the group thought it would be just as easy to get it out of the way and not have to come back into the school on a Saturday morning. Stacey danced with Hugh as she promised she would. Three times. The first time out of a sense of obligation, but Hugh wore an earthy, captivating scent, so the second and third dances took place because she wanted to get close enough to smell him.

They went to Morgan's after, and because of the late hour, Stacey phoned home to explain. Morgan's house had a basement and a room they could call their own, so they played Twister there. Amber volunteered to manage the spinner while Stacey, Morgan and Hugh became contortionists. Stacey was wearing a skirt, and when her next move required her to be compromised, she pretended to slip and was disqualified. Morgan and Hugh kept going until Morgan said he couldn't do it anymore. He had to pee.

Morgan and Amber then cuddled on the couch while Stacey and Hugh lay down on the rug in the corner. As usual, the lights were off, which made it difficult to maneuver intelligently. Stacey let him kiss and fondle her. His scent captivated her, and she wanted to know the name of it but didn't dare ask in case he thought it was the main reason she lay beside him, which it was. His hand gently rubbed the inside of her leg, and the sensation, happening while he kissed her, overwhelmed her. His hand slid up her leg, and at first she felt separated from that leg, and she lay there curious about what might happen next. The higher the hand worked, the more evident it became that the leg belonged to her and she had a visitor, not one she wanted to let in the front door, but one she might be willing to visit with on the porch. Hugh wanted to be like Morgan, everyone could see that he emulated everything Morgan did, and one thing Morgan had going for him was a steady girlfriend who invited him in once and a while. Hugh kept his hand on her leg and moved his lips from her lips and whispered in her ear. Stacey heard him whisper but didn't respond because she needed to take in what he had said. Hugh thought she hadn't heard him so he repeated his request. *I think we should do it sometime.*

Stacey had been enjoying herself, and she wished he hadn't said a thing. Sometimes words only got in the way. I've got to go, she said and stood up and traced her hand along the wall to find the door.

I've got to go too, Hugh said and got up to follow her. By the time Hugh made his way out to the street, Stacey had disappeared, which made him think she hadn't walked home but had run.

During Sage's second monthly checkup, the doctor, for the first time, expressed concern. After month one, his vital signs had remained the same as at the hospital, but after month two, he had high blood pressure once again. The doctor directed his comments to Della more than to Sage because she was the one, he felt, who could do something about it. Sage was not over-weight and never had been. If anything, he had lost weight since his stroke. Exercise would help, and while nurse Belle put him through his paces Mondays, Wednesdays and Fridays, for the rest of his week, his exercise amounted to shuffling to the bathroom and back to his chair. He told Della to guide her husband, whenever possible, around the living room before he went back to sitting in his wheelchair. Della asked if a walker would help, and he said it might but she would need to be constantly at his side, as his balance and coordination were poor and having him rely on the walker might pose more risks than benefits. He said to find a squeezable rubber ball that would allow him to strengthen his left arm. Then he mentioned salt. Della said Sage liked salt on everything he ate and always had. This practice had to stop immediately. The doctor prescribed a regimen of diuretics and beta-blockers that would help. He asked if anything had changed in his daily routine, and since Sage had made nightly visits to Fort Whoop almost from the beginning,

Della said she didn't think so. Stress is a major cause of high blood pressure, the doctor said, so Sage should avoid scenarios that might trigger tension in his life. After they left the doctor's office, Della thought her leaving the house nightly had been one change from month number one, but she couldn't imagine Sage getting worked up because she needed to get away for an hour a day. When they got home, she asked him if her evening outings bothered him, but he grabbed his pen and pointed to no. The doctor had also asked if Sage smoked, and she had answered no for cigarettes, but his sessions with Hart *were* smoking and she thought she should have mentioned it. It wouldn't matter in any case. Sage would learn to get by without salt because she would see to it, but if anyone suggested he stop smoking pot, it would be a sure source of instant tension.

Della left Sage in the car when they stopped first at the drugstore and then the hardware store. She found only a few toys there but bought a small rubber ball that had some give to it. Next she took Sage out for coffee and a treat and had to load him into the wheelchair one more time. She could tell Sage didn't like having his clipboard away from the wheelchair for the trip. She thought he might not want to appear helpless in public, but she carried on with her plan anyway. He didn't want a treat of any kind and drank only half his coffee. A few people came up to him in the restaurant and said polite, innocuous things to him to which he nodded his head.

Molly had been minding her kids through it all, and the outing took longer than expected.

Is everything all right? Molly asked.

I think so, Della said. The doctor's concerned his blood pressure has gone up. He prescribed some drugs that should help.

Molly helped get Sage back into his wheelchair, which made that easier. Later, when Della took him to the washroom, he pointed to the bedroom. Della didn't know how much exercise the doctor thought Sage capable of, but he tired and fell asleep before she closed the bedroom door.

Della knew Oli Hardwick from church, a member of the congregation from when she first attended, and he never missed a Sunday. Rose and Molly had filled her in on most of the congregation over the last few years, and because of her fastidious informers, Della knew Oli as a widower. He's a gentleman, Rose said. A stamp collector, Molly said, one who spent his days bent over his hobby or walking his dog. He'd retired young, having sold his lucrative sign-painting business, and Molly said sometimes he wished he hadn't sold when he did. On several fronts, he seemed a lonely man. One fall, Hart had taken a trip without Molly, a search for artifacts for Fort Whoop, and Oli Hardwick and gone with him. Hart said all the way there and back, he talked about how much he missed his wife.

One night, due to heavy rain, Della took the car downtown for coffee, and Oli Hardwick sat at a corner table reading the newspaper. Not the local paper but a thick one from out of town. He looked deeply involved in it so Della didn't bother him, just ordered a coffee and sat by herself. Oli looked out over his newspaper and saw her there and suggested she bring her coffee to his table and join him. She did.

Oli had heard about Sage's fate. Everyone in town had. Despite this, he had Della explain the chronology of her husband's condition, and he listened intently to all the details as if he wanted to pass some later quiz with flying colours.

You've had a tough go of it, Oli said. When he spoke these words, Della felt the impulse to mention Sage was the one who had it tough, but then she thought about it and realized Oli identified with her circumstance because he too had an assumed part of his life wiped out. And he was right. Life would never again be what it once was.

They both ordered a second coffee, and Oli offered to buy her a Nanaimo bar. Della said she had better not, and Oli said if maintaining her figure concerned her, she had nothing to worry about, and he ordered a Nanaimo bar for them to share. Della told him she knew he was a stamp collector and wondered what that entailed. Oli came to life then, you could see the spark in his eyes when he spoke. He'd attended the Great Western Stamp Show in Richmond last year, and he was planning a trip to Bayside, New York, for an even bigger show coming this summer.

I collect stamps from anywhere I can if I think they have value. That doesn't just mean older stamps, it means rare stamps. My collection focuses on Canada and England, but I dabble in American stamps too, mostly to trade. Next year I'm thinking of going to England. They have huge stamp shows there, and I haven't been back for over twenty years.

Oli went on about stamps for close to an hour. Della imagined such a thing might bore her, and it might have if she were reading about it, but Oli's enthusiasm made it sound like a thrilling adventure.

Years ago, in England, Oli said, mail cost a fortune to send and was sent "collect," and since it often required a day's wages to receive it, thousands of letters would travel the country with no hope of being delivered. Then they adopted the penny stamp, which made it cheap for anyone to send a letter, and the stamp worked to send a letter anywhere in the world. I have three or four at home in varying condition. Stamps aren't just items, you see. They bring with them a sense of history.

My dad had a collection, Della said. A small collection, nothing like yours. There's a lot more to stamp collecting than most would think. I can see that now.

One more thing I'll bet you didn't know. The Queen has a stamp collection.

You don't say?

I do say. And John Lennon collected stamps as a boy.

Well, I'll be.

You're welcome to come over and view the collection sometime, Oli said.

I'd like to do that, Della said. I'd like that a lot.

This happened on a Wednesday, and Della went back to just walking around the neighbourhood for the next while, but when Wednesday rolled around again, she took the car and went back to the coffee shop and saw Oli, newspaper in hand, as if he'd been waiting for her all week. This time they each ordered their own Nanaimo bar. Oli's hair looked different, and she saw he had it combed over to the side with what looked like a wave-set. They talked again. For a long time. Not just about stamps but about the church they attended and Fernie and what the future might hold for the town. Della had ended up in Fernie because of Sage's job, and they'd stayed put partly for the anonymity of the place, so she hadn't considered the town's future but thought maybe she should. They talked about some of the people in the church and some, like Hart, that didn't attend. Oli said he envied Hart because of his passion for collecting things and because he had a wife who didn't object. When Della heard this assessment, she thought maybe Oli's stamp collection had begun in earnest after his wife died. A natural progression, that was. When something that substantive in your life falls away, something is bound to take its place.

25

TOWARD THE END OF MARCH, Hart had his first bed and breakfast customer, a couple on holiday from Toronto in town to catch the end of the ski season. They'd read his notice in the laundromat. Once he got his customers settled, he went next door for Sage because he'd been busy the night before and he didn't like to leave him two days in succession. He couldn't take him to Fort Whoop, so he grabbed an extra Hudson's Bay blanket and wheeled Sage to the back of the woodshed, like the old days. From where they sat, they could hear the man out at the well drawing water with the hand pump.

That's good, Hart said, referring to the couple sleeping in his fort replica. I only put up the one notice, and I've got a taker already. I think I'll put together a pamphlet and put them in the visitors' center. This could be a nice supplement once I bow out of the insurance business. Someday I'll be one of those old farts hanging around the coffee shop giving free advice. Free because no one would pay for it. I guess you're never too old to sell insurance, but it gets tedious after a while. I imagine you know all about tedious.

Hart told Sage anything that came to mind, just as he would have wanted if they switched roles. He would want to know everything going on in town. I see Stacey dyed her hair, he said. She's a redhead now. I saw her walking down the street, chatting it up with a boy she knows. She's getting to be quite a looker, that one. I can see why the boys would be interested. Do you ever think what it would be like to be that age again? With your whole life in front of you? I don't often. Just when I see someone like Stacey starting out. That's when I think about it.

In the middle of June, it got hot. Everybody said it was hot earlier than usual, but Stacey couldn't remember if that were true or not. She and Amber were about to finish grade ten. Morgan was graduating, and Amber felt uneasy about what that would mean. He would go to UBC in the fall, and he would have a room in residence, so Amber said she'd think up excuses to go to Vancouver because Morgan said he could sneak her in and nobody would know. Amber said the uneasy part of it all was that if she could sneak in with no one knowing, so could other people. She trusted Morgan, she said. They loved each other, and as soon as she graduated, the two of them would get married and Stacey would be the maid of honour.

Amber and Stacey wanted summer jobs, something other than babysitting or walking dogs. Amber's dad knew someone who ran the golf course, and she thought there might be two job openings. Stacey knew Della wouldn't like it, but she wouldn't stand in her way either. She'd noticed a change in her mother lately. Della didn't interfere as much as she used to, and Stacey felt like her equal somehow. She was studying for her driver's test, and Della took her out to practise at least twice a week. It wasn't clear to Stacey what had engineered the difference in her mother's treatment of her. They owned a VCR, and every Sunday night, Della and Stacey rented a video to watch together, and Sage could watch if he wanted or close his eyes. *Hannah and Her Sisters, Pretty in Pink* and *An Officer and a Gentleman* were some of the movies they'd viewed. Sage watched them all, but she couldn't tell if he had enjoyed them or not. Stacey had to remind herself that the people in the movies were acting, but it didn't feel that way. They magically appeared in your living room like real people.

On Wednesday, Della told Stacey she'd be out for most of the evening, meeting members of the congregation to study. Only the word members being plural was a lie. Don't expect me until after ten, she said.

Oli Hendricks lived just out of town in a house that looked too big for one person. She pulled into the driveway, and Oli was at the window, waiting. The few flower beds in the front yard looked like they'd been let go. Oli wasn't much of a gardener by the look of things.

Well, I made it. I always said I'd pop over to see your stamp collection, and low and behold, here I am.

Della had a light coat folded over her arms in case it cooled on the way home, and Oli took the coat from her and hung it in the hallway. All the times the two had met for coffee, Della had come away thinking Oli brimmed with confidence and charm. He didn't look as confident now she had arrived at his doorstep. Possibly he didn't have many visitors.

I got some Ethiopian coffee we can try. I'm glad you could come. Can I show you around the house first? It's an older house, but it has its charm.

Della got the tour. The old cuckoo clock in the living room had belonged to his grandfather and was the only artefact passed on to him from that generation. The clock didn't work, he said, but he liked having it around. She saw the updated kitchen had a dishwasher, something Della wanted but couldn't yet afford. The bathroom had a jetted tub. Della didn't know anyone who owned a jetted tub. The main floor had two bedrooms, with one of them converted to a study of sorts. A desk squatted at an angle in the corner, and a large table dominated the middle of the room. For laying out his stamp collection, she guessed.

The upstairs is much the same, Oli said. There's another bathroom up there and two more bedrooms. That's where I sleep.

They ended back in the kitchen, and Oli showed her the coffee before he made it. I wanted it to be fresh, that's why I waited, he said. And look, I bought a half dozen Nanaimo bars to go with it.

This is a big house you have, Della said.

It is. Sometimes I think I should buy something smaller, but you get used to a place. You know how it is.

Della wandered to a back window and looked out at three trees that had finished blooming and were vigorously green. She couldn't say she was all that used to her house. Familiar was as far as she could go. Oli may not have an interest in gardening, but he kept the inside of the house immaculate. Of course, he didn't have kids parading through the house all day long, and he didn't have an invalid to take care of. She felt bad for thinking so. Oli may well have had plenty to cope with before his wife died. He never mentioned his wife in all the times they'd been together. Molly had said his wife had taken almost four years to pass once they got the prognosis. Molly wouldn't have made up something like that.

The coffee he made was delicious, stronger than the coffee they had downtown. He opened the box containing six Nanaimo bars, and Della blushed. They sat in the living room and listened to the old clock that showed the wrong time but ticked obediently, and even though the eating and drinking didn't take long, it felt late to Della, and she thought maybe she wasn't there to see his stamp collection after all, but Oli rose to his feet and asked her to follow him into his office. He opened a large cupboard she hadn't noticed when she first viewed the room. From the hundreds of photo albums inside, Oli selected a few and brought them to the table in the middle of the room.

Storage is an issue for a stamp collector. As soon as I come upon a stamp, I file it where it belongs. If you don't, you end up with envelopes or bags full of stamps you know nothing about after a while. I have some of those too, but they're duplicates. Countries, including Canada, issue stamps that reflect something about their culture. This book, for example, holds Canadian stamps that honour entertainers, this one has literary legends. All my Canadian stamps are in yellow binders. Not sure why. The green binders like this one are British, and you can see here stamps issued during Queen Elizabeth II's reign. He pointed. This one features castles.

He handed Della a magnifying glass and had her bend over and peer at certain elements that differentiated one stamp from another. Take a close look at this one. It comes from Mauritius, and it was meant to say *postage paid*, but it says *post office*, 1847 that one.

Oli opened up as he showed his collection, but then they went back to the living room for a second cup of coffee. They sat down on opposite ends of the large olive-coloured couch, and with no prompting, he spoke about his wife, his voice not much stronger than a whisper.

I thought my life had ended when she died. I couldn't do anything for a long time. When she died, it was like a glass had smashed and scattered across the kitchen floor, and it wasn't just my wife who had died, but our togetherness went missing too, and I could see the thousands of pieces everywhere, but I had no way of putting us back together again.

It must have been hard, Della said.

You have no idea. And I'm glad you don't. You're the first woman to set foot in the house in four years. That's how hard it's been.

He stopped talking, and Della stared across the room at the cuckoo clock. The clock had been ticking earlier but was now frozen in time, and she wondered if it had stopped at the exact minute his wife had died. She turned toward him and saw him crying. Without a thought, she moved over on the couch and put her arm around his shoulder.

Would you do something for me? he said.

I will. Just name it.

Oli stood up, held her hand and pulled Della from the couch. He held her hand tightly and led her upstairs. She hadn't felt the need for a cigarette all evening, but she wanted a cigarette now. When they entered his bedroom, he explained what he wanted.

Would you lie down with me for a few minutes? Just lie down on the bed and hold me?

He lay down on the bed as if it were something that needed demonstration. Della looked at him, turned on his side, his head sunk into a soft pillow. She kicked off her shoes and climbed onto the bed beside him. She put an arm around him, and he sobbed. Over his muted emotion, she told him everything would be okay. She didn't say it with much conviction, but she said it because she felt the ache of his hunger, though she wasn't convinced it would ever go away.

Until after ten, she had the house to herself. Her mother had said so, and she figured she could count on 9:30 being safe. She phoned Hugh right away, and he was thrilled she had phoned. Are you busy tonight? she asked, and Hugh said, Never too busy to spend time with Stacey Howard.

Good, she said. Come over tonight about 7:30. Make sure you shower first. I think you're right. You and I should do it.

Stacey rarely drank beer, but she got two out of the woodshed and put them in the fridge. She had a quick shower and put the diaphragm in place like she'd practiced several times already and now felt what her aunt would call savvy like a pro. She put on a short skirt and a loosely fitted diaphanous top and didn't bother with socks or underwear. She saw Hugh drive up early in front of the house in his mother's green Ford. He sat in the car, waiting for the right time. Stacey reconsidered and went to her room and put on a pair of black underwear. She left a dog biscuit for Lucky in her room and closed the door. When he knocked, she opened the front door, and he stood there with a small bouquet held in both hands.

You didn't need to bring flowers, she said, then leaned her head upward and kissed Hugh on the lips. He looked over her shoulder after the kiss, after his eyes opened, and he saw Sage sitting in his chair, taking it all in. Stacey leaned forward and kissed him again, only longer this time. Hugh followed her and the flowers into the kitchen, and she asked him to open the two beer while she put the flowers into water.

He doesn't mind I'm here?

Don't worry about him. He sits there just like he is now.

They kissed again and then sat down at the kitchen table and drank their beer. Hugh had shaved before coming over and had a small nick on the end of his chin. He kept putting the back of his hand there, as if he didn't trust it. Stacey drank her beer fast, and he tried to catch up.

This is my first time, Stacey said. I want everything to be perfect. You only fuck for the first time once in your whole life.

I want it to be perfect too, Hugh said. I brought two safes with me.

Don't worry about a thing. I have everything under control, but you have to do it just as I say or the whole thing's off.

At eight o'clock, *Highway to Heaven* would be over. Sage liked the show, about an angel descending to Earth to help people out. It didn't seem like the type of TV show he would like, but he watched it every week. Tonight, Hugh was her angel and would help her get what she wanted. The show ended, and Stacey turned off the TV.

First she turned off the overhead light and lit what remained of a Christmas candle she'd found in the cupboard. She sat on the couch and pointed to a spot where Hugh was to sit so he wouldn't have to stare at Sage the whole time. She grabbed his shirt and pulled him toward her and kissed him with all her might. Hugh looked over his shoulder just once and then slid his hands under her blouse, and he soon forgot that Sage was in the room. Stacey helped him out and pulled her top over her shoulders. She undid the fastener on her bra and let Hugh do the rest. He leaned in and nibbled each of her breasts as if this was what someone like Morgan had told him to do. He paid attention to each breast equally, and Stacey thought that was fair. His hands slid up and down her legs, but he hesitated each time he touched her panties. After the third time, she stood up and slid them off and threw them onto the rug in the middle of the living room floor. She grabbed his right hand and guided him to where he needed to go. She told Hugh he should take his clothes off, and he did as she said. It was sticking up, pointing right at her from where she sat on the couch, but then Hugh turned to look at Sage one more time. Stacey offered a small kiss on the end of his penis. She wished he had two penises to pay attention to, but he only had one, so she licked it twice. She'd learned that get-ready trick from Amber, who had explained it as foreplay. He wore that scent again, and she stroked him, and all his attention came back to her. She slid onto a bath towel that lay on the thick rug in the middle of the room and pulled Hugh on top of her. Are you sure I don't need a rubber? he said. Morgan told me—

Trust me. Just trust me.

Stacey wasn't sure she could remember all that happened next. She guided him inside her, and he pounded his body on top of hers, frantic, like the world would end soon and only he knew about it. It didn't take long. That's the part she remembered long after. It didn't take as long as she wanted it to.

Are you okay? he asked.

Yes, she said. Thanks for asking. She leaned forward and saw Sage sitting in his chair, his face all scrunched up as if he had a bad toothache. She didn't want Hugh to see his face. That would ruin everything. She wrapped her arms around Hugh and held him right where he was when he'd groaned like an animal that had given up on life, a position she would remember forever.

26

STACEY HADN'T FALLEN ASLEEP right away, and then she fell into a deep sleep, which explained why she woke late, in a panic to get to school on time. She had a quick shower and washed her diaphragm. The song "Puff the Magic Dragon" was inside her head and wouldn't leave her alone. She thought of her Aunt Sadie and wished she were around now so they could discuss all that had happened, and Aunt Sadie would be the perfect sounding board. She considered what to wear to school and wished she had some new clothes because she felt like a new person. She chose the same top and skirt she'd worn the night before. It would encourage her dreamlike state to continue. She made a tuna sandwich for lunch and cut it into four equal sections as usual, then threw two pieces of celery into her lunch bag. The house became a crossroads then, her trying to leave in a hurry, Belle the no-nonsense-nurse arriving earlier than usual and Della welcoming her wards at the front door. Della hadn't had time to get Sage to the washroom yet, and when Belle arrived, Sage was worse than usual. He'd messed his adult diaper right where he sat, which didn't impress Belle. Stacey left immediately, leaving her mother to answer the nurse's pointed questions.

She felt a slight movement of air as she walked down the street, a gentle breeze that made walking effortless. Though she wore the same clothes as the night before, it felt like she wasn't wearing clothes at all, as if people could see inside her in a way never before possible. Mr. Partridge, her biology teacher, would notice for sure. He often went on about the angst animals feel before rutting season. He would notice a difference in her, and when he did, she would smile back with a controlled smile, one that suggested that yes, he was right, but she had everything under control. She found it thrilling, this new way of knowing the world, one that took away forever a younger self that could slip in and out of serious scrutiny. Power bestowed and innocence lost.

Part of her wanted to see Hugh, but another part of her wished she were on her way out of town for the summer so she wouldn't run into him for months. She didn't feel what Amber and Morgan felt, not even close. Hugh would want to do it again and soon, but Stacey didn't feel that way. It had been an experience bound to happen, and now she wanted the waters to calm once again. Aunt Sadie told her that people are more like dogs when it comes to sex than most people think. Male dogs are always on the lookout for females in heat, and when they find one, they're relentless. She would be friendly around Hugh, work with him in the Environmental Club, but he would get the message loud and clear she wasn't the young woman in heat he wanted.

She would enjoy her first day after in her present elevated state of mind, one that left her head feeling empty but not completely empty, occupied as it was with all she now knew. On a whim, she could turn her attention to her recent history and feel a sense of exhilaration all over again. That was her plan for the day, and it might have worked out that way except that as soon as she walked through the school doors, she saw Amber by her locker, waiting for her. Amber said, You and I have something to talk about, so I hear.

For most of her life, Stacey had listened to her mother offer the wisdom of her years, sometimes spontaneously, sometimes in helpful sessions. Her mother knew what it was like to attend school for the first time, to sleep over at a friend's house, to have chores around the place that must be done. She had made a few mistakes along the way, and she wanted Stacey to avoid the same fate. With Sage back home, these sessions became infrequent, and when Stacey arrived late from school and sat down with her mother, it felt like their roles had reversed.

I shouldn't have gone off for such a long time, Della said. I shouldn't be trundling off like that and leaving him alone. Belle says something is wearing on him, something that wasn't there when they first brought him home.

So, Belle, who drops in three times a week for an hour, is telling you it's your job to stand beside his chair day and night? That's ridiculous. Is that what she's saying?

I guess that's what she's implying. It's hard on your dad, sitting there, watching life around him but not being able to participate. I'm busy most of the day, and most evenings he disappears with Hart. I think she's suggesting I need to do more.

There's not much he can do anyway, Stacey said. You know that. He sits there and watches TV and points to the word water. It's a terrible life for sure, but you standing beside him will not make it any better. If you tell Hart not to come and get him out of the house, it will only make things worse. Mom, stop thinking this way. You work all day. You've got to have a life too.

Della cried and Stacey watched her cry. It wasn't like her mother to cry about much of anything. She had being stoic down to an art.

He wrote something on his pad, Della said. After the nurse

got him cleaned up and exercised and sat down again. He wrote
I want to die.

Now it was Stacey's turn to become emotional. She rarely
cried, and she wasn't about to tell her mother why she had started now. For all the months Sage sat there, like a vegetable, she
had thought of him that way: a man with no feelings and nothing to say for himself. She realized now she had been wrong. He
may not have been able to express himself, but he was thinking
about everything that went on around the house, including his
observations of her. She hadn't fallen asleep for a long time that
night after Hugh had left. She had lain thinking about what had
happened. She imagined what he would have had to say had he
been tied down in a chair in the living room but not suffering
from a stroke, and she knew he would have yelled and sworn
so the entire neighbourhood would have known what was going
on behind closed doors. In the scene she imagined, she would
have had plenty to say back to him. She would have told him all
those years he leered at her, walked in on her having a bath and
climbed into bed with her after she'd fallen asleep were acts of a
deranged predator, and if he didn't like what he'd just witnessed,
it was too bloody bad. This was what people did, not with their
fathers but with someone of their own choosing. The vehemence
of her thoughts that night felt justified, and she'd fallen asleep
regarding what had happened as more than reasonable. Now,
watching her mother emotionally muddled, Stacey realized she'd
gone too far. She sensed questions in the air, questions she felt
unprepared to deal with.

When summer began, both Stacey and Amber secured jobs working at the golf course. Stacey drove a refreshment cart from hole
to hole and found if she wore a short skirt and a tank top, her
tips almost equaled her wages. Amber worked inside, sometimes
signing people in and other times working in the back of the

kitchen. For the first few weeks, both girls felt like this was the life they were intended to live. They had crossed over into the working world, they had money in their pockets and the esteem of other adults. Within a matter of days, Stacey's ebullient state came to an abrupt halt.

Several meetings had taken place regarding Sage's state of ill health. Both Della and Stacey met separately with his doctor. Della implemented changes and asked Stacey to cooperate. They agreed that on Sunday nights, designated as movie nights, the three of them would take turns picking out a movie to rent for the evening. One week, Sage, after being presented with a list, asked for *Top Gun*, and they invited Hart and Molly over to watch it with them. Once, when it was Della's turn, she rented *Crocodile Dundee*, and Stacey knew it was because she thought Sage would be interested. Stacey wasn't as patronizing, but her choices avoided movies with lavish sex scenes. Della took her nightly walk but shortened it to a half hour at most. Stacey told her it was an absurd sacrifice because on many nights, by the time she got back from her walk, Sage had already gone to Fort Whoop. Della's cooking became plainer than usual, after the doctor suggested that rich foods were more likely to upset Sage's stomach. On Sunday nights, they ordered pizza. Sage didn't appear to get any better with the adjustments around the house, but he scrunched up his face like a prune less often than he had. Because Stacey was having the time of her life with work and friends, it wasn't until one night Della asked her to cook supper in her stead that she noticed her mother slowing down. Two days later, she went to see her doctor, who ordered tests run. They found blood in her stool, and ten days later the doctor informed Della she had stomach cancer.

Della's local doctor gave her the news after days of medical consultation with doctors from Calgary where the tests had been conducted. The cancer had spread to her liver, so there would be nothing to gain from an operation. Stage IV cancer, they said, a term that sounded definitive but meant nothing to Della. They recommended chemotherapy but she refused. She knew people who had gone through chemo, and unless she saw hope at the end of it all, she wasn't interested.

The babysitting business shut down, and parents scrambled for daycare. Stacey said she would quit her job at the golf course and stay home and take over with the babysitting, but Della said that would only offer a temporary solution. Della felt weak but able to carry on when she returned from Calgary. Stacey cooked most of the meals and stayed in most evenings to be with her mother. Sage became the big concern. Stacey would soon return to school, and Della couldn't provide for him much longer. Della knew she would have to find an alternative, and soon, because Stacey refused to be in the house with Sage unless Della were with her.

She informed Molly and Hart, though it was plain Molly the Nose got wind of their circumstance before they volunteered the information. Molly came over to chat every afternoon, brew green tea for Della and spearhead a search for someplace suitable for Sage. Within two weeks, she had a list of two places in town that might work, and she drove Della to view them both. Tom Uphill Memorial Manor offered assisted living, but it would take all of Sage's company insurance payment to cover it. Della explained to Hart that she didn't have life insurance coverage of any kind, and he looked down at his feet when he heard the news.

It wasn't until a direction had been decided, with only a time-line yet to be determined, that the news reached Sage. He knew something was out of kilter, but each time he asked a question with his writing pad, he received only a pat and evasive answer. Finally Della realized he deserved to know what was happening to his wife.

I have to tell you something you don't want to hear. It's bad news, and I know you've had enough of that already to last a lifetime. I'm not well. I have cancer in fact. Cancer of the stomach. The doctor says there are things they can do to ward off the pain, but there's nothing to be done about it otherwise. It's spread. That's what they say.

Stacey stood in the kitchen listening to her mother's explanation. Her mother said what she had to and then became emotional. Stacey went to her room and closed the door.

I can stay home, at least they think I can. They'll have nurses come by, and there's a chance Sadie will come. I haven't asked her yet. I know you would do what you could, but you can't do anything, and soon I won't be able to help you much at all. That's why it means you'll need to move out of here, but to a nice place. I visited it myself, and I think you'll like it. It's called the Tom Uphill Memorial Manor. I know you've driven by it before. They'll take care of you there.

Della watched her husband's face. He understood everything, that much was clear by the tears that trickled down his cheek. His one eye wasn't much for seeing but was still capable of showing grief.

I'm not sure what will happen with Stacey at this point. It's best she stays here, of course, but that will depend on whether Aunt Sadie can come to live. All the money from your insurance will be needed for Uphill Manor. I know it's hard to face all of this, but some hard decisions must be made for Stacey's sake. We promised to bring her up, and she's almost there, but we're going to need some help. We both thought she'd grow up and move away and we would grow old together. That's not going to happen now.

Lucky was lying prone on the rug while Della explained. Part way through, he got up and put his muzzle on her leg, as if hoping that might help. By the time she had shared all her information, he had moved over to lay his head on Sage's left leg, the one place he would be petted.

27

IN SEPTEMBER, SCHOOL BEGAN as it always had, but Stacey wasn't as excited as she should have been about the prospect of clearing away one more of life's hurdles. As much as she disliked getting up every morning to go through the routine of school and saying goodbye to her mother, school was a haven and a chance to clear her mind, sometimes for an hour or two at a time. They moved Sage to Uphill Manor before the long weekend, and Della stayed home alone, and day by day, less of her lived there. Stacey came home one afternoon from school and found her mother out in the backyard watching the leaves fall to Earth.

They had seen no sign of Aunt Sadie, and Stacey thought that odd. Despite the differences between the sisters, she felt certain that, at a time like this, previous missteps would be set aside. She questioned her mother every day or two until Della admitted she hadn't yet written to her sister to ask for help. Sadie would be busy, Della rationalized. And besides, she said, Sadie's life is enough of a burden, and there's still time before I go adding to it.

The time part bothered Stacey. It kept her awake at night. She didn't know how many days her mother had left, but it was scary to see her losing weight and growing more frail by the day. One night, after Della had fallen asleep early, she rifled through their most recent address book and wrote a long letter to Aunt Sadie, explaining everything and asking her to help immediately. Five days later, Stacey arrived home to find a red Mercedes convertible parked in front of the house.

Aunt Sadie had been in the house less than an hour. There had been tears spilled during that short time, but after that she became indomitable in her care for Della. In the average-sized bedroom where Della slept, the double bed, when pushed against the wall, left room for a motorized hospital bed that Sadie rented month by month. This allowed Della to get up when she felt like it and rest in various elevated positions when she wanted to stay in bed. Aunt Sadie said she would sleep in the bed against the wall and be there if needed in the middle of the night. Her second night there, after Stacey cooked supper, Aunt Sadie suggested Della lay down for a while and went into the bedroom with her and closed the door. They talked for a long time, just the two of them, while Stacey did her homework.

Well, kiddo, not the way anyone wanted life to work out now, is it? Your mother says you've been such a help, and she's so proud of you. I guess you learn soon enough that shit can appear on both ends of a shovel. I will be staying here and doing whatever needs doing. It's good you wrote when you did. Your mom worries about your schooling. She's right, you know. These are tough times, but if you don't graduate, you'll be halfway down the rabbit hole before you can blink. I'm not the world's greatest chef as you're about to find out, but I'll have supper ready every night so don't worry about hurrying home from school. How's school going by the way?

Fine.

Well, that's good. If you need me to go to the school for anything, just ask. I've never had kids, as you know, so this is all new to me.

You know what sucks so much about all this? Morgan's dad

says we're one or two generations away, maybe less, from not having to die. He says scientists will have vaccines that people get every ten years, and they'll get to stay young for as long as they want. If we lived in that world now, Mom might only be twenty-five and not have gotten sick at all.

Well, the way I see it, there's no use wishing for what we can't have. Things will be different in the future, but right now our only choice is to be practical. That nurse Belle is something, now isn't she? I like no-nonsense people when I can find them. I think she would have excelled in the army, that one. Anyway, I think I have your mom's medications down, and we will see she's in as little pain as possible. We'll do what we can, the two of us, to make sure she gets what she needs for however long she's got. You up for it?

Yes. And thank you for doing this.

One thing you'll find out eventually: there's neglect in every family. The way things worked out, this family had more than its share. I can't make up for the years gone by, but I promise to do what I can now.

Della insisted she wanted to live life as close to normal as she had the energy to accomplish. The three of them went out at least once a week for the first while in Della's car so that Stacey could practise her driving. Della sat in the back seat and let Sadie sit up front. Chances were it would be Sadie who would witness Stacey getting her licence, and she might as well learn what she was up against.

Every Wednesday, Della wanted to visit Sage at Uphill Manor, so Sadie and Della made a point of arriving about three in the afternoon and spent a half hour telling him anything new they could think of, mostly updates on Stacey's school performance, and they avoided any talk about how Della faired. Sage could see by her gaunt appearance that Della was fading quickly, and he got emotionally wound up if Della and Sadie didn't keep talking to distract him. One day, as they were about to leave, he held out his hand for them to wait and grabbed the pen and wrote three words on his pad. *Sorry for everything.* Della cried with her head on his shoulder, while Sadie rubbed her back. Della composed herself and told Sage they would be back next week as usual, but it felt like a lie. She knew her goodbye would have to last forever.

By mid-November, spiralling flakes of snow blanketed not only the surrounding mountains but the valley below. Most days Della experienced the onset of winter only through her bedroom window with the curtains parted in the afternoon. She seemed mesmerized, watching the snow's inevitable descent, her mind filled with memories of fourteen winters where a powdery blanket insulated everyone in the small town from the outside world. Some kids were taking advantage of the snowy street before the snowplow showed up, and she watched a little girl in a snowsuit fall off a toboggan and lay in the snow like a slug. Della had always felt the most safe then, in the middle of winter, her husband stewing about a life he couldn't quite grasp, her daughter wiser with every passing day. Under the cover of thick winter, less room existed for questions of honesty to seep in, and above all, she had cherished the silence of snow. They felt impervious then, complete, a family in motion with her at the centre of it all, being the mother she'd yearned to be.

Unless Hart or Molly knocked on the front door, no one did. Until a Tuesday just after dinnertime. The man who knocked called himself Mr. Winters, which gave Stacey a chuckle when she met him at the door because no snow had fallen all day, and now it had started up again. He was the son of the couple who'd perished on 9th Street months earlier. He had come to town to deal with insurance and the sale of the lot, and he heard from neighbours that his parents' dog was alive and being kept by someone in town. He had been told that this might be the house. As if willing to offer testimony, Lucky noticed someone at the door, barked once and trotted into the living room. By the time Stacey invited the man inside, Della, having heard the interchange, had struggled to a standing position and held onto the doorframe.

Hello, Brutus, the man said and reached down and ruffled the dog's head.

His name is Lucky, Della said. We're sorry for your loss. It was terrible, and there's nothing more I can say. When we went by many hours after the fire, Lucky was out in the yard at night, his paws burned to the point he could only limp. No one cared about the dog then. Just us. We brought him home, and he's been checked out by the vet. He's healthy and he's Lucky now. That was months ago, I might add. Some people would have shot him to put him out of his misery.

I know, Mr. Winters said, but when my kids heard—

Mr. Winters, listen up. It's too late for that. This dog was practically dead. Stacey wanted to rescue him, and we did. He gets walked twice a day, fed twice a day, and he's part of *our* family now. I don't want to be rude, but there's not a snowball's chance in hell this dog is going anywhere. End of story.

Mr. Winters seemed to understand the conviction. I'm sorry for the upset, he said, and closed the door behind him.

Well, Sadie said, I think you missed your calling all these years. You should have been a lawyer after seeing that performance.

Thanks, Mom. You were great.

Della didn't seem to take in the compliments. She shuffled back to bed and didn't budge until morning.

One Sunday night, because Della wasn't up to making it to the couch, Sadie and Stacey dragged the TV and VCR over so it filled up the doorway to the bedroom. Della wanted to see *Mary*

Poppins, and the three of them lounged in bed to watch. The next morning, life resumed with everything back in its place, and Sadie said she would take a run to the store to get groceries, and Della agreed that she should. Lucky, who spent most of the day outside regardless of the weather, snuck into the house when Sadie left. She got home and found that Lucky had climbed into bed with Della. She ordered the dog off the bed, but he didn't flinch. He had his head resting beside Della's hands laced together on her stomach, a dog's way of doing his best to pay his respects to the dead.

It was cold the day they buried Della. Clear and cold and a wind along with it to make sure you noticed. They had no indoor service, as Della had requested. A few, including the parents of those children Della had cared for over the years, stood at the graveside while Reverend Munson said a few words honouring Della and the life she'd led since coming to Fernie. Reverend Munson thought highly of Della and knew some of her family circumstances. He might have gone on longer had it not been so cold. Amber, Morgan and Hugh showed up, and Molly and Hart appeared as expected, and they'd offered to pick Sage up, and he sat wrapped in blankets in his chair beside the cavernous hole about to accept his wife back to the earth. Oli Hardwick also attended. He stood off to the side, as if not eager to explain his interest in coming.

Most memorable to Stacey that day was her dad beside the grave, swaddled in so many blankets he was almost beyond recognition as a human being. Once the service ended, those in attendance made their way to their cars that had cooled already but would offer sanctuary from the wind. When it came time to drive away, Hart and Sage sat and stood, stubborn against the elements, the last ones to leave.

Aunt Sadie had made sandwiches, and Molly had baked

squares, and they invited people to stop by but few did. Sage didn't want to go back to the house, with so many memories fresh in his mind, so Hart took him back to Uphill Manor. An hour after the service, the only people in the house were Stacey, Sadie, Molly, Hart and Oli Hardwick, who explained that he'd met Della at church and said she was the kindest woman he'd met since his wife had passed away.

Even with five people in it, the house felt empty, and when it got down to just two people, Stacey felt as if no one occupied the house, not herself and not her aunt either. They nibbled on and off at the sandwiches left behind and sat in the living room. Stacey didn't feel like talking and neither did Sadie, but she felt a responsibility to do so.

Your mom and dad didn't plan for much, but they each had a separate bank account set aside for their funeral service. I guess your mom didn't want you to have to worry about such a thing.

Stacey felt a tightness in her chest, as if her heart wanted to shut down suddenly, the sort of feeling she expected to have at the gravesite but that only now was upon her. Even if she had wanted to speak she couldn't have managed, and she realized her mother had done whatever she could to shelter her from anything bad. She'd done the best she could.

Neither of them considered turning on the TV. Finally, Aunt Sadie said, Your mom always liked to go for a short walk after supper. I know it's cold out, but let's go. I think she'd like that.

The wind had died down to a whisper, but it was even colder than before. Lucky zigzagged back and forth on their route, leaving yellow punctuation marks in the snow at every corner. The snowfall from days before had been ploughed, and walls of snow, curled at the sides of the road, stood like frozen banks of ice. The snow that remained on the street crackled underfoot as if the two of them were walking on glass.

I will stay with you. Your mom said it would be up to me, but that's what I've decided. You have a little over six months, and guess what? You'll be finished grade eleven. I was thinking about Christmas. It won't be the same here, that's for sure. I thought maybe the two of us, once you're out of school, could make our way down to San Jose for two weeks. Don't tell me if you think it's a good idea right away. Best to think about something like that.

They walked around the block, a shorter walk than Della would have taken, but at least they got themselves out of the house. When they returned and had cleaned the snow off their boots, Stacey turned and gave her aunt a desperate hug. I do want to go to San Jose, she said.

28

EVERYONE DESERVED A FRIEND like Amber. She talked with Stacey when she wanted to talk and just hung out with her when she didn't. They were both focused on school and on getting good grades, and now that Morgan had gone on to university, they had more responsibility coming their way with the Environmental Club. Hugh was the official leader, but he didn't offer the leadership they'd been used to. Amber never hitchhiked to UBC, but because Morgan's holidays were longer than those in public school, he would be home in a week. Amber planned a surprise party to celebrate, and Stacey pretended to be excited. Someone must have told Hugh that Stacey liked the scent he often wore because he wore it anytime he thought they might be together. She felt thankful for Hugh and what they'd done together, but it had nothing to do with the future. He had rescued her from the fate of Angus Bland, but she would spend the evening warding him off if she went to the party.

Stacey found it hard at first to keep her mind on school. She had two exams to prepare for, and she wrote them, and because the last bit of school before the holidays was lame at the best of times, Aunt Sadie wrote her a note, and they flew to San Jose two days before school got out, ensuring that Stacey didn't have to worry about Hugh and his endearing aroma after all.

Hart, thrilled to do it, took care of Lucky. Molly didn't want a dog in the house—she said she was allergic—but Hart said it wouldn't be a problem because he would keep Lucky in Fort Whoop and it would be like having a huge dog house for the two of them.

The flight from Calgary to San Jose marked the first time Stacey had been on a plane of any kind. The details of the journey occupied her wholly. Soon after they sat down, she asked the flight attendant if she could meet the pilot. When she met him, she relaxed; the pilot was about fifty years old and had a warm, trustworthy face. It didn't feel right to be on the plane for such a dramatic experience without her mom present. Stacey had never asked, but she thought it likely her mother had never been on a plane and now she never would be. Aunt Sadie relaxed once they boarded and grew excited as she told her about all they would see in San Jose. Stacey had heard of Los Angeles and San Francisco, but this was different, her aunt said. The people who lived and worked there were different.

Do you think we could drive to San Francisco? Just so I could see it?

I'm sure we could do that. It's not far. But believe me, there's lots to do in San Jose.

All Stacey knew about San Jose was the Dionne Warwick song Sage used to sing when he got drunk. It was cloudy when they arrived but much warmer than Calgary had been, and Aunt Sadie hung up their winter coats as soon as they got to her house. You won't be needing that for the next two weeks, she said.

The house Aunt Sadie had lived in for less than a year was in Willow Glen. Her friend Martin picked them up at the airport and drove them to a large Spanish-style ranch house, guarded by trees, with sidewalks on both sides of the street. The property had a pool in the backyard covered up with something blue, and it looked neglected. Martin stayed long enough to have a drink then phoned his son to come and pick him up so he could lend Aunt Sadie his own car for the next two weeks, a Cadillac with leather seats. When he left, he gave Aunt Sadie a kiss and told Stacey he hoped she enjoyed her time with her aunt.

Is Martin your boyfriend?

No, not really. Just a friend. Hey, what do you say we order in tonight? I don't feel like cooking and after maybe we can catch a movie. Sound good?

If it's okay with you. Thanks.

Your mom did a good job, you know that? You're always so polite. You must have a lot of friends.

I have some friends. I don't like having too many friends. And I wasn't always polite you know. I was stubborn when I was a kid. If I didn't get my way.

That's good though, don't you see. It means you have standards.

Stacey didn't know how to respond. She'd never thought of herself as a person with standards before.

I got to put the diaphragm you gave me into practice.

You did? How did that go?

I guess you could call it a once in a lifetime experience.

Do you like the guy?

I wish I did, but I don't. He's not my type.

See what I mean? Aunt Sadie said. You've got standards.

They woke to fog on the first day, but a breeze came up, and by the time they embarked on a walk to the city centre of Willow Glen, the skies had lifted, and it felt like paradise to Stacey. The weather reminded her of an early summer day back home. The little town was quaint, not that Fernie was without charm, it had plenty, but the low-lying buildings and sidewalk cafes here felt magical, and Stacey felt as if she were floating about the town instead of walking. She noticed day spas and boutiques on every block, and Aunt Sadie wanted to walk into every store they passed. In most she knew someone who worked there, and she introduced Stacey as if she were a prize she'd won in Canada and brought back to gloat over.

We'll come back here and get our nails done later in the week. Would you like that?

I've never had my nails done. Amber did them once, but never in a nail place.

Well, that settles it. I'll book a manicure *and* a pedicure, and you'll have proof when you get home that you've been to California. Remember when the two of us went out for lunch and ate mussels?

That was great, Stacey said.

Well, in two more blocks, there's a seafood restaurant to die for. There's nothing in the world you could imagine eating for lunch you couldn't find around here somewhere.

After lunch they went to a bookstore called Hicklebee's that Aunt Sadie said was famous for kids' books but they had books of all kinds. Stacey only had forty-two dollars in Canadian money to spend, but her aunt said she would pay for any book she picked out. Stacey chose Stephen King's *It*.

That must be the shortest book title in the world. Are you sure you want that one? It sounds violent.

I like Stephen King. He has a great imagination. Don't worry, I don't plan on killing little kids or anything. Sometimes it's good to go places where you know you could never live.

After a week, Stacey couldn't stand it anymore, she had to phone Amber and tell her what she'd been up to. Aunt Sadie said that wouldn't be a problem, and she let her phone in the privacy of her small office.

Stacey started in with a synopsis of all the things they'd done and all the places they'd been to. We saw the mall my aunt owns.

It's not a huge mall and not all that modern, but it's a money-maker according to Aunt Sadie. We drove to San Francisco and drove over the Golden Gate Bridge and ate crab at Fisherman's Wharf and had a ride in a trolley car. I wish you were here with me. We'd have so much fun.

The most outrageous thing Stacey saved for last. She told Amber about the day it had warmed up and Aunt Sadie had suggested they hang out by the ocean, and they took a blanket and towels and went off to Bonny Doon Beach.

We used the blankets to lie on and the towels for headrests because the water was too cold and no one was swimming, but there were fifteen or twenty nude sunbathers, and Aunt Sadie staked out a spot in the middle of them all. From kids to old people, it was wild. It's the most freeing feeling you can imagine, Amber, honestly. You would have felt like an idiot if you left your clothes on down there. The feeling of the sun on your skin is so soothing.

Stacey didn't get the gasps of astonishment she expected from the other end of the phone. When she asked what was wrong, Amber explained that Morgan had decided to move on. They would be friends, whatever that was supposed to mean.

The days of the last week slipped by one by one like a death sentence approaching. One night, Stacey offered to cook supper, spaghetti and meatballs, and Aunt Sadie invited a friend to dinner, someone called Nathan. The meal was delicious, Stacey thought, and so did Aunt Sadie and Nathan, though it occurred to her that part of its success was because they were well into the wine before she had dinner ready. She made a salad to go with it, one with fresh shrimp. After dinner, it seemed obvious Aunt Sadie wanted to spend time with Nathan, so Stacey watched TV while they stayed in the kitchen and played Yahtzee. Stacey had wine too and grew tired and went to bed. When she got up in the morning, she was alone at first, and then Nathan and Aunt Sadie came into the kitchen in matching housecoats.

The next night, Aunt Sadie said she would cook, and she invited Martin for dinner. Martin was older than Nathan, which maybe explained why he asked so many questions. She couldn't tell if what he asked about, such as what it was like to live in Canada, were serious inquiries or if he was just kidding around. He wanted to know how old, on average, Canadians were when they first learned how to snowshoe. Stacey said she had no idea. She'd never snowshoed once in her life.

In the morning, she got up first again. She ate half a banana and went for a walk. It was a good neighbourhood for walking. Every tree a chorus of birdsong.

29

MOLLY THE NOSE WAS SWEEPING her front porch when Stacey and Aunt Sadie arrived part way through what should have been the first day back at school. Molly took Stacey to Fort Whoop where Lucky lay sleeping on a rug he'd adopted. When he saw Stacey, he barked and performed a dance he may have been rehearsing in her honour. Molly said, as if to deflect the dog's zealous welcome, that they allowed Lucky to sit in the living room every evening to watch television for one hour.

The house smelled dank and musty and depressing after California. According to Molly, it hadn't snowed for almost two weeks, but snow remained at the side of the road. Aunt Sadie said she would get groceries the next day, and they ordered in pizza and watched a movie, Stacey snuggling with Lucky on the floor the whole time.

We're going to be busy, both of us, Aunt Sadie said, and that turned out to be true. Aunt Sadie paid the mortgage and the bills needed to keep the house running, but Stacey knew it wasn't what her aunt had in mind, living life in a small town, bogged down in snow with all her friends in California. To keep herself busy, she accepted a job as a booking agent for the ski hill, and part of the time, she worked from home. Stacey, on top of her school work, got a job at a clothing store where she worked Saturdays, and Aunt Sadie turned out to be the store's best customer. Not only that, she taught Stacey how to be a salesperson. She learned to welcome those who entered with only a hint that the purpose of her presence was to sell them something and engaged them by commenting on something most would agree with, or by asking a question that could serve up a conclusive answer without being the least bit contentious. The weather always worked, be it fair or foul. Customers rarely admitted what they were looking for, often because they didn't know. Stacey encouraged them to try things on, never just one thing, because what suited a person was always a mystery and one just never knew. They only came out of the change room wearing a new outfit when the item had passed the biggest barrier of all, the client's initial grudging acceptance, and at that point, they wanted confirmation of their preliminary verdict, and Stacey learned to offer validation without going overboard. *Oh my*, often did the trick. It hurt no one to suggest they might want a matching scarf or pair of socks. The trick, her aunt assured her, was to have the customer leave the store with goods in hand they felt deserving of.

Aunt Sadie took Stacey driving a few times and told her she was more than ready to pass her test, so Stacey got her driver's licence in late February. As the months rolled over, it felt less and less to Stacey like she lived with an aunt, but instead, with one of the colourful birds she'd seen at the Calgary Zoo one summer, birds that could talk, though who knew what would come out of their mouths. Twice in the spring, once to replace her mall manager and a second time for undisclosed reasons, Aunt Sadie flew back to San Jose. The second time she left for two weeks, during which time Stacey held an Environmental Club party at her house. As the party wound down, Morgan showed up and took Amber away. By eleven only Stacey and Hugh remained. Hugh had changed in the last year: his once lanky figure had grown solid and muscular, and he now wrestled on the wrestling team. He rarely wore the scent that had enticed her to walk across any room to be near him, but he coated himself with it the night of the party.

I need to take Lucky for his late-night walk, she said. Want to come?

When they got back, they needed no negotiations before they spent the night together in Aunt Sadie's queen-sized bed. Not quite the whole night. Stacey woke before six and realized it would soon be light out and Molly the Nose would see Hugh drive away. Hugh agreed he would get up and drive to a truck stop and drink coffee until he could reasonably go back home, but only if they did it one more time. Stacey found that a reasonable compromise.

Martin said he might like to visit Fernie for a week. You liked Martin, didn't you?

He seemed fine.

You can help me show him around. I think he'll like it here. Maybe he can fix the drain pipe at the back. Martin's good at those kinds of things.

With grade eleven complete, Stacey wished more than ever that her mother could see how well she was doing. Aunt Sadie congratulated her on her performance but with the same enthusiasm she would have bestowed upon her had she taught Lucky a new trick. Stacey could remember one afternoon, in grade seven or eight, when schooling had been the topic that surrounded a tea party with Molly the Nose and her mother. Because of Molly's encouragement, the tone of the dialogue suggested that an education was the only safe ticket out of Fernie. Stacey hadn't considered what it might mean to leave the only town she had known. She liked Fernie and its familiarity. But a year away from graduating, the world looked so much different. She felt restless, and her Aunt Sadie's constant reviewing of her worldly travels didn't help.

Martin hadn't come, but he planned to. Aunt Sadie grew antsy in anticipation. She needed something to do.

Your mother said near the end that if the house ever sold, to be sure to clean out the attic. Any idea what's up there?

Nope. Never been there. I'm surprised mom would have put anything in the attic. She couldn't stand spiders.

Aunt Sadie hated spiders too, but after lunch she put on some old clothes, fitted a toque over her head and got the stepladder and a flashlight and opened the hatch in the spare bedroom that led to the attic. She handed three sealed boxes and one open box down to Stacey, then took one last look around.

That's all there is. Insulation and spider webs.

The open box contained a photo album, one Stacey had never seen. Most of the pictures weren't inserted but lay like bookmarks inside. A picture of Sadie and Della when they were about twelve or thirteen showed them leaning against a car, and a few pictures of Della suggested places she'd worked, like the fish packers and an orchard filled with apples. Three or four pictures commemorated her wedding to Willy Hoffner, and two pictures showed Sage by himself, both with palm trees in the background. The rest was junk: an old lamp with a flexible head, a figurine with a head decapitated, a partial set of silverware tarnished the color of old shoes. Things, Stacey imagined, Sage hadn't gotten around to throwing out. A second box contained old clothes, including a bathing suit Della must have worn or wished she could have worn when she was young, and a third box contained an assortment of old books and a tax return from 1973. Aunt Sadie said she wondered why Della had bothered to mention looking in the attic. Then they opened one box and found four books that contained Della's diaries.

Well, will you look at this. Your mother must have spent hours filling all these. I'm guessing this must be why she mentioned the attic. She wanted to leave these to you. Don't you think? Anyway, as much as I'm tempted, I think she meant them for you. But promise me one thing: if there are any juicy tidbits in there that mention your Aunt Sadie, you'll let me in on it. Promise?

Sure.

The phone rang, and Aunt Sadie came back ecstatic. Martin is at the airport. I'm going to pick him up in an hour. We can go out for dinner tonight, the three of us. Do you want to come to the airport? Just for the drive?

No, it's all right. I'll stay home and wait.

Yes, of course. That makes perfect sense. It's not like you don't have reading to catch up on.

Aunt Sadie and Martin arrived home late, and Stacey was in her room with the door closed. Aunt Sadie knocked on the door but got no response.

Stacey? You in there? Sorry we're late. Martin had to go through customs. Have you eaten yet? We can still go out to eat.

She knocked one more time and opened the door to find all the boxes and their contents scattered around the room. Stacey hated anything messy. Only her shape indicated where she was wrapped in covers.

You remember Martin?

Hi, Stacey, Martin called from the doorway.

Let's go, kiddo. You can pick whatever restaurant you want. What do you feel like?

I'm not hungry. I'll stay home. You two go.

Are you sick or something? What's going on?

I'll be fine. I just can't eat now. You go.

I don't blame you, Aunt Sadie said. I've felt that way many times. See, Martin? That's what I was telling you. That niece of mine has high standards.

As soon as they left, Stacey phoned Amber and asked if she would come over. Amber said she would bring Morgan with her. Stacey said she only wanted to talk to her, and Amber heard something in Stacey's voice. She told Morgan she would be busy for the rest of the evening.

The first diary chronicled another life: their wedding, living somewhere out in the country that wasn't named and the years Della and Sage spent in Vancouver. What she read interested her, but then it occurred to her she hadn't been mentioned once. The second diary began in Hope. She read Della's words quickly the first time, as if reading a suspense novel, then she started again and reread the words that caused her stomach to tighten like a fist. She searched for ways to see the diary as nothing more than a cruel joke. But it wasn't the least bit funny and was as cruel as cruel could be. All she had come to think about herself was as false as the premise of the life she'd been living since she could remember. Nothing in the writing suggested that it wasn't real; Stacey could remember the events mentioned, either because she remembered them or they'd been discussed so many times she felt like she knew them. Her whole life had been a betrayal, which made even the events she knew she'd experienced feel like encounters she had only heard about. She wasn't the Stacey she thought she was. She might not be Stacey at all. She might be Madeline or Jennifer or Montana. Her mind felt severed from her body. She traced her fingers over the letters. The only thing in the room that felt real was the dog she'd named Lucky, who climbed up onto her bed as if he sensed he wouldn't be reprimanded.

She needed someone like Amber near her so she could cry. Amber would understand her role in what was happening. Cry is what they both did. As soon as Stacey opened the door to let her in, Amber cried, even before she knew the reason why. They sat on the bed, and Stacey explained everything. She read excerpts from Della's journal aloud.

I told Sage to keep driving. If there's one thing that will settle a child it's driving around in a car. Sage was concerned about the dog. He rolled the window down as if that would help find him. The little girl was all played out. Kept her eye on us until her head finally flopped to the side. She looked so peaceful, asleep like that. Sage kept driving around and around, and I'm thinking if you're going to burn gas, you might as well put it to good use. I never told him that. He must have thought of it himself because he soon pulled out onto the highway, and it felt like we were a family heading east.

Amber sat beside Stacey on the bed, their backs to the wall. Lucky lay beside Stacey, his head on her leg. With every entry read, Stacey kept one hand in motion, soothing the dog on his head, around the ears. Amber had an arm around Stacey, her hand rubbing her shoulder.

Sage being tall and on the narrow side with the features he has, mostly angular, and me being more of the rounded variety, gives people we meet in Fernie pause for thought when they meet Stacey. People are used to saying things like: She's the spitting image of her mother, that's for sure, or She has her father's eyes at least. With Stacey holding your hand, you can almost see the thought process people go through until they conclude, as Molly did eventually, that a child can be a blend of two very different parents and not look much like either one.

Every word felt like a knife digging deep inside, and it got worse the more she read, and she wanted to stop but couldn't. As she read the words for the third time, violence became part of it all. The suffering felt like a direction, the only direction she could take.

He doesn't often get raging drunk, but when he does, he gets braver and loses sight of how to play with Stacey. He cherishes her though, but

I sometimes wonder if he had preferred a boy. He likes to get down on all fours and crawl around the house with Stacey riding on top. Stacey loves playing horse this way, but when Sage tells her to hang on and starts bucking, it's not always the safest activity just before bedtime. Sage feels sorry when she takes a tumble. He offers to give her a bath and read to her in bed. Sometimes he tells her stories, and he's good at it. When he tells her stories, she believes him.

Stacey tried to see and feel what Della had written. With each sentence, the world became darker and darker. With every word that melted into the past, she expected something egregious to happen. But it wasn't something going to happen. It already had.

We both kept waiting for the other person to say something. Something that made sense. After we left Hope behind, it was too late. The little girl cried most of the first week, her blanket balled up in her fists. It was what I wanted, and that's why Sage kept quiet. This was what we both wanted, to make a family, but Sage couldn't do it. Now there was a way, and it made no sense and all the sense in the world.

This is too big, Amber said. It's too big for both of us. You need to sleep at my house tonight. We can talk until we're done talking. My mom won't mind. You need to bring these with you.

Stacey left a note. Her aunt would worry otherwise. Walk and feed Lucky, it said. She addressed the note to Aunt Sadie, but even this had become a lie. Sadie wasn't her aunt at all, only a woman playing a part in a bad dream.

30

THE NEW DIAMOND GRILL WAS BUSY, and Martin and Sadie had to wait, which was fine because Martin wanted to walk around town. The air was clear, the mountains almost showing off, and he was impressed.

What do you think's wrong with Stacey? he asked.

I don't think it's anything like the flu. She rarely gets sick. But she worries a lot, and it's been hard for her with her dad in a care home and her mother gone now. Just before you arrived, we went through the attic and found three or four journals Della had stored there. She's been reading them is my guess. You can imagine coming upon things your mother wrote about all the years she was alive and you sit down to read them. It must be emotional for her.

She's got one more year in school, right?

Next year's the finale. She's a good student. She'll want to go someplace after she graduates, I'd bet on it. She doesn't belong here. You know what's sad about the situation?

No, what?

She says she wants to grow up to be like me. She's so much bigger than that, but I don't know how to tell her.

How long do you plan on mothering her? Are you staying

here another whole year?

I'm guessing. What would you do if your only brother had a kid in the same situation? It's not an easy decision, is it? I took off when I was about her age. I owe it to my sister not to let that happen to Stacey. It feels like the right thing to do.

Amber's mom and dad always treated Stacey with kindness, and with what had happened over the last year, they checked up on her whenever they saw her. Amber's mom knew something wasn't right when they arrived for their impromptu sleepover. She pestered them both with questions and got nowhere. Amber knew how to get her mom to back off if necessary, and they found sanctuary in the bedroom.

Your mom or dad never said anything about how it all started? Amber said.

Della and Sage, you mean. No. I asked her once why there weren't any pictures of me as a baby, and she said they were lost in a house fire or the movers lost them. Something like that. You hear people talk about what their kids were like as babies, problems they might have had, but they did none of that. That's because they didn't know me.

So, they adopted you somehow?

I wish. They stole me. In the town of Hope. I've never seen the town, but that's where they stole me. In broad daylight.

Amber left to make them both a hot chocolate and grab a bag of potato chips from the cupboard. Her mother asked if everything was all right in there, and Amber said they weren't as good as they could be.

They sat quietly, drinking hot chocolate and nibbling on chips. Amber considered how she'd feel if a few hours ago she'd found out her mom wasn't her mom and her dad wasn't her dad and that the two of them had stolen her and drove her to Fernie to live. She would stomp into the kitchen kicking and screaming and throw things until she got an explanation. Maybe she would phone the police or run away. But for Stacey, her make-believe mother had died, and her fake father was as good as gone himself.

Maybe there were circumstances, Amber said.

Oh, there were circumstances all right. They couldn't have kids. They'd tried for years, and they wanted one so they grabbed me in the park and drove away. It's all here. I'll show you.

Stacey found the section near the end of the second diary, where Della admitted everything, so Amber could read it. How they couldn't have kids and how desperate Della had been. Even Sage, loser that he was, had tried to get her to reconsider.

So what are you going to do?

I don't know what to do. I don't even know who I am at this point. All I know is where I didn't come from. I could be anybody.

So you were a little kid walking around crying, and they found you, right?

Exactly. Even if people find a dog on the loose, they know enough to take him to the pound. That's the first place people look if their dog goes missing. If we found a lost kid crying in Fernie somewhere, we'd call the police or something. Think about it. Fifteen years ago, someone lost me, and for fifteen years they didn't know where to look. They probably think I'm dead by now. Isn't that what most people would think?

Maybe they're still looking, Amber said. Remember when we were younger and we tried to become investigators? We need to do that again. We're older now so we can figure this out.

I'm almost an adult. Imagine giving birth to a kid and not meeting them until they were an adult. If we found them, they might not want to meet me. And how can I prove I belong to anyone after all this time?

They have experts for that stuff, Amber said. They could do genetic tests to make sure. I think if I lost my child, I'd want to see them as soon as possible, grown-up or not. What we need to do is find out where you came from. Until that happens, you'll feel like you do now, which is awful.

Amber and Stacey had shared many sleepovers, but never one where they talked so far into the middle of the night. They had hot chocolate three more times and ate a ham sandwich after midnight. They made two lists, one with what they knew from the diaries and the other what they needed to know. The latter was shorter, but when the lists sat side by side, they seemed equal. They discussed how much Stacey didn't look like Della and Sage and what her real parents might look like. The dad wouldn't be as tall as Sage, and the mom would have lighter hair. Freckles maybe. Stacey thought maybe they were poor and let her wander off because they couldn't afford to keep her. Amber said maybe, but they might also be rich, maybe famous, and once found her life would change for the better.

They agreed not to tell anyone else about what they knew. Not Amber's parents or the police or anyone. Not until they could figure out what had happened.

Amber said, This is a tragedy for you, and anyone would see it that way. But there's one good thing. You live in Fernie, and I live in Fernie, and if none of this had happened, we wouldn't be friends.

I'm thankful I have you to help me think everything through, Stacey said. It felt like keeping her private thoughts to herself but in a bigger room. As they both faded into sleep, Stacey realized she still needed to tell one other person about everything that had gone on. She mentioned her by name, but Amber had already fallen asleep and didn't hear her.

Martin had never fished in his life, and he met someone in town willing to teach him. He would do anything for the chance to skirt the arterial waterways that flowed between what he referred to as serious mountains. He used Sage's fishing gear without asking, but Stacey didn't care in the least. This left Aunt Sadie home alone a lot, sometimes for an entire day, unless Stacey was there, which wasn't often. She always had something to do, like picking huckleberries, a good enough reason to be somewhere else.

Hey, kiddo. Where you off to? Aunt Sadie asked.

I'm going to meet friends downtown.

Don't go yet. We need to talk. Something's going on, and I know your mother wouldn't leave you to stew like this. I thought we could go somewhere. Just the two of us.

Stacey hadn't cried since the night she and Amber had gone through the diaries, and she thought she had finished with the emotional part of it all. But she was sobbing now, unable to control her breathing. More than anything, she wanted to run out of the house and up into the mountains to be by herself, but she knew better. She had to face reality, and this marked the beginning. After days of rehearsal, she had almost stopped thinking of Della and Sage as mom and dad. Almost. Now, standing in the kitchen in confrontation, she couldn't think of the woman in front of her as anything but her Aunt Sadie. Stacey hadn't revealed what she knew for the most pathetic of reasons: Aunt Sadie was all she had left from the life she used to have, and once Sadie learned the truth, that would end too.

She gave her aunt the briefest of book reports, then went to her room and brought out the four volumes Della had written and pointed to the second volume as the one she should read first.

You're mentioned in three or four places, Stacey said, as she headed for the back door. She said you were nuts but a lot of fun to have for a sister. It could be way worse, you know. At least you had a sister for a while.

The golf course rehired Amber for the summer, but Stacey, too confused to think about working anywhere, didn't apply. Besides, her aunt would pay for everything. Stacey and Amber pretended they were writing a play about missing children and went to the library to ask questions. They kept a list of missing children, all of them Canadian, and two from B.C., but the list only went back two or three years. The librarian, a kind and helpful woman, wore her hair in a braid that funnelled all the way down her back. Stacey couldn't keep from staring at the braid. She imagined pulling on it to lead its owner to someplace else in the library that would have all the answers.

These children have all gone missing recently, Amber said. There must have been kids missing before this.

Oh yes, there were plenty. Every year new ones disappear. If the child isn't found in the first month, they often never are.

What happens to the children that aren't found? Stacey asked.

Well, dear, I guess you have to use your imagination for the answer to that. It's not the sort of thing most people want to talk about.

Amber persisted. But if they were missing, even if they weren't found, they must be on a list somewhere.

I bet they are, the librarian said. I think you'd have to go to the police to find that out.

With no one home at Amber's house, they went there to chart out a plan. They would go to the police but not in Fernie. They would drive all the way to Hope and ask there. The police must have records that went back fifteen years, and if they asked questions there, no one would know them or know why they cared. Amber would take a few days off. As many as necessary. Stacey would borrow money from Aunt Sadie. She would get the oil changed and take the green car, which was her car now. It was a long way to drive, but they would take turns. Amber had her licence finally, and she had a cousin that lived in Midway, so they could stay one night there. Amber would tell her parents they wanted to visit Stacey's relatives in Hope, and Stacey didn't need to offer any explanation because no one would care. The librarian had said that, after a month or two, the chances of finding a child were slim, but even though fifteen years had melted away, it made sense not to let any more days or months or years go by. Maybe she had a brother or sister, older or younger it wouldn't matter, and they would be getting older just like her. If she had a sibling, Stacey wanted it to be a boy. It would be even that way. One boy. One girl. Besides, it already felt like she had a sister named Amber.

I think I might head downtown to play pool with some fishermen I met, Martin said as soon as they finished the dishes. No one said anything about the diaries, but Stacey understood Martin's exit had been preplanned. I won't be back until eleven he said, as if reading from a script.

Molly knocked on the front door as soon as he left. She said she and Hart had a movie to watch and did anyone want to join them. Aunt Sadie said no so definitively that Molly left without bothering to argue.

Stacey sat on the couch, her head leaning forward, staring at her hands, her lower lip between her teeth, trying not to show emotion. Aunt Sadie sat beside her and put a hand on her shoulder.

I can't believe it, she began. I don't think anyone would believe it. All afternoon I've tried to imagine what you are going through, and I can't. It's horrific and disgusting, and no one deserves to go through something like this. I can sit here and tell you I'm sorry, but that's a pissy thing to say. Of course, anyone would be sorry. And mad too. I can't believe my own sister would do something like that.

Aunt Sadie got up and paced back and forth in the living room. She didn't know what else to do with herself, but she had the urge to smash something. She'd never understood unwarranted violence before, but she understood it now as she lifted a black vase from the bookshelf, one Della had taken a shine to before she passed. Sadie had bought it so Della would have something to feel good about. She held it in her hands for a long time. Stacey looked up and saw her holding the vase, and it was as if the two of them had a part in its journey to the floor and the hundreds of pieces that scattered across the room. What remained after was a silence that left no room for words, only feelings. Outside, Lucky barked, a sound filled with yearning, one that not even a loyal dog could fill.

31

NOTHING IN STACEY'S EXPERIENCE had suggested that cars don't always run when you want them to, and her naivety served her well on the two-day trip from Fernie to Hope. Late the day they arrived in the village of Midway, Amber's cousin took them up into the hills, before the sun went down, to watch the turkey vultures soar over the windswept, oat-coloured fields. Amber and Archie talked about relatives they had in common, a conversation Stacey envied and endured.

When they arrived in Hope, they stopped at the tourist information building to determine the cheapest motel in town. Neither of them had a credit card, so the owner insisted they pay up front and also pay a fifty dollar damage deposit on the room. Amber said they could do that, but Stacey insisted that they see the room first. She could hear her Aunt Sadie's voice off in the distance confirming that her niece did indeed have high standards, but it had nothing to do with standards. Stacey wanted to make sure the room wasn't already trashed so they would get their deposit back. When they returned to the motel office, Stacey had the owner itemize the following: one bureau handle loose and almost falling off, no rail in the small closet provided, a small red stain—probably nail polish—on the rug, and the hot and cold water handles to fill the sink were functional but reversed. Her list seemed to allay any concerns of the manager until Amber asked where they would find the local police station.

Stacey wanted to walk around the busy town before they did anything, and even with people on every sidewalk, she found it easy to differentiate between tourists and locals. The tourists wore startling colours and got out of their cars to stretch their legs and point at things, whereas the locals sauntered from one shady spot to another, often seated beneath large trees in the park. Two men played chess using a stump as a table. Some sat hunched in groups of two or three over coffee or water, wearing clothes that suggested the better part of their available wardrobe might be in the wash. The park in the centre of town held a grove of ancient trees, and Stacey recognized it as the park Della had described in her diary. She found an older man sitting by himself at a park bench.

Is this where a big fair comes every August? she asked.

No, the man said. She looked at him, and he kept staring straight ahead as if examining the past like he hadn't for years.

Did they ever have a fair down here?

Used to, the man said. Stopped it a few years back. Bunch of crooks run those things. Nothing but chaos and dust.

Stacey wondered what it would take to make a man like that smile. She couldn't think of anything.

I think we should find the police station, Amber said. While it's still open.

Police stations don't close, Stacey said. They fight crime twenty-four hours a day.

I know, but the people who might have files on missing children eat supper. I say we go now and get something to eat later.

The police station was on the Old Hope Highway on the way out of town. They parked the car, and both sat deep in thought. Stacey thought that Della and Sage must have driven right past the police station on their way out of town. It wasn't like the police station was hidden or anything.

Better if we say we're doing research on missing children, Amber said. The writing-a-play excuse was kind of lame. I brought a notepad and pen. We can take notes.

This is harder than I thought it would be, Stacey said. I want to find stuff out, but I'm afraid at the same time.

A woman sat in the shape of a C, curled over an electric type-writer behind a counter. She wasn't wearing a uniform, and at first they thought she might be the only one there.

Yes? May I help you?

Hi. We would like to talk to a constable please. One who's been around for a while, if possible.

One who's been around?

Yes, that's right. If there's someone who worked here fifteen years ago, that would great. We're doing research on children who've gone missing.

Anyone in particular?

No. Just children.

Well, police officers move around. You know that. I'll see if Constable Hereford has a minute. He's been here for three years.

When she went into the hallway, Amber said, You've got to say something. I'm doing all the talking.

Constable Hereford came to the counter. He was tall and slender for a policeman, Stacey thought. He didn't look mean or capable of handling rowdy or criminal types, but maybe he made up for his insufficient brawn by being smart and that's why they'd hired him. Stacey introduced Amber and herself and explained that they were doing research on missing children for school. She said they were from Fernie and were on their way to Vancouver but thought it would be wise the check out the records of missing children in smaller towns too. She told Constable Hereford that they attended Kootenay College and that they hoped to interview as many people as possible about missing children.

Constable Hereford towered over them at the counter, intimidating Stacey. He listened patiently and then appeared lost in thought. When Amber pulled a notebook and pen out of her purse, he told them to accompany him to his office.

So, why your interest in missing children?

Well, we both want to be social workers one day. It's part of our study to choose an area of public concern, and we thought this would be a good one.

Well, it's an important one, that's for sure. Last year we had 57,233 reported missing persons in Canada. Most people don't know that. Sixty-five percent of these cases were solved within twenty-four hours. Children wandering off, that sort of thing. Eighty-seven percent found a solution within a week. Of course, that leaves many that haven't been solved. Sometimes these cases remain open for years.

Amber kept busy taking notes. Perfect, Stacey thought. If they could keep the man talking, eventually they could close in on what they wanted to know.

Are some of these children missing at a young age? Stacey asked.

People go missing at all ages. I've heard of cases as young as a week old. Some people go missing when they're elderly. Almost half of those categorized as children go missing when they're fourteen or fifteen. That's another stat most people don't know.

Does it happen in the town of Hope? Amber asked.

It happens everywhere. We had an eleven-year-old boy go missing about a year back. He was out fishing and fell off a ravine and hurt his leg. Fortunately his parents knew he'd gone fishing. He had to spend the night in the wilderness by himself, but we found him the next day.

We want to do our fact finding as far back as 1970. Has anyone else gone missing in Hope since then?

Constable Hereford heard the question and busied himself in a filing cabinet for a few minutes, then he left and said he'd be right back.

Just as I thought, he said. Marjory, the lady you met at the counter, has been here for twenty-three years, and the only other case in Hope was the one I'd heard about. A four-year-old boy wandered off from his parents. A fisherman found his remains on the banks of the Fraser River a week later.

What the fuck? Stacey said as soon as they left the police station. No one reported a missing child. What the fuck?

I know, Amber said. It's brutal. She watched Stacey warily. Stacey did not normally swear. But who wouldn't? So what do we do now? Try a different city? We both need to eat something first.

They ate a hamburger and a sundae at Dairy Queen and went back to their motel. Stacey said she needed time to think so she had a bath. Amber turned on the TV and watched the news. A child had gone missing in Elliot Lake, Ontario. The weather would be hot again tomorrow. Stacey got out of the bathtub so Amber shut off the TV.

We didn't find out much, did we? Stacey said.

Well, I've been thinking about what we know. It's true we didn't come to Hope and find your parents wandering the streets with a sign saying they'd lost you, but we know a lot more about missing kids, that's for sure. And we know that no children of any age went missing in Hope back when you were here. Not reported cases. Only two this whole time. So even if your parents, or whoever was looking after you, weren't from here, like say you were from Vancouver but you went missing in Hope, that's where the loss would be reported. But yours wasn't reported. Nobody knew to look for you. The question is why.

Amber liked to make lists. She got out her notepad and they threw ideas back and forth.

Something horrendous happened to her parents.

She didn't have parents—she was a ward of the state, and the loss was covered up.

It was grandparents looking after her, and they were really old and forgetful, and they forgot they owned her.

It was a single mom looking after her, and she couldn't take it anymore, and when Stacey went missing, she never reported it, just moved on and changed her identity.

The dad wanted a boy, but Stacey was a girl, and he was not mentally stable and killed the wife that gave him a girl instead of a boy, and then he killed himself.

It was an aunt looking after her at the fair, but she had a brain aneurysm and collapsed somewhere and left Stacey as easy prey.

Someone who didn't want kids came with her to Hope, then dropped her off in the park, and that's why she wasn't reported missing.

Stacey belonged to someone who worked at the fair, and by the time her absence was noticed, they had moved on to another town.

You know what all this means, don't you? Stacey said. She felt herself getting emotional, and she stopped and forced herself to take a deep breath. It means whoever owned me a long time ago didn't care enough to find me. If you come from something like that, what chance do you have? Now there's no one.

No, Amber said, hearing her friend say what might be the truth. She tried to come up with an argument to challenge what had been said, but she couldn't think of one. She thought of mentioning that Stacey still had Sage but thought better of it.

We need to get out of here. We've been sitting for two days. Let's go for a walk.

Stacey agreed. Part of her wanted to sit and wallow in self-loathing, but it would be better to go somewhere and do something. She almost felt itchy.

Just before dark, they made it down to the river, so powerful that Stacey couldn't help but think of the little boy the constable had mentioned. Anyone who fell into that river would be on their way to Vancouver, like it or not. Had one of her parents fallen in the river that day? Did the other try to help and fall in too? But if so, why was she found in the park, and not here? They heard someone singing behind them and looked around to see two boys with a sport bag in hand walking the same way at the side of the road. It didn't take long for them to catch up.

Hi, one boy said. Just the word hi. Nothing else.

Hi, Amber said.

We're heading down to the river for a beer. Care to join us?

Amber looked about to say they were just out for a walk and had to get back, but Stacey beat her to it and said they had nothing better to do, so the four of them walked another two or three minutes until they came to a path that led down to the riverside.

Is it safe here? Amber asked.

Absolutely safe, one boy said. Then he introduced himself as Mike and said his friend's name was Wayne. Mike and Wayne in the town of Hope. A chance to meet the locals.

Nobody ever comes down here, Mike said. Just us. Come on, we'll show you.

They sat against the riverbank and drank their beer. They were nice enough, Stacey decided. Soon the surfaces of their lives had been traded, then Mike and Wayne explained, while they had grown up in Hope, they didn't plan on living there forever. Stacey asked them what was wrong with Hope, and Mike said he guessed there was nothing wrong with Hope, but when you'd lived in Hope as long as he had, you know it's time to move on. Both had taken a prospector's course, and they had all their gear and would soon be up in the mountains seeking their fortune. Gold and silver and copper all ran throughout the mountains, and they only needed to find it before anyone else did. Stacey talked to Mike mostly, and after they were on their third beer, he said there was a really cool spot just around the corner. Did she want to see it? She did. It was hard to see where they were going so Mike held her hand as they made their way along the river's edge. When they got to the appointed spot, it wasn't much different from where they had started, so far as Stacey could tell, but Mike said if you sit down between the logs and focus on the river some nights, you'll see the canoe races pass right before your eyes.

At one point, Stacey remembered hearing Amber somewhere on the bank behind her, calling her name. Stacey didn't answer because she didn't want to be disturbed. She didn't have any pants on for one thing, and she felt dizzy suddenly, maybe from the beer, and Mike was standing on a log wearing her bra over his eyes like they were the latest rage in safety goggles.

Stacey didn't know where she was, only that she wanted to give herself up for consumption, be transformed and away from all she had learned.

You're on the pill, right?

The words tilted her world toward sobriety, and she heard Aunt Sadie speaking off in the distance, and while she couldn't understand the words, she knew she was talking about the diaphragm she'd introduced to Stacey, the one back in Fernie, because when they started out, she could never have imagined being in the situation she was in now.

I've got to go, she said.

Wait. You can't leave. What about your pants? Where are you going?

By weaving her way between the side streets and away from the last of the late-night revellers, she found their motel, receiving one cat whistle as she made her way through the yellow fluorescent glow of the town. She had her own key, but she had left it down by the river. She didn't know how exhausted she was until she knocked on the door and Amber opened it. Then, no matter what questions Amber asked, she could only respond with laughter.

32

THE NEXT MORNING, THEY GOT their deposit back and left early. Amber had to wait in the car while Stacey cleaned up the motel room, despite Amber's insistence that the chambermaid would do it. Amber drove and Stacey sat beside her, the waist of her pants inside the car and trapped by the window, the legs flapping out of control at highway speed. They'd driven back to their rendezvous from the night before, and Amber had found Stacey's pants, the legs floating in an eddy at the side of the river, soaked. No sign of her bra. Either Mike had kept it as a souvenir or some fisherman later in the day would find a memento of one who had gotten away.

Do you believe in fate? Stacey asked.

Fate?

Yeah, you know. The life you're living was predetermined somehow, and you couldn't escape it if you wanted to.

I don't know. Do you?

I don't know either, but I'm thinking about it. I somehow got lost in Hope. That can happen, I guess. But there must be ten thousand people there in the summer, and I had a two in ten thousand chance of Della and Sage finding me and deciding what they did. I could have been found by nine thousand nine hundred and ninety-eight other people.

That's true. You could have.

But I wasn't. Don't you see? Strange things happen to people all the time, and when they do, you hear them say, Well, what are the odds? It's like my destiny was just a matter of time.

Amber drove past a policeman parked at the side of the road. I'm glad I wasn't speeding, she said. It's possible he wasn't looking for speeders. It may have been Constable Hereford on the lookout for missing kids.

Then Amber said, I know what my mom would say. She'd say when things happen that we can't control, it's an opportunity to learn something. She's into tarot cards and horoscopes, that's why she thinks that way. I never question her about it, but it seems obvious to me. Of course you're supposed to learn from it. You learn something when you walk into a brick wall. At least you'd better.

When they got to Midway, they filled up with gas and kept driving. Amber could get an extra shift at the golf course if they didn't stop. Stacey didn't want to go anywhere. She wondered if her Aunt Sadie would be there when she arrived. She might have taken their road trip as an opportunity to head back to San Jose and pretend none of this had happened. Stacey felt small, sitting there. She had to slow her mind down and wait for one thing at a time. Thinking took time, and there were always options, but for now she didn't know what to do next. Her pants were drying. That would be something. To put on dry pants.

Less than three miles from home, the Valiant stopped running. Stacey, now driving, pulled off to the side of the road. They considered walking but instead went to a house up the road and phoned Hart. He showed up a half hour later and tied an old tire onto the back bumper and pushed the car slowly into town and to the front of the house.

That was illegal, he said when they had finished. What they don't know won't hurt them.

Amber walked home, but before she did she gave Stacey a hug that meant something. They didn't say anything. They didn't have to. Hart could feel it too and turned back into his own house.

Aunt Sadie stood with the front door opened. You made it, she said. Lucky squirmed between Aunt Sadie's legs and jumped up on Stacey, almost knocking her down. Stacey had trained him not to jump up on people, but she held his head and ruffled his ears.

Barely made it, she said.

Stacey hadn't told Aunt Sadie why she and Amber had driven to Hope before they left, but she told her now. She told her everything they found out and what remained unanswered. She told her she needed another bra.

On the long drive back, the two of them hadn't talked like they had on the way to Hope. Amber, tired herself, seemed to understood that Stacey needed time to sort out her thoughts, and during the ponderous stretches of highway, a lot of thinking took place. Stacey hadn't learned what she wanted to, and the more she thought about it, the more she understood that it was unlikely to be any other way. She felt wiser now than she had been before she'd gone, as if she had gained a sense of perspective that prepared her for what she knew her aunt was about to say.

I read all the diaries while you were away. I hope you don't mind I did that. Martin had to head home, and I had the house to myself, and when I read through them, it was like Della was in the room with me. I could hear her voice the whole time, and she kept trying to explain what she meant by what she'd written. The whole thing is incredulous, don't get me wrong. None of this should have happened, but it did and that's that. What they did was stupid and illegal on top of it all, and the whole time, they were thinking only of themselves. My sister especially. I was mad as hell when I read them the first time, and that was how I felt when I went through them again, but there was something... a kind of feeling...

She was my mother, Stacey said.

What?

She was my mother. Everything she did that I can remember she did for me. The only reason she put up with him was because she was afraid we couldn't survive without him. We never know all the reasons things happen. She looked after me, and she didn't have to. She wanted to. A lot of bad things happen to kids before they grow up, but none of them happened to me. I don't like everything about the way things turned out, but in the end, I have to consider myself lucky.

The dog was lying at Stacey's feet. He heard his name and got on all fours and put his head on her lap. Stacey had said her piece. Her aunt just sat there and didn't respond. In the awkward silence, Stacey thought maybe she'd said too much. Been too honest.

I'm going to tell you something, Stacey. This is the wrong time to tell you, but there might not be a better time.

Can we turn out all the lights first?

We can, but why?

Words are truthful when spoken in the dark. It feels that way. Stacey got up and turned off all the lights and pulled the drapes at the front of the house. Then she sat down prepared to listen.

The thing is I'm not your aunt. Not really. But I feel like your aunt. If that sounds stupid, I can understand that, but the thing is... the thing... is I'm less your aunt than you think I am.

What do you mean?

Our parents, Della's and mine, were older when they raised us. That's because they weren't having any luck making children. Your mom, Della, they adopted, and two years later, they had me. This often happens to couples. Anyway, Della and I were raised as sisters, but we weren't biological sisters. You may have wondered why we don't look much alike. That's why.

Stacey kept petting Lucky on the head, over and over. She didn't look in her aunt's direction while she listened, and in the darkness, she wouldn't have been able to see much of her if she had. It was her turn to be silent, but this time it didn't feel difficult to bear.

If you have any of that rum left, I think I'd like some.

Martin left two beer in the fridge for you.

I think I need rum.

There was a quiet to the heat of summer that reflected the life she now lived. A still life. She didn't have a job and didn't have the energy to look for one. She went to visit Sage once and left him a box of shortbreads at reception but didn't go in. Aunt Sadie had to return to San Jose for two weeks to deal with her business leases, and during that time, it would be up to Stacey to think about it. *It* being the plan her aunt had outlined.

A plan felt dangerous. A plan suggested the intention to move from something you knew to something you didn't. Her aunt had been drunk when she outlined her proposal, while Stacey sat on the couch and watched what looked like two of her aunts, waving their arms in the air, explaining. If she absolutely had to, her aunt would stay in Fernie until Stacey graduated. Eleven more months. She didn't want to live in Fernie. She liked the town, but her home was elsewhere. So she suggested to Stacey that she move to San Jose with her and graduate there. They could sell the house, since Sage would never return home, or rent it out. The rent would help defray the cost of things, though Aunt Sadie made it clear she would pay whatever Stacey needed no matter what she chose to do. Martin said, with what had happened to her family, it wouldn't be a problem getting her into a good school. Martin owned three fashion boutiques and could get her a part-time job if she wanted one. During parts of the explanation, it sounded like Martin's plan, but her Aunt Sadie seemed genuinely excited about the prospect. She'd never stayed in one place long and had never had kids of her own, and this was a chance to change things. Lucky could come if she wanted. Some people in the neighbourhood had dogs. She'd have to walk him in the morning and again after school, but it would be doable. Or, Lucky could stay with Hart. Stacey could decide. After she graduated, there was Santa Clara and San Jose State right there. She could be anything she wanted to be. This was a chance to think about the future. To decide what she wanted out of life.

And so her aunt set her up for two weeks of torment and misery. She wouldn't ask her aunt to hang around Fernie against her will. Even if she stayed, as she said she would, it wouldn't feel right. Once again she thought of Della as Mom, and she wished her mom could talk her through it. She thought about the times her mother had explored her own family history, how Della's dad wasn't one to do much of anything, unlikely to take a chance, while Della's mother would try anything on for size. Her aunt and her mother didn't look much alike, but the real difference was how they'd patterned themselves after different parents.

The few times Stacey got together with Amber, she pretended everything was fine. If she explained what she felt, she knew Amber would champion her cause and petition her parents for Stacey to stay with them through grade twelve, an option Stacey wouldn't consider. Amber's brother still lived at home, and the house was small, and she wasn't willing to take a chance on destroying what she and Amber had cultivated over the years. Some things you couldn't ask of even your best friend in the world.

Hart said he would look into getting her car running. He'd been at it for a week with no luck. One day while he worked under the hood, Stacey asked him if he'd like a cup of coffee. He said he would, and the two of them sat on the front step. Stacey had baked him some cookies and put them in a plastic bag, and she could see that, at the present rate of consumption, Molly the Nose would be lucky to sniff the crumbs.

Is everything all right? Hart asked.

I'm good, she said.

You've been through plenty this last year, what with your dad failing and your mother passing. I want you to know if there's anything we can do, you just let us know. Molly loves coming to people's rescue. Not that you need rescuing or anything. But you know what I mean. Any time, night or day, just ask.

Hart got back to work on the car, and Stacey went to lie on her bed. Growing up, there had been ample opportunity for her to think things through from her bedroom. A bedroom remembered everything you'd been through. The walls were patient listeners and didn't ask questions.

She took Lucky down to the dikes by the river. He loved it there because of the other dogs that he could play with. She sat and stared at the grey current, and Lucky sat beside her and did the same. She loved the way the trees along the river offered a verdant curtain, as if to cover the shy river sliding behind them. Sage had come to the river often to fish, but one time Stacey walked along the dike and saw him sitting on the same rock she was on now, just staring out at the persistent flow, trying to figure out something in his narrow life that wasn't clear to him. Lucky was smiling, Stacey was sure of it. In a few hours, he would be hungry, but for now he had everything he wanted.

August 3rd the sun rose, diminished by cloud, but warm, the day humid for such an early hour. Stacey left a note on the kitchen table. She needed a walk but wouldn't be long.

She wanted to go by herself.

Through town and up the hill to St. Margaret's Graveyard. Hundreds were buried up on the hill with no grave markers, miners who had passed away outside the reach of relatives of any kind, but Stacey stood in front of a modest flat stone that read: *Della Avery Howard, 1933-1987*. People raved about the views from St. Margaret's, but Stacey didn't see how that would benefit her mother now. People have plans when they're alive and able to think up plans, and then they die and everyone understands they were plans that only work for people who are living. Visitors standing tall could see the mountain glory from the ridge. Maybe the cemetery wasn't designed for the dead at all.

Stacey knelt down, not in prayer, but reverently. She conjured up dozens of memories of her mother, like how she always made sure Stacey had a new outfit for the first day of school every September. She said these thoughts out loud. No one else was around to hear, but it didn't matter anyway. Where one went when they died wasn't obvious to her, but it was possible her mother could hear every word she said. She hoped so, anyway. As sad as it had been, she thought of how, only days before her mother had passed, she'd struggled to get out of bed to tell off the man who tried to claim Lucky. Her heart felt swollen as it did every time her mind travelled back to when she was in her mother's care. She would take the feeling with her wherever she went.

Martin had everything packed in his new SUV. If they flew there, she would have been allowed a suitcase at best, but with driving, they had room for anything she could think of that meant something. Boxes filled with her vast collection of stuffed animals and the books she had been raised on. She'd packed her mother's teapot, old and cracked but able to manufacture the best-tasting tea ever. And clothes. She didn't have that many clothes, and pretty much anything in her closet seemed valuable. On the way back from the cemetery, she tried to imagine what it felt like that summer, two years old, walking frantically between large trees and total strangers, walking without direction, seeking a solution to being alone. No one could remember the exact nature of their thoughts and feelings at such a young age, but she thought the experience must have left a residue of some kind. Everything that happens leaves some kind of history, recorded or not.

The front door to the house was open and so was a door to the back seat of the car. Martin and Aunt Sadie were still inside. Lucky stood close to the car, anticipating instructions to hop in. Martin came out with something wrapped in his arms and headed to Hart and Molly's house. Aunt Sadie stood at the front porch looking uncertain, the way people do when it comes time to move on.

I think we've got everything, Aunt Sadie said.

I know, Stacey said. Come inside for a minute. We need to talk.

33

PEOPLE WERE PRONE TO MAKE COMPARISONS. One day to the next, a month, a year. A neighbour who had just moved in and had a yappy dog might be compared to the previous owners who played piano. August had always been a month when foul weather ruined someone's camping trip, and when the plangent sound of rain filled the valley, people found comfort in it. This year it had rained only once in August, a windy month, though the wind presented only a hollow threat and didn't bring much if any cloud cover over the valley. The forests posed a fire hazard—something people worried about even when rain fell. Most felt a certain discomfort, an uneasiness when things changed from what they expected. Why hadn't it rained more? Did this mean more snow than usual in the winter? Could it be there wouldn't be enough snow to coat the surrounding mountains? How long did one wait before one spoke to the new neighbour about that dog that found any excuse to bark: a crow, a cat, a pedestrian, a passing car, an apple obeying gravity and thumping to the Earth? Time clothed in routine had a deliberate quality, but change caused time to break; it became harder to account for, and perspectives changed, as if it were natural to keep resetting one's internal clock. August was a long month.

The money at Stacey's disposal mostly equaled what she'd had years previous, but she had to think about money in a finite way now. She bought herself a new outfit for school. Flared puffy skirts didn't work for her. Glitzy fabrics and ornamentation were the order of the day, but denim was, mercifully, still possible. The ad in one magazine she'd thumbed through said: *Don't be mad at me because I'm beautiful.* Tanned skin looked healthy and beautiful, but she had spent little time in the sun all summer. Still, she found an outfit she liked, something she suspected even her mother would have approved of, and she dressed purposefully, ready to start her last year of high school in a way unlikely to cultivate enemies.

Most of what she'd packed up from the house remained in boxes, and she had no immediate plans to unpack anything other than the clothes she needed. In the end, she hadn't been able to get in the car and drive to San Jose to start what would have been a completely different life. When friends, neighbours or classmates asked why she had not gone with her aunt, and several did, she couldn't furnish an answer that made any sense to anyone but her.

Aunt Sadie had offered to take her in and give her everything she needed to graduate and chart a new path in life. Her response to Stacey's decision turned out to be hardest part of all. When Stacey had made up her mind that she couldn't leave Fernie, she expected her aunt to be relieved. Instead Aunt Sadie wanted to explore her trepidation from every angle possible. She tried every plausible argument she could think of to reverse Stacey's decision and even got Martin involved for support, though Stacey had the feeling that he, at least, felt relieved. Not until mid-afternoon did Aunt Sadie and Martin drive their SUV south, after everything loaded had been unloaded and the dog blanket set for Lucky to lie on returned to the floor beside Stacey's bed. It had been important for

Aunt Sadie to take her in and help her, that much was clear.

Molly the Nose kept appearing on her front porch while Stacey sorted out her life, and she watched as all Stacey's belongings made their way from the car back to the house. Although she couldn't easily articulate why she had to stay, Stacey felt clear about it all. It was Lucky who was most confused. He knew something was changing, and he wanted to know how it involved the life of a dog.

Probably at Hart's insistence, Molly the Nose kept her distance that first night. Stacey made a toasted cheese sandwich and sat on the couch with her dog at her feet. She had a journal of her own, a new one, in which she intended to record the events of her life. She wasn't sure what to write first. Lucky always understood her thoughts, or she felt that he did. When her breathing became uneven, he knew something was up. She wrote: *I love my dog.* A perfect, short sentence that expressed how she felt, and it had an even number of words, letters and syllables.

At eight-thirty, Aunt Sadie called from Spokane. She wanted to know if everything was all right. Was there any chance she'd changed her mind? No, Stacey said, it was better this way. You'll consider coming to San Jose for Christmas like last year? Yes, Stacey said she would consider that. A consideration of the future was as much as she could promise for now.

Six hundred and fifty dollars had been Hart's guess, and it turned out that was exactly the monthly rent Stacey could get for the house. A teacher and her husband moved in the first of September. They owned a small black and white dog with a pug nose that barked during the day if left alone and any time, day or night, if they let him out in the yard. Hart was away most of the day, so while he despised the dog, he said he could put up with it. Molly the Nose wouldn't admit it, but she was getting deaf in her old age and hardly noticed the dog. Stacey found the constant barking irritating, but she coped by imagining that every time the dog barked a twenty-five cent deposit went into her bank account. She'd moved into Fort Whoop and paid Hart a hundred dollars a month for the privilege. Hart said he didn't feel right charging her anything. She told him to get over it. She had enough money left over to pay the mortgage and the taxes, and she worked on Saturdays at the clothing store so she would have a little extra to put into a savings account. She had no idea what to save for, but she knew her mother would have insisted she save something, just in case.

At first, Hart and Molly the Nose wanted to take responsibility for her situation and help her out. They offered a room in their house, but Stacey wanted her independence, and she also wanted clear lines drawn. Growing up she had learned the importance of drawing the line. Unless she did something eventful on Sundays, she ate supper with Hart and Molly and watched the Sunday night movie on either NBC or ABC, depending, while the two of them hunched over cups of Darjeeling tea. The rest of the time, Stacey kept her distance from all the neighbours. Thursdays she walked to Amber's house, ate supper and watched the *Cosby Show* after. She missed watching TV at first, and Hart said if it meant a lot to her, he would figure out a way to hook her old TV up at Fort Whoop. Stacey knew how important it was for him to keep his fort as authentic as possible and said she didn't want a TV. Hart recognized her intention and accepted.

Once she crawled out of the cave called August, life became illuminated once again. August had been a month of resolution, and her focus turned to coping with the next ten months. She felt older, busier and more in control of her life. She had needed August more than she'd realized, and now she could move on.

Hugh had also moved on. He was volunteering at a kibbutz for a year, then he planned to backpack in India for a while before returning home. Stacey thought he was working on his sense of humour when she first heard about it, but he was dead serious. With him so far away, she knew they might never see each other again. When she thought of him at all, she remembered what he smelled like.

She worked every Saturday, all day, and got to like meeting the people who came into the store. Every customer represented a story or a cartoon about life, and they were diversions she looked forward to. If she went anywhere, it was on Saturday nights, to house parties mostly, though she didn't drink much and wasn't fascinated by drugs like many of her peers. Plenty of boys attended these parties, and she had plenty of offers, but it had been months since she'd put her diaphragm to good use. Lucky was her most steadfast companion, and she took him everywhere she went. The dog had slowed down noticeably, and she guessed she should expect that. Hart had her car running again (it was the solenoid, he said), and some Sundays she'd take Lucky for a drive somewhere, if for no other reason than to say they got away.

She had assimilated everything her mother had written in her diaries, and most of it she accepted. In her weaker moments, she found time to feel sorry for herself, and sometimes felt rage surfacing from what had gone on, but she had learned how to quiet her mind when these ephemeral bouts arrived. She avoided the temptation to pick away at the scab of regret. She no longer had the diaries; she had insisted that Aunt Sadie take them with her, and she didn't want to know what she did with them. She didn't have a phone, but on the first Sunday of every month, she phoned Aunt Sadie from a pay phone. Her aunt sent her letters and postcards almost every week with pictures of San Jose and the beaches of California on the postcards, reminders of what she'd turned her back on and what she could embrace once she'd graduated. Every letter arrived with American money stuffed inside, and Aunt Sadie said she was putting two hundred dollars a month into a special account in case someday she wanted to attend San Jose State. Christmas came up in every correspondence. Don't forget about San Jose for Christmas.

A routine would create the grid she needed to see her through to graduation. Amber and Stacey managed the Environmental Club. They still did some of the work, but mostly they trained a group of grade tens and elevens so they could carry on the following year. They both felt like parents in their new role. Parents who, like it or not, would leave a legacy behind.

People around her were all preoccupied with events that didn't consume her. The Winter Olympics were coming to Calgary in a few months, just up the road a few hours, and people acted as if it was the event of a lifetime. It wasn't often she thought about such things. She had only one issue on her mind that had not been resolved. It had taken months for her to decide what, if anything, she would do about it.

She asked Hart if he would go with her. Throughout the fall, Hart sporadically visited Sage at Uphill Manor. He chose sunny days and wheeled Sage in his wheelchair out to the corner of the grounds where the two of them would smoke a joint or two before they got too cold. Hart said he would take her, not a problem. What day did she want to go? She wanted to take Lucky too, and one Sunday they went as an entourage. I don't want to stay long, Stacey said. I just want to see him and go.

They stayed more than half an hour. Stacey brought him a box of his favourite cookies, which delighted Sage, but he also wanted to visit and ask questions and pet Lucky the whole time. On the way there, Hart told her how Sage liked to hear news, so she told him about her living in Fort Whoop and renting out the house. Hart had already told him that, she could tell, but he pretended to hear it for the first time.

That wasn't so bad now was it? Hart said on their way back home.

No, she said. It was good.

It's the right thing to do, what you're doing, he said. I don't need to tell you why. You wouldn't have gone there to see him if you hadn't already figured it out.

There's something I've lost, Stacey said.

Lost?

His voice, she said. I can't remember his voice. It's been only a year since the stroke, but I can't make myself hear what he sounded like.

Stacey went on her own after that. Every second Sunday, she and Lucky drove to Uphill Manor and visited Sage. Every second Sunday was about right. With the life she was living, she could only hand over so much that could be deemed news. Some Sundays Molly helped her bake cookies to take. She always brought cookies, but she also thought of something else that would capture his interest. She brought a picture of them as a family, several years back when they still owned the purple car, and he liked that, she could tell, by the contorted half-smile that unfolded on his face. One week she read him a short story she'd written for her English class, a story about a mining disaster, fictitiously set in Fernie, though there had been many mining disasters in the town that might have been close. The walls of a horizontal shaft had collapsed leaving seven miners trapped. The town worked in twenty-four-hour shifts trying to get to them, and on the third day, they found six of the miners. One was dead, but the other five had lived. Every day that the miners toiled to rescue those missing, a dog came along, and every day he moved away from where everybody else worked and sat at the mouth of a mine shaft abandoned for almost a year. The man who owned the dog finally noticed the animal's behaviour. After the fourth day, having still not located the last of the seven missing miners, the dog's owner insisted they pursue the abandoned shaft. Many thought of the old shaft as too risky and didn't want to lend a hand, but enough agreed to follow the dog owner's insistence, and halfway down the cavern, they heard a tapping sound. Always three taps in a row. Tap, tap, tap. Then nothing for a long time, and later they would hear it again. The rescuers mimicked the tapping, and when they did, the tapping would start again. They drilled into the rock wall and wedged a thirty-foot plastic pipe through the rock. The trapped miner made the pipe move. They fed soup through the pipe for the next two days and eventually rescued the man who had a leg badly crushed. The last of the seven miners survived, and the dog became a legend. A few years later, the dog died, and some thought there should be a monument or a statue on the mountain in his honour. The mining company wasn't in favour, saying it provided a reminder of what had gone wrong in the past, so the seventh survivor said he would pay for it himself. A statue carved from anthracite coal paid tribute to a dog who had put his instincts into practice.

By the middle of November, the visits became weekly affairs. It wasn't much of an effort to drive there, and Lucky looked forward to it every time. If the air wasn't frigid or windy or filled with yet more snow, Stacey would wheel Sage outside so he could stare at the mountains. Once she brought her camera and had a nurse take a photo of the three of them. She lifted Lucky up so he could sit, however awkwardly, on Sage's lap for the photo. She wasn't sure why she wanted the image. She just did.

Her visits to Uphill Manor grew more comfortable over time. She avoided discussions of the past, and the nebulous future garnered little attention. She related what was going on in her life now, almost eagerly. When the week leading up to her visit had been close to uninspiring, she made up events to give him something to think about. When she explained things to him, she called him Sage if she felt she had to use a name of any kind. She wasn't ready to use the word "Dad," but she imagined that someday she would.

About the Author

Bill Stenson was born in Nelson, B.C., went to a one-room schoolhouse on Thetis Island and grew up on a small farm in Duncan. He became a teacher because he loved literature and taught English and Creative Writing at various high schools, the Victoria School of Writing and the University of Victoria. He and Terence Young founded the well-known *Claremont Review*, an international literary magazine for young adult writers that is still going today. As well as editing the magazine for many years, he wrote a short story collection, *Translating Women*, and two novels, *Svoboda* and *Hanne and Her Brother*, published by Thistledown Press. He has also published stories in many magazines, including; *Grain, The Malahat Review, The Antigonish Review, filling Station, Blood and Aphorisms, Wascana Review, Prairie Fire, Toronto Star, The New Quarterly, Prism International* and the *Nashwaak Review*. Stenson was a finalist for the 2nd Great BC Novel Contest (2013) and a winner of the 4th Great BC Novel Contest (2017). He was also a finalist for the Prism International Fiction Contest and the Prairie Fire Short Fiction Contest. He lives with his wife, poet Susan Stenson, in the Cowichan Valley and writes every day.

Acknowledgements

Research for this novel was helped along by Rosalee Fornasier and the Sparwood Historical Society, Terri Tombossa and Ron Ulrich and the kind folks at the Fernie Museum and also David McCoy whose insights into mining were invaluable. Thanks to all of you.

Thanks also to John Lent and Audrey Thomas for their belief in the manuscript and to Mona Fertig, Pearl Luke, Mark Hand and Judith Brand at Mother Tongue Publishing for their patience and insight. I have been blessed by you all.

PREVIOUS WINNERS OF THE GREAT BC NOVEL CONTEST

Everything Was Good-bye by Gurjinder Basran (2010)

Lucky by Kathryn Para (2013)